For indomitable spirits.

These Ruthless Deeds

TARUN SHANKER
KELLY ZEKAS

Swoon
READS

SWOON READS | NEW YORK

A Swoon Reads Book

An imprint of Feiwel and Friends and Macmillan Publishing Group, LLC

These Ruthless Deeds. Copyright © 2017 by Tarun Shanker and Kelly Zekas. Excerpt from Duels and Deceptions copyright © 2017 by Cindy Anstey. All rights reserved. Printed in the United States of America. For information, address Swoon Reads, 175 Fifth Avenue, New York, N.Y. 10010.

Our books may be purchased in bulk for promotional, educational, or business use. Please contact your local bookseller or the Macmillan Corporate and Premium Sales Department at (800) 221-7945 ext. 5442 or by e-mail at MacmillanSpecialMarkets@macmillan.com.

Library of Congress Cataloging-in-Publication Data is available.

ISBN 978-1-250-12795-2 (trade paperback) / ISBN 978-1-250-12796-9 (ebook)

Book design by Liz Dresner

First Edition—2017

10 9 8 7 6 5 4 3 2 1

swoonreads.com

Prologue

THE DOOR WAS locked. The door was always locked, no matter what room she woke up in. But she tried the handle anyway, jiggling it as quietly as possible, trying desperately not to disturb her captors.

She sighed. At least there was no foul-smelling fabric stuffed in her mouth this time. No ropes tying her to the small room's dingy little bed.

And this time she was in a room with a window that one could, perhaps, escape through. She crossed the room with halting, uncoordinated steps—something was wrong. It was almost as if she were learning how to walk again, with no knowledge of where her limbs ended. But no matter—escape was her first and only priority.

She looked out the window and frowned. Surely it was London, but there was something . . . strange about the view. The buildings appeared a bit newer, neater. The roads wider. The carriages different. She'd never been to this part of the city before.

She listened hard; no sounds came from the rest of the house. Slowly she pushed on the windows, which softly squeaked open. The street noise made her cringe, and her heart pounded. She sent up a quick prayer that no one inside would hear. She climbed

onto the sill, slid outside onto the ledge, and closed the panes behind her.

Ah yes, the drop. It wasn't too high but high enough to worry about broken limbs. Fortunately, below the sill was the overhang of the ground-floor window, jutting out just far enough to step onto.

Delicately, she gripped the sill and dipped her body slowly downward. One of her slippers slid off and fell to the street, but her toes just managed the next ledge. Her feet tested her weight, and then she let go and sank down into a crouch, afraid to trust her balance standing tall. Goodness. Was it to be this easy? Would she simply be able to find a carriage and get back to her family—to her home?

She looked down. Getting around the ground floor window was more terrifying than falling. She couldn't risk her captors seeing her from inside—not when she was this close to escaping. Gathering her courage (how little she seemed to possess!), she leaped off to the side of the window, falling the few feet to the hard ground, scraping her knee upon landing. She let out a hiss and contemplated her dirtied skirt. A small laugh escaped her as she realized a musty skirt might now be the worst of her problems.

The girl began to walk purposefully, still unsure of her steps, but winding up and down the streets, farther and farther from the house she escaped from, looking for anything the least bit familiar. Bills and advertisements for strange products were posted outside one pharmacy. A young boy shouted about the day's events and tried to sell a newspaper she'd never heard of, *The Sun*. The city smelled different than she remembered. And when she glanced inside a bank, searching for a clue, movement in the corner of her eye stopped her dead in her tracks.

Staring at her was a black-haired woman with a few pockmarks dotting her skin and a Mediterranean look about her. The strange woman was a few inches taller and a little thinner. The curiosity in her gaze matched the girl's own—as did the subsequent look of understanding and horror when the girl realized there wasn't a woman on the other side of that glass window. It was her own image being reflected. And she looked nothing like herself.

Her stomach twisted, hands began to shake. Was any of this real? Had she even escaped? What if she was still trapped somewhere, drugged and sleeping? She was on the verge of breaking down, turning around, and asking the newspaper boy where she was, what year it was, and whether she was dreaming. But as she desperately searched around for something to calm her panicked questions, the answer hit her in the form of a building across the street.

Or rather its sign, which said NEW YORK CITY POSTAL OFFICE.

As unbelievable as that was, it did solve some mysteries. Why an advertisement said an elixir was "the best in America." Why the boy was shouting news about a factory fire in San Francisco. Why she felt so lost. Somehow, she'd been transported across the Atlantic without noticing. How many days had she been asleep?

It didn't explain what had happened to her, but when she saw the signs advertising trans-American and worldwide telegraph services, nothing mattered more than getting home.

England.

Home.

She hurried across the street toward the postal office. She didn't have any money, but she might beg the operator to send the shortest message to her family. Then she could go to the police, safe in their presence, until her family arrived. A giddy smile overtook her face as she thought about her sister, who would surely find her way here without even waiting for their parents.

As she opened the door to the postal office and heard a voice she'd hoped she'd never hear again, her stomach dropped. "*Tsk, tsk*—you know you can't be wandering around like this. What if they found you?" he scolded.

She had been so close. She tried to run but her first step didn't even reach the ground. A wail left her throat as a crackle rent the air, her stomach lurched, and the floor opened up, swallowing her whole.

Chapter 1

FEBRUARY 1883
BELGIUM

"THIS WAS A terrible plan."

"Evelyn, it's your plan."

"Yes, but you've escaped from far more asylums than I have. Why wouldn't we choose your plan?"

"Because yours was better. There's no need to worry yet. He hasn't even been inside for more than five minutes."

Miss Grey was right. But her reassurances didn't make me feel any less responsible for Oliver Myles, our slippery new friend. Since he was the only one with a useful power for a secretive rescue, we'd saddled him with every difficult task. He had to memorize Miss Grey's complicated map of the asylum (which was somewhat vague, being from memory), steal the keys from a nurse, find Emily Kane's quarters, and sneak her out a side door, where we'd be waiting, doing absolutely nothing to help. If his powers failed him, he could easily get caught by a guard, get stuck in a locked room, or fall down through the floor toward the center of the earth and we wouldn't be any the wiser.

I hated feeling this useless.

I hated feeling the weight of this plan on my shoulders.

A shiver escaped me along with a long-held breath, its white mist barely visible in the faint light of our covered lantern. The night sat cold and silent. There was nothing else around us for miles except the oppressive blackness of rolling hills and woods. I pulled my wool cloak tighter around my shoulders and tried to imagine where in the building Oliver would be at the moment. He should have reached Emily by now, sliding through walls as easily as I stepped through a threshold. Perhaps I could convince Miss Grey to take a quick nap, check his progress in her dream, and assuage my—

Oliver's head burst through the wall. I jumped, still not quite used to his head popping out of things heads shouldn't pop out of. The rest of his body followed and he gave us a disgruntled look.

"What happened?" Miss Grey whispered, uncovering the lantern slightly. "Did you find Emily?"

"I did," Oliver said, "but she wouldn't come."

"Did you tell her my name? Did you remind her about the dreams?" Miss Grey asked.

"I tried to—she wouldn't listen to me and when I kept trying, she said she would scream."

Miss Grey let out a sigh. Over the last few days she had tried to prepare Emily for this escape by entering her dreams and calming her fears. But this seemed to be just like the last time Miss Grey was here, when she had escaped the asylum herself. Emily had refused to come and Miss Grey had had no choice but to leave her behind. Judging from the dark look on my former governess's face, she was not going to let that happen again.

"I'll have to speak with her," Miss Grey said. "How many nurses have you seen in the corridors?"

"Only one. And she's easy to avoid because you can see her light."

Miss Grey turned to hand me the lantern, her face pinched and white. "Evelyn, would you wait—"

"No," I said firmly. "This is still *my* terrible plan. I'm coming with you."

"Very well," she said, extinguishing the lantern's flame entirely.

Oliver disappeared through the locked door before realizing we could not follow. A second later, he came back with a smirk and handed us the stolen keys. "Sometimes I forget you have to deal with doors," he said.

"Well, you don't have to be smug about it."

Miss Grey unlocked the back door, slid it open as quietly as she could, and followed Oliver into the abyss. With one hand on my governess's back, I closed the door behind us to shut out what little guiding light remained. The pitch black was utterly disorienting, but the two of them seemed to know the way well enough. The building smelled of damp linens and pungent chemicals. I could feel Miss Grey quaking and wondered if this was conjuring up horrors from her time here before. I couldn't get the images out of my own head and I'd only heard them from her. The stories about the nurses' cruel treatment, the beating, the drugging, the starving, the freezing, the electrocuting, the isolating. The way they pushed patients deeper into madness to keep them here.

I stayed close behind, concentrating on keeping my footsteps soft, steadying my breathing, and trying to quell the rising sense of fear that we'd be discovered and I'd experience those punishments firsthand. That my parents would decide to leave me here forever for our reputation's sake. That I would fail again, fail like I had failed my sister.

I swallowed hard, pushing down the thoughts that made my needy heart beat faster. We proceeded at a slow, methodical pace for a minute or two, taking a right turn and two lefts, pausing at one corner upon the distant echo of steps and the faint flicker of a flame. Oliver scouted ahead and waited for the corridor to descend back into complete darkness before leading us forward again. When we found ourselves at our destination, Miss Grey's body shifted as she groped for the wall, the door, and the keyhole. With the faintest scrapings and a click, she managed to unlock the door and lead us inside.

"Emily?" Miss Grey whispered into the darkness. "Please, don't be alarmed. It's me, Alice."

Silence.

A match ignited and a thin candle seemed to materialize in midair, followed by another in Miss Grey's lantern. Oliver blew out the match and handed me his candle. "I'll watch the corridor," he whispered, closing the door behind him.

Miss Grey took a hesitant step farther into the room, raising and turning her lantern to bounce the light against the walls. It was unfurnished and tiny, making it easy to find Emily. A slim girl with ropes of dark, thick hair tumbling down over her shift was huddled on the bed, knees to her chest, staring at us from deep-set brown eyes, huge in her small, pixie-like face.

"Emily. Do you remember me?" Miss Grey asked, shining the lantern on her own visage. "Alice. Your friend."

"Alice, Alice, Alice, Alice," Emily muttered to herself as if she were reading a list in her head. Then she stiffened. "Alice! You shouldn't be here!" Her voice had an Irish lilt.

"Don't worry, dear. My friends and I have come to help you escape," Miss Grey said gently, aiming the light at me.

At those words, Emily shook her head furiously. "But I can't escape! I already told that boy."

"Why can't you?" Miss Grey asked, eyes flicking back to the

door. I felt my own nervousness grow, ready to be gone from here.

Emily turned away from us. "I don't wish to speak with you. Please leave. Thank you."

"You don't belong in here." Miss Grey tried again. "Just think, when we get to London, you will be able to move about freely, to do whatever you please—"

"I can't!" Her back was shaking. "I can't! The ghosts! They find me wherever I go."

"But, Emily, there are no ghosts. Believe me. There are no ghosts." Miss Grey looked at me helplessly, but I did not understand any more than she did. Emily believed ghosts were after her?

"Emily, my name is Evelyn Wyndham," I said softly. "Can you tell me about the ghosts?"

She still did not turn, but I could hear her voice clearly in the dark, little cell. "They—they do things. They hurt people."

"How do they hurt people?" I asked. Did she mean the nurses and guards here? Or did she really see ghosts? Was that somehow a part of her power?

"They knock people over and they drop things and they break down walls and they ruin everything!" Her voice rose on a frantic pitch and Miss Grey rushed to the bed, shushing her quietly.

"It's all right, Emily. It's all right." Miss Grey put her hand on Emily's shoulder and the girl jumped slightly.

"Don't—they'll hurt you. P-please. Don't make me leave," Emily said, shivering pitifully.

Oliver looked in through the small opening of the door. "We should go!"

I looked down at poor Emily on the pallet and joined Miss Grey, kneeling on her other side. "I promise, there are no ghosts where we are going."

She shook her head repeatedly. "They make things fly and they follow me. Always."

Miss Grey put her hand to her mouth, stifling a small gasp as she finally realized where Emily's fear came from. "Dear, do you mean you think there are ghosts who control the objects around you?"

She gave a tight nod.

"Oh, Emily!" Miss Grey was smiling in relief, happy to explain everything to the younger woman. "That's just your special ability to manipulate the things around you—I have mine, to see into your dreams. Evelyn here can heal sick or wounded people—and oh, there are so many others. You are not alone!"

The girl peeked at Miss Grey through a sheet of hair. "I don't have any special ability. It's ghosts."

Oliver spoke again. "Miss Grey! We have to go!"

I exchanged worried glances with her before deciding that getting Emily out of here was more important than not lying. "Emily, please, I promise I will cure you of the ghosts."

At that, she finally turned uncertainly. "You can do that?"

"I can," I said, making a promise I did not know I could keep. "But we have to go—now."

Miss Grey tugged lightly on Emily's hand and she uncurled her limbs hesitantly. We gently pulled her to standing and I squeezed her palm as she shivered against the dampness of moldy sawdust under her feet.

"It's all going to be all right," I promised again.

We crept out of the room, Miss Grey and I each holding one of Emily's hands, and found Oliver, rapidly dimming candle in hand. Emily shrank back but Miss Grey calmed her. "This is Oliver, our friend. He is going to lead us out."

Oliver barely spared Emily a glance as he gestured to the blackened passage on the left. I breathed easier with every step, more and more sure of our success. Slowly we crept along, and all seemed well—until we reached the end of a passageway and Oliver slipped through the wall to see if our next turn was free of guards.

But Emily didn't know that was happening. All she saw was our guide slipping through the wall. A cry erupted from her tiny frame, rumbling the floor, the walls, the entire building.

"Oh, Emily, please, stop, that's just his ability!" Miss Grey pleaded with the girl. "He's not a ghost!"

The shaking stopped.

Emily's screaming stopped, too, but not because of Miss Grey's convincing explanation. Emily had fainted into our arms. We stood frozen for a moment of fragile silence, listening, hoping earthquakes were an everyday asylum occurrence.

An alarm began clanging. At once, Miss Grey and I rushed to Oliver, Emily's body supported between us. We passed rooms where frantic voices spoke with curious or fearful tones. Every door we passed we willed not to open upon a group of burly guards and nurses.

"Just one more turn," Oliver whispered back to us. But I could feel a sense of doom creeping upon us as we rounded a dark corner that looked like every other.

This one led to a nurse whose eyes bulged at the sudden sight of us. "Stop! Stop right there!" she yelled.

We spun around and broke out into a full run, heading in the opposite direction. Emily's extra weight was wearing on us, slowing Miss Grey and me down. Oliver quickly passed through our bodies, making us gasp at the oddness, and he led the way, turning left down another dank corridor. The piercing sound of a whistle followed us, calling more nurses down, the light of their lanterns brightening our paths.

Another left and we found ourselves headed straight for an

intimidating woman blocking our escape. I hesitated, but Miss Grey pushed me and Emily forward, shouting desperately, "Keep going. More are behind us."

In a full sprint, Oliver tossed his candlestick straight at the nurse. She barely dodged it and it clanked and clattered onto the floor behind her. Oliver used the distraction to melt through the wall to his right, disappearing completely, and before she knew what was happening, he launched himself out of the wall right beside her and brought her down with a whoop and a thud, allowing us to pass.

"That's right—I did that!" he yelled triumphantly at her. I couldn't say what kept me moving, but we were at the end of the hall before I stopped to look back for Oliver, yelling and struggling with two more nurses who had arrived to restrain him. *He should have slipped out from their grasp and caught up by now*, I thought.

"Wait!" I yelled to Miss Grey. "There's something wrong with Oliver!"

She stopped and we dithered in the shadows. I couldn't leave him. A sharper panic was cutting through my general anxiety now.

"We have to go—his power will return soon enough!" Miss Grey said, pulling Emily determinedly away from Oliver. I took a step back to him, and another to Miss Grey. My mind sped, knowing that I would be unlikely to free Oliver from three different guards. Whichever way I went, I would be failing someone. I felt sick, but finally rushed back to Oliver. I would not leave him behind.

"Let go, you bloody bastards!" he was yelling.

"Let go!" I joined in. "Stop it!" I tried to break them off him, but there were too many.

One of the nurses pulled my arms tight behind my back, and

thick palms gripped my ankles. I could feel the calluses through my stockings. I flailed wildly, but they easily pulled me down, experienced in controlling disorderly patients. One grunted and sighed before slapping me hard across the face with the back of a fetid hand, and I stopped struggling for a moment, disoriented by the shock of it.

"Miss Grey!" I looked around through the sea of guards, hoping she'd managed to miraculously solve the problem. But her only response was a shriek as they restrained her and took Emily.

As they dragged us away, I heard my companions' screams and pleas as though underwater. They rushed over me but did not seem to sink in.

A crackle rang out, a new sound amid the grunting of the guards. I turned to see a guard disappear through a strange sliver in the air that materialized out of nowhere. My heart dropped and I screamed.

It couldn't be.

I began to struggle again but another crackle split the air, and the guards' hands released me. I fell but did not hit the ground. Instead a solid arm found my waist, reaching through from a new world, pulling me away from the asylum and into a dark-paneled room with a blazing fire.

I looked up, caught in his embrace, bewildered and gasping.

"Hello, Miss Wyndham. I always *did* want to rescue you."

Chapter 2

MR. KENT'S FACE WAS inches from mine, his brown eyes glittering, his smile uncontainable, his familiar scent of spice and smoke bracing. My head swam as I stared at him, unable to comprehend what exactly had happened.

The smile turned into a frown. "Are you all right?" he asked.

"I . . . don't know yet." He pulled me to my feet but kept one arm around my waist and I forced myself to reorient. Just seconds ago I was screaming and fighting through a dark endless corridor and now Mr. Kent was embracing me in a cozy study. Some part of me worried I was back in the asylum, drugged up and dreaming. "Where . . . are we? Is this real?"

His mouth twisted with pleasure, dimpling one side of his cheek, and he drawled, "As thrilled as I would be to appear in your dreams as a daring, dashing rescuer, this is most definitely real. We're in London. You're safe now."

"How did—"

That same crackle interrupted me with the answer to my question. Oliver and Miss Grey stumbled out of thin air, followed by two strangers, one carrying Emily, who appeared to be sleeping. I felt my breath leave me. The last time I'd seen someone travel like that was when Mr. Hale had come to help us find my sister, then cowardly disappeared into one of his doorways that could take him anywhere in the world.

But neither of the strangers was him. One was a compact, well-built man in his thirties, wearing a threadbare, olive jacket that clashed with his bright-blue waistcoat and plaid maroon trousers. His dark hair was pulled into an old-fashioned queue and he sported a neat little mustache accompanied by an air of general disinterest.

The one holding Emily was a very tall, slightly portly man in his forties. He set her down gently (if awkwardly) on a settee. She murmured and turned, eyes still closed. The man who carried her had a kind, square face that suggested a grave, trustworthy demeanor. "Is anyone hurt?" he asked, looking the rest of us over.

I looked, too, and blood caught my eye. Slipping out from Mr. Kent's grasp, I hurried to Oliver and Miss Grey, trying to assess their injuries.

Oliver shook his head stubbornly. "Those guards don't know how to punch," he said, though his cuts, bruises, and bloody nose said otherwise. "I just don't know what happened. . . ." He frowned hard and pushed at my hand, trying to slip through it. I frowned back. Perhaps he was just overtired.

Miss Grey's injuries were less severe, but I grasped her and Oliver's hands tightly. Their minor cuts and scrapes began to fade before our eyes, while Oliver's deeper cut started to close at a glacial place.

"Marvelous," the tall man murmured, eyes wide with reverence. He stepped in front of us. "Miss Wyndham, may I? I believe I can help."

Mr. Kent smiled over the man's shoulder. "Captain Goode here can raise the strength of your power."

"Oh yes, we didn't even introduce ourselves. How rude," he

said, removing his hat. He gave a small bow and offered his hand. "My name is Captain Simon Goode and my brother, Mr. Felix Redburn over there, is the one who brought us back here."

"I . . . thank you," I said, leaving one hand on Oliver and taking Captain Goode's proffered hand with my other. At his touch, a strange, calming glow filled my body from the center out. By the time I turned back to Oliver, his cut was fully healed. For one lovely moment everything seemed . . . safe.

I moved to Emily's side and touched her shoulder gently. She was breathing easily, and seemed to be in a deep sleep. Still, I kept my hand on her in case she had an injury I couldn't see.

Behind me, Captain Goode spoke again. "Please allow us to welcome you to the Society of Aberrations."

A chill cut through me, despite the warmth of power flowing through my veins. I whirled around to see Miss Grey's tight expression. She'd heard him, too.

"I know, Miss Wyndham," Mr. Kent put in hastily. "I thought the name impossible myself. But it's true: He really *is* called Captain Goode. Please go ahead and make what jests you will about it, but I believe I have covered most of them." His joking did not mask the fact that Mr. Kent was very aware of why I had gone so cold.

"The Society of Aberrations," I echoed, feeling numb. How *dare* Mr. Kent bring us to them? The mysterious society that had funded Dr. Beck's research on powered people. With their support, he'd kidnapped my sister and put her through his horrible experiments. Even if Sebastian and his fatal touch had unwittingly killed Rose in his attempt to save her, Dr. Beck and his patrons were the ones responsible for it.

We were better off back in the asylum.

Captain Goode's slow voice came in starts. "Is there . . .

something wrong? I don't know what we've done to alarm you . . . but I'm sure—"

"They've heard of us already," Mr. Redburn interrupted, sauntering around the edge of a large desk and hopping up onto it. "And it doesn't sound like they were pleasant things."

Captain Goode frowned. "I can assure you, we have only the best intentions."

"That's what you call working with a deranged murderer?" I asked. I turned to Mr. Kent, barely able to look at him. "And now you're working with them?"

His face fell slightly. "Miss Wyndham, I'm sorry, I just—you disappeared for almost a month. Miss Lodge claimed you were sick, which I knew was impossible. So when these gentlemen approached me to join, my first thought was to ask for help finding you. But I would not have agreed to work with them if they hadn't proven themselves. I asked them, in every way possible, of their motives."

Captain Goode was looking uncomfortable, shifting his weight in front of the fire. Mr. Redburn looked deeply unconcerned as he picked at his nails. Fine. Let them prove it once again.

I turned back to Mr. Kent. "Then they shouldn't mind if you ask them why they helped Dr. Beck kill my sister."

Captain Goode didn't flinch. In fact, he gave a regretful nod. "Of course. I can't begin to tell you how sorry we are about the fate that befell her—"

"Did you support Dr. Beck's experiments?" I interrupted, forcing away the bone-deep sorrow, not wanting an apology. Mr. Kent repeated my question.

"Yes, with funding," Captain Goode answered. "But we were unaware of the . . . horrible specifics."

"You didn't suspect anything despite the fact that his patients were very often dying?"

"Not at first," Captain Goode said, shaking his head. "He kept his research very private—he was worried another scientist would steal his discoveries. We believe he only told us about a select few of his patients."

Not good enough. Perhaps they were able to resist Mr. Kent. "And how do I know your power is even working on them?" I said to him.

He raised his brows for a moment before turning to Captain Goode. "Captain Goode, what is the first mildly embarrassing secret that comes to mind right now?"

"I find Miss Grey rather pretty," Captain Goode answered, pursing his lips in embarrassment.

"Kent." Mr. Redburn jumped off the desk. "I told you, the next time you decide to amuse yourself—"

"He is proving his power is working, Felix," Captain Goode cautioned, then gave Miss Grey a nod. "My apologies, Miss Grey."

Blushing, Miss Grey scrambled for a question to ask. "I—if you had known the specifics about Dr. Beck's experiments, would you have let it continue?"

Captain Goode shook his head vehemently when Mr. Kent asked the question for Miss Grey. "No. When we started to suspect the truth, someone was sent to watch over him."

"And that someone was Mr. Hale, yes?"

"It was."

"Then why was Mr. Hale terrified of the Society of Aberrations?" I put in. I remembered Mr. Hale's fear vividly. Because of Rose's charm power, he'd grown to love her while she was Dr. Beck's captive—so much so that he gave us the information to find her. But when we asked for his help to rescue her, his fear of the Society outweighed his love. He warned us to pray they didn't learn of our powers.

And here we were.

"Because Mr. Hale was a criminal and he knows we don't tolerate powers to be used in harmful ways," Captain Goode answered.

"When I first dreamed of powered people, I did see him steal from a man and drop him in front of a carriage," Miss Grey said, reminding me of her story. "I don't know that the man survived."

"I'm not surprised," Captain Goode said with a sigh. "We made it clear he would be put in a prison if he continued like that. We tried to set him on a good path, teaching him to use his power to help people. But it's been deeply disappointing that he's run away. We're trying to locate him again."

"Why?" Mr. Kent asked.

"His power to create portals can be incredibly useful or incredibly dangerous. We want to find him before he hurts anyone. We're concerned about what he's done to warrant running away. And what he might be doing next."

"But by all means, continue to throw more wild accusations at *us*," Mr. Redburn said, lighting a cigar. "Perhaps our rescue wasn't up to your standards?"

Captain Goode shook his head at his brother. "Your worries are perfectly reasonable," he reassured me. "I will answer anything you wish."

He seemed to have an answer for everything. Even though it should have assuaged my fears, it only bothered me more. Miss Grey and I had spent the last few months dreading the Society of Aberrations, trying to imagine how they could be worse than Dr. Beck and how they could scare Mr. Hale. We hadn't ever considered they'd rescue us and claim to be the good ones.

I gave Mr. Kent another question to relay. "Does the Society of Aberrations want to hurt us?"

"No, of course not," Captain Goode answered, looking a little wounded himself.

"Does the Society want to or have any plans to experiment on us?"

"No, we would never let Dr. Beck's work continue."

"Then what do you want from us?" Miss Grey asked.

"We want to invite you to join us," Captain Goode said after Mr. Kent played the parrot's role again. "Because I believe we want the same thing. There's a reason you risked your safety to rescue Miss Kane. Why you sought out Mr. Myles. You want to help others with these powers. Teach them, protect them, guide them. And you want to help the world with those people. Is that correct?"

It was. I had spent months trying to find some goal, some purpose that I could cling to in the dark haze of Rose's death. Miss Grey and I had talked at length and I finally believed that this was what Rose would have wanted. She would want me to help everyone I could.

If only they hadn't killed her.

"It is. . . ." Miss Grey was answering Captain Goode, looking torn between hope and caution.

"That is exactly what we do here. It's what we've been doing for more than two hundred years. As a quiet, rather secret branch of the British government."

At that we all paused. "You are part of the government?" I asked slowly.

"Indeed." Captain Goode nodded after Mr. Kent asked the question for me.

"But . . . Dr. Beck spoke as if these powers were new." I felt entirely confused and annoyed, as if I'd finally accepted that the sky was green, only to be told it was yellow.

"He didn't trust us with some of his findings, so we didn't trust him with some of ours. And the past didn't concern him because there wasn't proper scientific evidence. But I think the past concerns you."

"What do you mean?" Miss Grey asked.

"It would be easier if I showed you," Captain Goode said, gesturing to the door. "Felix, will you watch Miss Kane?"

"Gladly," he responded, blowing out a puff of smoke. "She's the most appreciative of the lot." He gave his brother a mock salute and threw himself onto a settee across from Emily. She was still breathing easily, a slight huff as she exhaled, and I cautiously left the room, Mr. Kent giving me a reassuring nod.

We followed Captain Goode up a set of stairs near the front of the building. Miss Grey was stepping neatly at Captain Goode's side, cocking her ear up to him as he pointed out various pieces of interesting artwork. Oliver kept testing his power, shoving at the walls, but it seemed to have disappeared entirely. He grew more and more frustrated as we continued the tour.

I did not know what to think. The Society of Aberrations was actually a part of our government? It made no sense at all, but how could the two men lie with Mr. Kent here to test their responses? I took a deep breath, trying to calm myself, to think rationally. I glanced around and at first there didn't seem to be anything revelatory about the place. It looked much like other societies I'd visited before, furnished as a cozy home away from home, with paintings, sculptures, and significant items to display the Society's illustrious members, accomplishments, and history.

Except, as I peered closer at a lovely portrait, vibrant against the dark paneling, I realized that the young woman featured wasn't contemplating a book of poetry or sighing at her vanity—she was concentrating on a ball of fire held between her hands. Farther down the passage, a scene that could be illustrating *The Tempest*: an old man reaching at a stormy sky swirling above him. Even in a small frame, a young man posed next to a simple vase full of flowers had something strange and unique featured—all the flowers seemed to be encased in a layer of gold.

"I would much prefer that gent's talent," Mr. Kent said from behind me, his voice warm in my ear. A few strands of hair fell over his brow as I turned and saw him smiling confidently. He offered his arm and I took it, continuing down the gallery watching the styles of artwork and the fashions portrayed change with the times.

"I haven't forgiven you yet," I said.

"I'm looking forward to convincing you," he responded with a soft chuckle.

Finally, we passed through the seventeenth-century works and found ourselves in the main foyer of the building. Captain Goode stopped in the center of the room and gestured up above the open stairs to a large portrait of a domineering man in a splendid cape and jaunty hat. It even had a feather.

"That is Jonathan Reed," he said. "He founded the Society of Aberrations in 1688 after assisting King William and Queen Mary. He and the three other original members were instrumental in the Revolution and were asked to work together as a special branch for the King and Queen.

"There was a woman who could fly, a man with extraordinary speed, and another like me, who could affect the levels of their abilities."

I stared in wonder at Mr. Reed's fading portrait, though there didn't seem to be anything visibly remarkable about him like the other subjects. "And what was his power?" I asked.

"The same as Miss Grey's. He could dream of powered people. And as the first known person born with powers, he was the one to bring the Society together."

He gestured to another wall of the foyer that displayed three more portraits. "And the other founders had powers vital to its growth. Without their flyer, they wouldn't have been able to reach new recruits. Without their runner, they wouldn't have been able to grow so quickly. And without their enhancer, they wouldn't have been able to discover the extraordinary limits of these abilities. But together, they were able to build a Society invaluable to our country. We would like you to join us. You would, in a sense, act as British agents."

Perhaps I had never really woken up this morning.

"I think he's trying to tell you that you are part of a long-lost prophecy, Miss Grey," Mr. Kent remarked.

"A prophecy would make matters much easier," Captain Goode said with a chuckle. "I simply try to understand the powers from a practical perspective, like our good founders did. Without the evolutionary theories we have now, they approached the question from the other side. They believed they were given these measures of power for a specific purpose. That there was a reason Jonathan Reed was born to one of our finest generals of the time. Our powers were meant to be used in service of the British Empire and, by extension, the rest of the world."

He led us out of the foyer in a different direction. One wall contained more portraits, while the other had doors leading to lounges, lecture rooms, and training rooms—each one unique in its own way. One contained targets, another held weaponry and hay-stuffed dummies, and there was even one with a long sequence of obstacles that resembled a steeplechase.

"Though we help the British Empire, the Society is dedicated to those with powers. We offer training to young women and men like Mr. Myles who are still developing their abilities," Captain Goode said, gesturing to the rooms. "We want everyone to find the full expression of their power." Oliver looked up at that, a bit of hope and eagerness softening the anger stoked by his failing power.

"Miss Wyndham, your healing works on all people, yes?" Captain Goode continued.

"As far as I know," I said in a clipped tone, still unable to believe this was the paradise for powered people that he would have us think.

"Which makes it rather easy for you to determine your purpose. You heal anyone who is sick or injured. Simple and pure. But, Miss Grey, you only dream of people with powers, yes?"

I shook my head at her, asking her not to tell them the truth, but Miss Grey paid me no mind, looking at Captain Goode as though he might know the answer to all her questions. "Yes."

"Then your purpose is complicated, much like mine." He gave her a small smile and she returned it. "Since my power allows me to alter the strength of another's, it rather limits my usefulness. Same, too, for my brother, Mr. Redburn. He hasn't always had the same power as Mr. Hale. His true power is the ability to copy someone else's power and hold it until he chooses to take another. It's useful now that he's part of the Society, but when our powers first developed, we weren't even aware we had them. It took many years to discover, as our powers depend entirely on other people with these extraordinary abilities.

"Which is why I believe in the Society of Aberrations. The

reason any society exists is for like-minded people to exchange and share their ideas for the betterment of all. Here, we simply do the same with our powers in service of our country. With my help, Mr. Kent can walk into a room and the truth will be spoken whenever anyone opens their mouth. Miss Wyndham, imagine healing anything in seconds if I doubled, tripled your healing abilities. How quickly you could rescue someone like Miss Kane if you had Mr. Redburn to take you across the world? What if I made your powers more stable, Mr. Myles? And as for you, Miss Grey, what if I said you could dream of specific people and target certain areas to find those in need of our help?"

I could see Miss Grey on the verge of joining already. They seemed to share the same conviction that their powers determined their destiny and duty. That we were chosen for a reason. There was a certain appeal, a comfort in believing that. A comfort I still couldn't quite feel, despite this seemingly benign tour.

"Mr. Kent, can you ask Captain Goode, if the Society of Aberrations is so noble and good, why all the secrecy?"

Mr. Kent repeated the question.

"For the sake of our safety—and the Empire's," Captain Goode answered. "Secrecy isn't always hiding something terrible. Can you imagine if it ever became public knowledge? It would be a witch hunt. It's the same reason you've decided to keep your own power a secret. It's why our current head is anonymous. Power begets danger. There would be no returning to any sort of normal life, even if we weren't persecuted."

I stopped short. "You don't even know who is in charge of the entire operation?" I asked, shooting Mr. Kent a look.

"I don't." Captain Goode answered the repeated question calmly. "And that is why everything has run smoothly for so long. Our head chooses his or her"—he smiled at Miss Grey—"successor by merit, not by title or wealth. It ensures the best of us is put in charge, but avoids the conflicts and unpleasantness that might arise from our more aristocratic members disputing the orders of someone they deem too lowborn. With the head anonymous, there're no power struggles or arguments about the Society's direction. Everyone works together to protect our country and one another because our head is one of us. Our members follow the directives, secure in the knowledge that we are moving forward and doing what's best for our Society."

We ended up back in the study room where we started. Mr. Redburn was dozing on the couch across from Emily, who had not moved beyond slinging an arm across her face. When had she last been in a warm room?

"What we're offering you and what we're asking of you are one and the same," Captain Goode said, smiling. "We want to keep building this society and we want your help. You want to heal the sick and injured, Miss Wyndham, and we want to help you do that efficiently, without drawing unwanted attention to yourself. You want to find other gifted people, Miss Grey, and we want to help you do that safely. And Mr. Myles, we'd like to offer our resources and teaching so you can better control your powers and assist us all in the future. It's as simple as that."

Silence greeted him as we looked at one another.

Mr. Kent turned to address the room. "Who here has another question for the Society?"

I had none. Neither did Miss Grey, Oliver, nor the sleeping Emily. But a muffled voice from the other end of the room, behind the curtains, did.

"I do! I mean . . . There's no one here—ahhh!"

Mr. Redburn jumped to his feet and flicked a hand out, sending a portal to open below the spy and drop her onto the rug right in front of us.

"Who are you—" Mr. Redburn's bark was cut off.

"Kit?" Mr. Kent exclaimed. "How on earth did you get here?"

Laura Kent, Mr. Kent's fifteen-year-old sister, looked up at us sheepishly, a tangle of brown hair, black skirts, and red curtains. "By being sneaky. I followed you here when you said you were going to find Evelyn and then I fell asleep and—oh! Evelyn!"

She sprang to her feet, enveloping me in a big hug. "Nicky told me about your amazing powers! I have so many questions! Can you heal broken hearts? Or love sickness? Oh, and I have so much to tell you! You've missed so many scandalous rumors!"

"And you're going to be one of them," Mr. Kent said, unlatching Laura from my person. "What made you think this was a good idea?"

Captain Goode shifted uncomfortably. "Mr. Kent, this is a breach of our—" But Laura was still talking.

"You did!" Laura whined. "When you were making the list of your favorite things about Evelyn, you said you admired her ability to sneak out!"

"Kit, you know not to listen to me!" Mr. Kent scolded. "I taught you better than that."

Laura crossed her arms and held her head up defiantly. "Well, if I had stayed home, then there wouldn't have been anyone here to ask the most important question."

"What is the most important question?" I asked, floundering as one often did under the assault of energy that was Laura Kent.

"You haven't even asked them if the Society is evil!" Laura said solemnly, shaking her head at our misstep.

"Why, young lady—" Captain Goode began.

"It's true!" Laura yelped.

Mr. Kent couldn't help but be amused despite his anger. "Captain Goode, is the Society of Aberrations evil?"

"No," he said, looking irritated before he relented. "Though to be fair, I don't think an evil organization would answer yes to that."

As absurd as Laura's question was, she was right to be blunt. His slick answers had not stopped me from feeling uneasy.

"Mr. Kent, we will discuss your sister in private. Miss Grey? Miss Wyndham? What will it be? Mr. Myles, you are welcome to stay here and learn to control that power of yours." He looked calm, confident, but with no aura of the zealot that Dr. Beck had possessed. He simply sounded like he wanted to help.

I looked around the room, thinking quickly, trying to figure out why I was still so unsure. Everything sounded perfect; we would be serving our country, and with my assistance and Miss Grey's, I could only imagine how much it would grow, how much we could do.

But maybe it was the secrecy, maybe it was the fact that I simply wasn't in control, maybe it was the connection to Dr. Beck, but it still didn't feel right, no matter how truthfully Captain Goode answered all our questions. I opened my mouth to decline.

"We are in your debt, Captain Goode. But more than that, I am so looking forward to working with you," Miss Grey said quickly, leaving me with my mouth half-open.

"Miss Grey, I am so pleased. We will find you your own abode, of course, as befits a lady of your status, but we will be spending much time together here, I am sure."

Miss Grey pinked slightly at that, but nodded regally, as though she were regularly gifted with houses.

"Mr. Myles?" Captain Goode walked over to Oliver and placed his hand on his shoulder. "Go ahead, try to slip through the wall now."

Oliver looked at him suspiciously, but put his hand up to the wall. He immediately slid through and turned to Captain Goode.

"How'd you do that?" Oliver demanded, shifting back from the older man. I couldn't help but smile. Oliver and his trust were not easily won. It had taken us months.

"Your power is still unstable, given your age. We can help you learn how to control it. You'll have plenty of training, a warm bed, and classmates your age here at the Society."

Oliver looked at all of us in turn.

"Oliver," I said, hoping to warn him off.

"Fine. I want to get better," he said, rough and determined. "I don't like getting stuck."

"Wonderful." Captain Goode smiled heartily and reached out his hand for Oliver's.

"But I'm right out of here if anything seems fishy," the boy said, crossing his arms, ignoring the proffered hand.

I felt suddenly panicky. Had I no one left who would believe that this was wrong?

A shriek rang out and for a second I wondered if it was me. But Emily Kane was sitting up on the settee, looking around wildly, her pale, thin hands held out in front of her defensively.

Mr. Redburn backed away slowly, muttering, "So, the mad one lives."

Miss Grey hurried over to the whimpering girl. "Emily, it's all right—" she began.

"No! The ghosts! They're going to hurt us!" Emily moaned, flinching and pointing at Oliver.

"It is quite all right, dear, they won't—oof!" Miss Grey gasped as she was suddenly shuttled to the wall. Captain Goode went to help her up.

"No, no, no!" Emily stood on the settee and began shouting at the air, "Stop it, ghosts! *Stop!*"

"Ghosts?" Laura marched over to Emily. "There are ghosts?"

Emily bit her lip, trying to hold back a sob. She nodded, wringing her hands, eyes darting. "They're everywhere."

"And you can talk to them?" Laura asked, trying to follow Emily's eyes.

"They—they don't always listen to me, though." Emily looked at her shyly, sadly. "I just want them to leave me alone."

Laura jumped up next to her on the settee. "It's marvelous!" Emily shrank back a bit, but Laura continued. "What a wonderful power! That might even be better than Evelyn's!"

"Actually, Miss Kent, Emily Kane has the power of telekinesis," Captain Goode put in. Both Miss Grey and I hushed him without turning away from the two girls. Laura was now pointing around the room, asking if there were various ghosts. Emily actually giggled!

Mr. Redburn looked at his brother. "Not sure we can keep that one. Seems batty."

"She is not!" I snapped. "She is distraught because she was kept in a dank cell for ages, a place she should never have been."

"Sounds like my stepmother's house," Mr. Kent put in.

"Oh! Do you think you could come to my house? I feel *sure* that we have plenty of ghosts you can talk to!" Laura crowed.

Emily looked at her hesitantly, through long falls of hair.

"She should stay here. I will assign her a guard. . . ." Captain Goode was mainly talking to himself at this point.

"I don't like this place." Emily was shaking as though she were only barely holding on to her control. The objects in the room rattled with her.

"Nicky! No, she *must* come home with us!" Laura had of course picked up on the one pertinent part of our conversation and leaped off the settee. "She is simply wonderful and I will never forgive you if you make her stay here instead of with me!"

Laura immediately ran back and took her new friend's hand. "Emily, you and I will have such fun together, only think on it!"

Emily was looking rather longingly at the idea of being with the one person here who didn't seem to frighten her. The rattling quieted as she calmed some.

I turned to Mr. Kent. "Do you suppose you could convince your stepmother to take her in?"

He smirked. "Oh, I would love to see what that woman would make of Miss Kane. It's a good plan—clearly the two girls will get along famously."

Captain Goode, however, was frowning at us. "We believe Miss Kane needs the aid and structure of the Society—"

"No!" Laura yelped, and Emily whimpered.

"It appears, Captain Goode, that neither of us will be joining you," I said, crossing my arms.

He sighed. "I am sorry to hear that, Miss Wyndham. Is there nothing we can say to convince you?"

I looked around the room, at Miss Grey, who was happy to have found kindred spirits; at Oliver, who could learn to control his power; at Mr. Kent, who had asked every question I could think of; at the two girls, who were now clutching each other's hands on the settee.

It could be a good place.

It could be everything we hoped for.

It could be our purpose.

But I was still unconvinced.

"I'm sorry, I cannot accept your offer."

Chapter 3

Mae Lodge's house looked as it always did. Sturdy, comfortable, inviting. A peaceful melody from the drawing room pianoforte filled the house and my body with a much-needed calm after the long night.

Mr. Kent had escorted me to Mae's before taking Laura and Emily to his stepmother's home, a place I was certainly not welcome. Emily and Laura had already decided that they were the best of friends and I felt better knowing that Emily was with someone who could raise her spirits. I was less comfortable about Miss Grey and Oliver's decision to join the Society, but at the very least we weren't stuck in an asylum.

Upon my entrance to Mae's drawing room, the music cut out abruptly. "Evelyn!" she said, sliding off the piano bench and embracing me at the doorway, enveloping me with striped pink silk and warm, easy goodwill.

"If I'd known you'd stop playing that beautiful piece, I would have found a way to sneak in through the window," I told her, trying for levity.

"Oh, I just do it to pass the time," she said with a sad smile. "You must be exhausted. Please sit, drink some tea, and rest. How were your travels?"

"Lovely, very well . . ." I started as she ushered me into a plush chair and set a cup of tea in my hand before I could finish a sentence. *Right. Explanations.* "I, uh—"

"I'm glad to hear it," she cut in, sitting across from me with a cup of her own. "Please don't feel obligated to tell me more than you're comfortable saying."

Even after living with her for the two months where I was not . . . the *easiest* houseguest, I still wasn't quite used to her limitless patience. "You don't wish to know what I was doing, mysteriously traveling to another country?"

She turned her gray eyes to meet mine. "I suspect it's rather important work, which leads me to believe that London society would have objections and a little discretion is necessary. I wouldn't want to cause any more trouble."

I nodded gratefully. "You know I would like nothing more than to take you into my confidence."

She smiled again. "It's quite all right. I enjoy imagining you traveling all over. I like to think you're helping to heal people, your talents in great demand by dashing princes and sheiks. It's rather exciting in my head."

"Yes, better not spoil that with the less-exciting truth," I said, forcing a smile. Her understanding, however, only made me feel worse. I couldn't help but wish I could share my secrets with her. Unload my haphazardly packed thoughts and worries. Treat her like the dear friend that she was. But even if I were to tell her only of *my* power, it opened up too many doors. She was far too perceptive. I could imagine her wondering about everyone else around her, figuring out Sebastian's power, and even guessing that he was involved in her brother's death. And his secrets were not mine to tell.

It was better to leave her with the fantasy.

"I did feel slightly guilty telling everyone who called that you were indisposed," Mae said, a touch of worry in her voice.

"I promise I was ill whenever you said it," I said, and finally took a sip of the tea. It was exactly as I liked it: strong, cut with a generous pour of milk and a half spoonful of sugar. As I watched Mae pouring more dark streams of fragrant tea into her cup, I appreciated the homey familiarity and a kind, smiling friend who did not know or care that I had an inhuman ability. For one crystalline moment, it was almost as if there were no such things as extraordinary powers or hideous asylums or secret societies or dead sisters.

"Tell me, what have you been up to since my departure? Other than spreading rumors of my 'illness'?" I asked, letting go of the tempting notion that I could tell Mae all my worries. She did not deserve that burden.

"Nothing as interesting as nursing royalty back to health." She smiled. "There has been little to disrupt our days since the New Year began." It was said placidly enough, but there was a tension that belied her words.

"However, there have been some . . . developments since your departure."

My heart raced slightly, a *dum-DUM, dum-DUM, dum-DUM* that felt like a miniature horse trotting along my chest. Mae's pewter eyes gave away nothing. Was it news of Sebastian?

"Your parents are in town," she said. "They asked me to contact them the second you are well."

My heart's premature gallop began to slow again. My parents. I had grown hard since the funeral, thinking about them as little as possible, spending the holidays with Mae and her family, choosing to pretend I had no home.

How could I forgive them when their negligence and care for

appearances had led to Rose's death? I stood up and began walking the length of the Lodges' drawing room. Sunlight streamed in through the gauzy curtains but I barely noticed. Mae studiously stared at a painting on the faded wallpaper across the room, giving me time to collect my thoughts.

"You told them I was sick?"

"Yes." Mae looked grave, for one moment reminding me of Rose's sweet seriousness. "However, it has been a number of days now, and your mother wants to see you. I said it was infectious but not life-threatening, but I don't think the excuse will last much longer."

"Oh, botheration and damnation—pardon me." I put a hand to my eyes, squeezing the pressure from my temples. "There is nothing for it, then. Do you know if they are staying with my aunt and uncle?"

"Your mother left a card. It appears they have let a London residence."

She went to a silver bowl on the marble-topped side table and pulled out a small stack of letters. Most of them were from Robert, still on a poetic mourning trip around the Continent. But on top was a creamy linen card from my mother.

Lady Wyndham, 43 Belgrave Square. My eyes couldn't help bulging at the ever-so-fashionable address. There was no way they could afford this extravagance after all that talk of debt.

"It . . . exhausts me even thinking of seeing them. I don't know what to say. Or how to say it," I murmured.

"You don't need to say anything," Mae replied, her sharp eyes following as I trod the silk rug. "I understand that there are many painful reminders there. But they are your family. They lost her, too."

I sat down hard on the settee near Mae. As much as I wished

to, it was hard to dismiss her advice. She'd been through this with her own family.

Though her parents had not betrayed her the way mine had betrayed Rose and me.

"Well. It appears I shall no longer be intruding upon your hospitality."

She gave me a small, true smile. "You have always been and will continue to be welcome to intrude. Oh! I almost forgot! I wanted to give you this, in case you missed them in your travels."

She walked over to a small table next to the piano and picked up what looked like a scrapbook.

"I collected as many as I could," she said with a small wink, handing me the book. I gave her a hug in return, promising to call soon. She rang for Cushing, and the poor servants quickly undid everything they'd done in getting me settled. As I made my way back outside, already dreading the journey to my family's new address, I heard Mae resume playing the same melancholy tune that had welcomed me inside.

Once I was in the carriage, I opened the scrapbook and felt my heart swell at the kind gesture. Mae had cut out and compiled the last two weeks' worth of Agony Columns from *The London Times* I had missed.

During my months with her, when my lying in bed and crying had become worrying, a very concerned Mae had tried to distract me with the collection of sad and mysterious advertisements from strangers. Brothers would write in pleas to their runaway sisters to return home. A secretive girl would write to her beau to arrange a romantic tryst. A lovestruck pedestrian would describe the exact time and location of when he met the eyes of a beautiful stranger, in the hopes she would see the note and feel similarly. I started out reading these half stories for the mutual misery, to see all the other people desperately reaching out with their hopeless problems. But somewhere along the way, I found myself appreciating the lack of resolutions. That way I could imagine my own happy conclusions. Mae had sometimes sat with me, laughing as we created fantastical endings to the most hopeless of situations.

I sometimes wondered if Mae read them in the hopes of finding a note from Sebastian.

We hadn't said his name once that entire conversation, but after everything she'd said about my mysterious travels and the importance of home, I knew he'd been on her mind the whole time. She was waiting for her fiancé to return, but from the look in his eyes the last time I saw him, I feared he might still be running. I tried to pretend that the thought didn't bring me pain. But it did. Losing Rose was hard enough. But I had lost the fragile, tentative thing that had grown between Sebastian and myself as well.

I sighed, leaning against the carriage seat. Perhaps I should take out a full-page advertisement that read: TO SEBASTIAN BRADDOCK: COME BACK, YOU BROODING FOOL.

The moment I stepped into my parents' grand townhouse, I knew I had made a mistake coming here. Despite everything we'd been through, despite everything my mother had said about our dire straits, despite her black mourning garb, she pleasantly sat in the bright morning room with guests, as if all were well.

"Evelyn! We were just talking about you," Mother said, her voice hitting that strident, cheery note that had always grated on me so. "You remember the Earl of Atherton, yes? And his mother, Lady Atherton?"

Across from her, a thin, angular young man stood up, eyeing me down his long nose, which was a feat, given that he was about my own height. A shock of springy blond hair flopped artfully over his forehead. As he bowed, I was strongly reminded of a finicky, high-strung lady's mare.

Next to him sat a familiar woman who had the same blond hair (though hers had lost some luster), the same thin-boned, long nose, and the same blue eyes, except hers were observing me with curiosity.

I made my curtsy, inwardly fuming. One daughter dead, the other "sick," and my mother still cared more about society. Of course, she would surely defend her actions with the fact that Lord Atherton was a young, eligible earl and his mother was one of the most respected matrons in London society.

Which begged another question: Why would they deign to be here? Hadn't Miss Verinder ruined my reputation completely these last few months? Even before that, we were not at such a level that Lady Atherton would pay us any notice. We had not traveled in the same sphere.

"I did not know you were acquainted," I said, taking a seat to the side of my mother.

"A recent friendship," Mother answered. Her eyes were bright and hard and giddy, as though she were perhaps drunk. She smelled of a cloying perfume that I had never noticed before. "Lady Atherton called to welcome us to the neighborhood."

"As my late husband said, 'life would be utterly lifeless without a friend.'" Lady Atherton paused significantly, nodding archly at me. "He always came up with such clever sayings."

Apparently, Lady Atherton had been married to Cicero. I was about to ask her about life during the Roman Republic, but her son spoke up.

"Miss Wyndham. You have been unwell. The weather has been cold lately." Lord Atherton sniffed as he made his proclamation.

Responding to such statements, which are not actual questions or inquiries of concern, is always difficult.

"Indeed, thank you, Lord Atherton. I am feeling fully myself again."

"Wonderful," Lady Atherton said. "We were just discussing the coming Little Season."

As if the Season weren't interminable enough, someone had decided there should be a two-month prelude. While most of the ton was still out of town, the more political families returned for the reopening of Parliament. "It's a shame to miss it," I said, beginning to wonder if I should perhaps panic.

"Well, you shall have more luck this year."

Mother gave her a darting glance. "With your kind offer, I am sure she will."

Both women smiled and I could swear the bones in my corset knitted themselves tighter.

"Offer?" I croaked.

"Lady Atherton has generously suggested she be your companion for the Little Season, as your father and I will still be in mourning."

Yes, definitely time to panic.

Lady Atherton continued before I could refuse. "Yes, the first step, Lady Wyndham, will be to take your daughter to my modiste. She's extremely exclusive. I have quite the list, Miss Wyndham. You'll need seven day dresses, and another eight should suffice for the evening gowns, with, of course, handkerchiefs, slippers, a variety of hats with trimmings—that should keep you through the next three months, but we will certainly need warmer-weather additions before the spring."

Mother bobbed her head furiously throughout, while somehow

managing to pour our guests another cup of tea. "As always, your help is invaluable."

"With the right hairstyle, neckline, and colors, we will draw everyone's eyes to her more pleasing features." Lady Atherton paused to sip her tea.

I seized the moment of silence. "I really don't think I am up to this yet, not so soon after my sister passed."

Lord Atherton blanched, looking deeply affronted at my boldness.

But Lady Atherton paused, fixing me with a simpering smile. "Indeed, it is so hard. Still, I am sure your sister would want you to find happiness!"

I refused to let the matter go, despite the cake my mother slid in front of me for appeasement. "I am truly not—"

"I do not mean to be forward," Lady Atherton interrupted. "But your reputation is still shaky. You have my deepest condolences, but we must reintroduce you to society and as soon as possible. The late Lord Atherton had a saying, 'Lost time is never found again.'"

I would give up cake if that saying was coined by Lord Atherton.

She beamed proudly at my mother. "It will be helpful, of course, with my chaperonage. We will call on many of my acquaintances and make a statement, of sorts. A ball, just before the Season begins in full, will strike the perfect chord."

I had to put my fork down, unable to take another bite of the cake. "We are all still very much in mourning. I don't think London society would approve of breaking such a custom."

Lady Atherton looked at least somewhat annoyed and Lord Atherton was staring at me as though I had just suggested that I run through the streets in my chemise. But still, his mother had an answer ready. "I believe you are nearly at the end of your mourning period, Miss Wyndham. And as for you, Lady Wyndham, you are very much in the same spot I was when my dear husband left us five years ago, and when I ended my mourning period early, it was regarded as brave, not heartless. It's unhealthy to mourn for so long. A ball, I think, held here in three weeks' time, with me as your guide, of course—it should be just right."

"Indeed, three weeks is exactly right," Lord Atherton put in, doing a remarkable impression of an etiquette book.

"Splendid," Mother said, and my stomach tied itself in further knots at the idea.

"Three weeks, then," Lady Atherton continued. "In the meantime, we shall take full advantage of the Little Season and you will make many new acquaintances as families return to town. By the ball, you and my son will be all anyone is talking about." Lady Atherton gave her son a slight smile at that.

Was this . . . a matchmaking? But no, he looked uninterested at best and fully disgusted at worst. He faced his tea as though it were a challenge to be withstood and only gave his mother a polite grimace. Surely not a man looking to marry?

And then I noticed the small cake that still sat uneaten next to him. And another in front of his mother. That was the last straw. I fully disliked them. How dare they leave perfectly good cake untouched?

I cleared my throat, wanting to be done with this, shake her loose. "What I never quite understand about the Season, though, is why does anyone want to get married? It seems to me very much like a slightly more pleasant prison, except the guard never changes."

Lord Atherton looked as if he might spit out his tea.

Lady Atherton simply sighed and stood up. "Miss Wyndham, you are tired and still recovering. We will leave you to rest. Lady

Wyndham, thank you for the pleasant visit. We will speak tomorrow about our shopping expedition."

Lord Atherton gave a bow and followed his mother out of the room.

Leaving me alone with my mother, glaring burning holes through me. "Well. I see little has changed." She walked to the door and rang the bell before turning back to me. "Have you forgotten what little civility you used to have, Evelyn? Lord Atherton is an earl and—"

A knock at the door came and cut my mother off. "Yes?" she said impatiently, and Pretton immediately appeared.

"Please ask Sir Philip to join us," she said, calling for my father. I barely managed to contain myself until Pretton left.

"Where is *your* civility? It hasn't even been three months and you're talking about marriage and the Season like everything is perfectly fine? Like Rose didn't—"

"I am trying to move forward and help you, Evelyn," she interrupted, her jaw tight. "I can't just wander around an empty house mourning her forever."

I didn't expect her to. That wasn't why I was angry with her. It was the fact that it didn't seem to have changed her at all. That she didn't seem to hold herself at all responsible. That she didn't bother to let Rose's death affect her in any way.

"You didn't need to come to London," I said. "How can we afford this house? You said there was no money left."

"Evelyn." My father appeared at the doorway. He seemed to have expanded as Mother hollowed. Crumbs from his breakfast still stuck to his mustache, which seemed somehow wilted against his fattened cheeks.

"Hello, Father," I said stiffly. He awkwardly approached and gave me a gentle hug. The smell of alcohol enveloped me.

Mother sighed. "Evelyn has just been quite rude to Lady Atherton."

He frowned as he stepped back. "Lady Atherton is not someone to make an enemy of."

"She would never have paid us any mind before," I said. "How did we come by this wealth?" I repeated.

"Your father's accountant. He discovered some investment your father had made that they both forgot about, it seems." Mother and Father exchanged a glance.

I stared, too flabbergasted to readily explode. "So . . . After Rose disappeared, after you told me that we had no money and that our reputations were all we had left, after you decided to do nothing to help find Rose in order to avoid a scandal, after Rose *died*—now you're telling me we actually had money and no one knew about it?"

She nodded, stiffening every time I said Rose's name. Father was looking vacantly across the room and I felt sure he was no longer listening. I wanted to keep repeating her name, to force their attention to me. But I had been awake too long and this took the last shred of energy out of me.

"Excuse me, the inimitable Lady Atherton suggested I rest." I shouldered past my mother, tired and furious and too tired to be furious.

"We are glad you are home," my father mumbled behind me.

I didn't turn around, just wound my way up the stairs, passing room after room. My parents had tried to move to this new house and fill it with all the heavy furnishings, paintings, tapestries, silk tassels, intricate fire screens, doorplates—fill it to the very limit so it wouldn't seem like anything was missing, so there wouldn't be that void. But it only made the problem more apparent. The meticulously arranged rooms were strained, artificial attempts at normalcy. The crowded furnishings looked like they were hiding something.

Or perhaps it was me. Perhaps grief was my companion now, to be dragged behind me as intrusive and burdensome as a heavy trunk.

The silent maid showed me into my room and I put my crushed hat down on the vanity, flinching, as usual, at my reflection. Haunted, bloodshot eyes peered suspiciously at me, blue-black crescents punched below, stark against my overly pale skin. Before, I thought myself capable of disguising my emotions, careful to be sure the world didn't discern my true self with ease. But the loss of Rose was written into every crease of my skin, every part of my body. Some days my right hand trembled ceaselessly. Other times my head pounded. Sometimes I woke in the middle of the night gasping for air, as if I had tried to stop breathing in my dreams.

But as miserable as it was, there was some comfort in the physicalization of my heartache. It almost seemed Rose was still here, pressing against me, refusing to let me go and forget her. As I ached my way into bed today, it wasn't just one part. I could feel it in every bone. She followed me to bed, curled up beside me, and hugged me tight until I fell into my dreams, where I saved her, over and over again.

Chapter 4

"Evelyn Margaret Wyndham! Wake up! I know you're here!"

The faint sound of footsteps stomping up the stairs vibrated into my room.

"Evelyn!" the voice continued yelling. "Show yourself this instant!"

Oh dear. She sounded angry. I shoved my head back under my pillow.

A distant door opened and slammed.

"Please, miss, I—if you wait downstairs—" a soft voice protested.

Another door opened and slammed. The footsteps grew louder, closer. My door flew open.

"There you are," I heard the intruder sweetly say. "Thank you, Pretton." And then the door closed.

A bounce shook the bed as the girl jumped next to me and yanked the pillow off my face. I squinted up at her chestnut hair, already falling out of its untidy chignon; the spectacles perched crookedly on her nose; the sprinkling of freckles and the slightly chipped front tooth that only made her wide grin even more endearing.

"I missed you!" Catherine Harding half shouted, grabbing me and hugging me.

"Mrrpph," I said back, but I returned the hug with equal enthusiasm. I had missed my best friend, too.

She reared back, adjusting her spectacles. "Do you know the number of letters I've sent to you in the past three months?"

"Um," I responded, very articulately.

"Thirteen. You received thirteen letters, ignored your best friend thirteen times, and threw away thirteen unanswered letters."

Too many reasons filled my head and I didn't quite know how to say them all. It was rather similar to the feeling I got every time I considered writing her.

"I just . . . ," I finally said.

"I know." She grabbed my hand and leaned against the headboard next to me.

"I couldn't sit at a desk and write a letter about it."

"I know."

"There was a lot . . . happening."

"You shouldn't have had to deal with her loss all by yourself." She squeezed harder and I tried not to cry. I just nodded as she continued.

"It's unfair and horrible and I'm so mad for you." She was almost crushing my hand now but it was exactly what I needed and I gripped back, hard. She didn't break down crying or offer platitudes or tell me there was a plan for everyone or say that Rose was in a better place. Instead, she looked fiercely ahead, jaw set, ready to fight through my pain with me. I took a few slow, deep breaths.

"Chocolate?" she asked suddenly.

"Chocolate," I confirmed.

I got up, pulled on my wrapper, and called for my maid.

"Now. Tell me everything. Who is Miss Lodge and why were you staying with her for so long?"

"I . . . There's a lot to explain," I said.

As I thought about how to begin, I finally understood why Sebastian had been so awkward when he tried to explain everything about these powers to me. It was a ridiculous thing to tell someone. With her pragmatic nature, there was only one way to convince Catherine. The same way I had been convinced.

"Catherine, I am going to show you something very strange. You must promise not to scream."

Her round eyes narrowed. "I never scream."

I padded over to my writing desk and took up a letter opener, shiny and new and quite sharp. I sliced it across my index finger. I thought it a small slit but there seemed to be enough blood to alarm Catherine, as she gasped and came over.

"Evelyn! Why would you do that?" She pulled out her handkerchief and hurriedly grabbed for my finger, but I pulled away.

"Just watch," I said, taking a moment before wiping the blood off and showing her the healed finger.

She stared at it, frowning, at a loss for words, then searched my eyes. "Are you playing a trick on me?"

I shook my head and put the letter opener down. "No trick. No joke. I know this sounds utterly mad, but while I was trying to—to find Rose, these few months past, I discovered something else. I can heal any wound, any illness in me or others."

Catherine stared hard at me, looking for a laugh that wasn't there. "Evelyn, I'm sorry, but you must be mistaken; this is impossible."

"You try doing it to me," I said, handing her the letter opener, which she reluctantly took while protesting.

"This is silly—"

I grasped her hand with the letter opener, pressed down hard, and dragged it across my palm. Blood dribbled out onto the rug and I winced more at the mess than the light stinging. I was getting better with pain. I'd tested my healing quite enough these last months.

With a gasp, Catherine dropped the letter opener and fumbled again for her handkerchief.

I stepped out of her reach and simply wiped away the blood so she could better see the miraculous healing.

"This sort of cut usually takes a few seconds," I said. "Just watch."

She did. She watched as the blood flow ebbed and my torn skin gradually closed and stitched itself back together. Besides the faint bloodstain, there was no sign my hand had even been cut.

"Good morning, miss." A knock came from the door—my maid. I shoved my hand behind me and positioned my feet over the bloodstains.

"Come in," I called, eyeing Catherine warily as she stared into nothing with a rather dazed expression.

Lucy opened the door and set down a tray. A long moment of silence reigned as she turned, curtsied, and shut the door. I decided to let Catherine continue her contemplation as I wiped the rest of the blood onto my handkerchief and poured the steaming chocolate into the two cups the maid had left.

I almost moaned after the first sip. If my parents *were* going to use their new wealth, I had to be glad for their cook.

Catherine didn't move for a long while. Then she pinched herself. "I . . . am having a lot of thoughts and questions right now."

"I imagine you must be." I poured myself another cup and led her to the chairs in front of the fire. "I will tell you everything. First, have you ever heard of something called 'saltation'?"

And so I explained. The theory that these powers were a jump in evolution. Dr. Beck, his associates. The people—good and bad—who had helped me. Mr. Braddock and Miss Lodge.

Catherine began to pace the room as I haltingly finished explaining Rose's death. She poured me another cup of chocolate and sat next to my chair, on the floor, as I told her about Belgium, Emily Kane, and the Society of Aberrations.

As if on cue, a slight crackling sounded and a piece of paper appeared in my hand. I opened my palm and Catherine gasped.

"This must be from them—our rescuers from the asylum," I murmured to her. I unfolded the note to read the short line. *We would be so grateful for your assistance, Miss Wyndham. There is a sick little girl who does not deserve to die. Please meet Mr. Redburn in your back garden as soon as you can.* It was signed by Captain Goode.

"Was that—did someone just . . . ?" Catherine was peering around the room suspiciously. We both jumped as a knock rattled at the door.

"Come in," I said, crumpling the piece of paper and shoving it behind me.

Lucy entered. "Um, miss, there is a Mr. Kent downstairs and he—well, he said to tell you that if it is at all inconvenient he is happy to come up here."

I rolled my eyes. "I apologize. He thinks himself very amusing. Please tell him Miss Harding and I will be downstairs shortly."

She bobbed a curtsy and left. I moved the gaudy fire screen and threw the missive into the flames. The sick girl was surely some play on my sympathies since their other approaches hadn't worked. I had told them I did not wish to be involved, and uninvolved I would stay.

"Catherine, will you help me dress?" I asked, taking off my wrapper. "Oh, and I should probably tell you, for all the time we've known Mr. Kent, he's had the power to reveal anyone's secrets."

Catherine was still gaping at me twenty minutes later as we entered one of the many parlors. This one was yellow. That is, the chairs, the banquettes, the rugs, the settee, the walls, the ceiling—all were the same shade of bright, buttery yellow. Mr. Kent, all in shiny black, looked rather magnificent in contrast as he stared up at a painting of some general who had, of course, a yellow sash.

"Curious, isn't it, how a painting could be quite this ugly," he said and turned, giving us both a brilliant smile.

"Good morning, Mr. Kent," I said wryly.

"Miss Wyndham, Miss Harding, you both look lovely." He bowed and was about to continue speaking, but Catherine was too overcome for niceties.

"You ask a question and people respond with the truth?" She interrogated him immediately. He glanced up in surprise.

"And here I thought we were supposed to keep our abilities secret," he accused me.

"She's my best friend. I wasn't about to leave her out." I sank onto a long banquette as Catherine circled Mr. Kent, observing him like a scientific experiment.

"Demonstrate, if you please, Mr. Kent—ask me a simple question so I can see how it works."

There was an amused glint in his eye. "Who would be an ideal husband for Miss Wyndham?"

"You would," Catherine replied automatically then clenched her fists and grimaced. I stared at her, stunned. I hadn't realized she thought of us in such a way. "Well, that settles it. Evelyn's solution it is."

"I hadn't ever realized there was a problem," Mr. Kent said mildly.

"Thank you, Catherine," I said, before turning evilly to Mr. Kent. "I propose that you be forbidden from asking any more questions. All your questions must henceforth be voiced as statements and if necessary, with an added clarification that what you stated was a question. This way, we can answer you freely."

"Do you know—" Mr. Kent shook his head. "It is very difficult to do that."

"You have a way with words. You'll figure it out," I said. Catherine sat down next to me, and I smiled at him sweetly.

Mr. Kent clutched his chest in mock pain. "I thought you were on my side, Miss Harding!"

"I am on our friendship's side," Catherine replied, waving her hand at him. "Not on the side of making people confess things better kept hidden."

"Why would you want to hide the fact that Miss Wyndham and I would make a marvelous ma—"

"Blast," I spat out, sitting up. Another piece of paper was in my hand. *The situation is truly dire. Mr. Redburn is waiting in the garden.*

Mr. Kent and Catherine both eyed the scrap of a note. "Is that from—I mean, one might presume that is the Society of Aberrations—end of question," Mr. Kent finished awkwardly.

Guilt curled in me. "Yes. I don't know what to do," I said, sighing.

Mr. Kent raised his brows. "What are they asking?"

"For me to heal a little girl."

"My God, the brutes, the monsters," he mocked.

I narrowed my eyes at him. "I told them no. I don't trust them. I don't believe they are telling us everything," I said firmly, sticking to my line. Besides, this was not my concern. Plenty of people died every day and I could do nothing about it.

"I never took you for one who would run away from someone who was hurt," Mr. Kent said mildly.

I looked up sharply. "I am not running away. I am already away. I don't want to go toward people I don't trust."

Catherine was peering at me through her spectacles with a mixture of pity and wariness. "Is helping one girl really so terrible?" she asked reasonably and annoyingly.

"It would never be just one," I said, feeling the curious combination of certainty that I was right and doubt that working with them would be as terrible as I feared.

"They have been nothing but helpful," Mr. Kent said gently. "And surely their being a government branch, with oversight, should assuage some worries."

I stood, staring at the rug, trying to think. It was truly garish. I stared at the equally awful walls instead.

"They simply wish to have a well-connected and very powerful girl on their team, and in response they reward you handsomely," Mr. Kent was saying, arms outspread.

I stopped. "How handsomely?" He looked uncomfortable and I pressed. "Handsomely enough for my reputation to be scrubbed clean and my family's fortunes to suddenly multiply?"

Mr. Kent replaced his pained look with a bright smile. "For the fortunes, I could not say. But your reputation . . . That credit is due to quite another party." He grinned broadly and smoothed his tie.

"What are you—" I paused and it hit me. "Oh heavens, what did you do?"

He shrugged innocently. "Let's just say . . . that I've been . . . in a sense . . . blackmailing key members of London society and editors of the scandal sheets into preserving your reputation."

I gaped at him.

"And by 'in a sense,' I mean that's exactly what happened." He smiled broadly at the room.

"You—you're serious?" I found myself half gasping the words but also not finding it terribly hard to believe. Mr. Kent never hid his worse qualities.

He wore them like badges.

"Come now, I can do some good on my own with my powers—I wasn't *so* irredeemable before the Society of Aberrations showed up."

"I think there's some confusion here about the definition of good."

"Why, Miss Wyndham," Mr. Kent replied, looking as chaste and good as a debutante at her presentation to the Queen. "I think we can all agree it's fair to punish these guilty people feigning innocence every day of their lives, all while helping a wrongfully accused innocent. I would certainly never ask you, but I suspect you agree."

"You cannot simply blackmail people into liking me!" I said, immediately thinking of the Athertons and groaning. "Do you know that a very prominent matron in London society was here with her oh-so-eligible son yesterday?"

Mr. Kent sniffed, unconcerned. "Which eligible son?"

"The Earl of Atherton."

"Oh my," he said, looking pained.

"Yes, he's quite the most stuffed man. And it's all your fault," I said, huffing as I settled back next to Catherine, who took my arm in commiseration. We fixed Mr. Kent with twin glares that seemed to wilt him.

"My deepest apologies, Miss Wyndham." He bowed.

I intensified my glare.

He said, "If only there were something I could propose to keep these suitors away."

Before I could ask him what exactly he meant by that, another paper appeared in my hand. *She is going to die. Please.*

"It's just helping someone live," Catherine said gently, reading the note over my shoulder.

Blast. I took in my two friends, people I trusted with my very life. "Mr. Kent, you really do trust them?"

"Not at all, I don't trust anyone," Mr. Kent said, shaking his head. "But I do trust everyone's self-interest. I can easily see how a society and its members being rewarded for performing miracles can lead to a pleasant and long-lasting cycle."

He gave me a half smile. "Though it seems you don't seem to trust my moral compass at the moment."

"You are right, but I do Catherine's," I said, turning to my always fair and judicious friend. "I told you all. You know how Mr. Kent feels. Is this the right course?" I would prefer to trust myself, but after the events of last year I was not at all sure I could.

Catherine's tongue poked through her lips a little as she pondered. "I cannot be sure, of course, but I do think helping some sick young girl today can only be a good deed. We can find out more in due course and decide whether you are better off without them." She brightened as a new thought came to her. "Oh, I shall do some investigating! There are sure to be some references to the Society of Aberrations at the Records Office. . . ."

And that was where we lost her. As soon as Catherine had a project, she could not focus anywhere else. She pulled out a pen and a worn little book of paper from her reticule, mumbling plans to herself.

Mr. Kent and I shared a raised eyebrow and smile. Catherine really was dear.

I sighed, standing. The Society's note was strangely heavy in my palm. I could never let the girl die. I had known deep down, from the first piece of paper that fell into my hand, that I would help her.

"Well then," I said to Mr. Kent. "I am needed in the garden, I believe."

Chapter 5

O F COURSE IT had to be a sick child, I was grousing to myself. Why couldn't it have been a sick factory boss who exploited children? Or a sick orphanage director who denied children extra gruel? Those I could have refused easily. But, of course not. It had to be wide-eyed, squeaky-coughing, shivering children plaguing my conscience.

Mr. Redburn deposited us on the drive of a lovely house and, to my surprise, Lady Atherton stood next to Captain Goode in front of the door.

"Ah, Miss Wyndham. Thank you for coming. I believe you know Lady Atherton?"

"Hello, Lady Atherton," I said, curtsying confusedly.

"Good morning, Miss Wyndham." She smiled at me as if this were a perfectly normal morning call.

"Lady Atherton is an associate for the Society," Captain Goode explained. "She is continuing her late husband's work with us. We have asked her to act as your chaperone if you continue to work with us, healing people around London."

A whoosh of understanding ran through me. It wasn't just my parents' money or Mr. Kent's blackmail that had brought Lady Atherton to their fashionable new address.

"My late husband spoke fondly of the Society's powers, so I wanted to help however I could," Lady Atherton said with a smile. "He always said power has a duty to secure the welfare of the people."

"I see," I said, tiring of the blatant theft. "Did he get that from Mr. Disraeli?"

"No, it was his own, I believe," Lady Atherton insisted. "Though I'm sure he'd have been flattered by the comparison."

"Miss Wyndham, may I?" Captain Goode asked, holding his hand out.

I nodded and gave him my hand. That strange warmth started to fill me.

"How long does it typically take you to heal a patient?" Captain Goode asked.

"Five to ten minutes," I said, feeling the warmth blossom out to my fingertips.

"Then this time it should take you one," he replied. He reached into his pocket and pulled out a small token. It was a dented old silver-looking piece with a strange marking.

"What is that?" I asked.

"A deception," he said, smiling and sending a wink to Lady Atherton. "We don't want everyone to know about our powers, so we use things like this. We will be telling the gentleman that we have a powerful healing charm in our possession. I will give it to you and you will pretend to check her temperature while actually curing the child."

I frowned but he was already lifting the heavy lion knocker. It rapped down hard against the door.

We waited a long moment. Behind me, Mr. Redburn sighed impatiently. Lady Atherton glared at him but he jumped forward to rap it again.

"I'd have thought Lord Herrington could hire a better house sta—"

Mid-insult, the door opened, revealing an impeccably starched butler in glorious livery and a look that was indifferent by most standards, but absolutely furious by a butler's. "Welcome to Newton House. May I—"

"We're here to see the marquess," Mr. Redburn said with carelessness, and ducked his way in. Pure shock overtook the butler's face (his eyes widened slightly), but he recovered and scrambled after the rude man.

"He is not expecting anyone at this early hour, and as such, I will have to ask you to return later."

Captain Goode followed with a calm-looking Lady Atherton behind him. "Please tell the marquess that the Society of Aberrations has come to—"

"She's here to heal his daughter," Mr. Redburn interrupted, edging to the stairs impatiently. How he expected to find a little girl's bedroom in this mansion without the butler's help was beyond me.

The butler looked torn between calmly speaking with us and chasing after Mr. Redburn. Confused, he split the difference, turned and puffed to his fullest. "Just one moment, young ma—"

"Rollins. What is going on down there?"

A red-haired, ashen-faced man stood partway up the foyer steps. His cravat was slung around his neck and even from this distance I could tell his eyes were swollen with lack of sleep.

"Your Lordship, these . . . guests—"

"Lordship! They're gonna make your daughter all better." Mr. Redburn gestured broadly toward me. "Though your butler—"

"My apologies, my brother has been up for many hours," Captain Goode said, closing his eyes for a moment as though in pain. "Please meet us outside, Felix."

Mr. Redburn smiled as if that had been his plan all along. He sauntered out the front door, leaving a very angry Rollins to close the door behind him.

"My apologies, Lord Herrington. I am here with Lady Atherton and Miss Evelyn Wyndham. We are here to help your daughter," Captain Goode smoothly said.

Lord Herrington hesitated.

"My lord." Lady Atherton curtsied. "I promise you will want to see what these people can do." She smiled a little and Lord Herrington softened.

"All right. Follow me. It certainly cannot hurt."

I clutched my skirts in one hand and slid past Rollins, who looked fit to burst. His mouth opened once or twice, but finally he just gave a tremendous sniff and stalked back to the doorway. I wanted to apologize, but how did one apologize for a man like Mr. Redburn?

Captain Goode, Lady Atherton, and I followed Lord Herrington up to the family rooms. He opened the door to a scene I had seen many times with Rose back in Bramhurst. I felt her with me as I focused on the fully drawn curtains, whispered tones, and the sense of delayed urgency in everyone's movements. All was centered on a pale child, hidden in the bedclothes. A shock of black hair over a pale arc was all I could make out from the doorway. At her side was a nurse, red-faced and thin-lipped. A lady, presumably Lady Herrington, the child's mother, paced the room, clutching a handkerchief to her mouth to keep in her silent sobs.

Lord Herrington rushed over to the bed. "Is she . . . ?"

"No, she is still with us," the nurse replied, voice gritty with lack of sleep and emotion. She gently swept back the dark locks. "We are trying to make her comfortable."

Lady Herrington scowled at us like we were disrupting a

horrible, intimate moment because, well, we were. "Lady Atherton? What is this? Who are these people?"

"They . . . They can help," Lord Herrington explained gently to his wife.

"Indeed, Lady Herrington, I beg you to allow this," Lady Atherton said, smiling encouragingly.

"More doctors, Richard?" The frantic woman tugged at her husband's arm. "Please, just let us spend these last moments with Pippa in peace! She doesn't have much time left."

"I know, dear, but they say they have something special." Lord Herrington gestured to us and Captain Goode stepped to the bed.

"How dare—" Lady Herrington started as she registered us as potential help for her daughter. "Her? She's practically a child herself!"

Her husband laid his hand on her arm placatingly as I reached the edge of the bed next to Captain Goode. The nurse nervously moved away and I took her place next to the child, noticing how translucent her skin was, veins and dark brows the only spots of color left on her face. Up close, she was so still and drawn it was hard to imagine her ever waking again.

"Be strong, dear," Lady Atherton said bracingly to her friend.

"I have a simple charm here that Miss Wyndham will place," Captain Goode said calmly. He handed me the silver token and I hesitantly put it on the girl's forehead. Captain Goode gave me a small nod.

"A charm? This is ridiculous!" The lady's voice was high and thin but echoed my thoughts perfectly.

"Miss Wyndham, if you would monitor the patient's heart," Captain Goode said, ignoring the woman.

I lifted the girl's hands from under the covers ever so gently. She was almost cold. A pulse beat lightly, slowly, under my thumb.

Lady Herrington looked at us in bewilderment and opened her mouth to protest again, but Lady Atherton spoke softly.

"There are miracles in this world. Believe in this one."

I took a deep breath and concentrated only on the girl's hands beneath mine. Though I did not know what difference it might make, I tried to send whatever power I had into her skin, hoping this wouldn't be the moment it failed me.

The room was quiet, expectant; just the elevated breathing of the six of us as we strained to see if the girl would revive. My eyes were fixed on her cheeks, wondering if there was a bit of color coming back into them, when the maid gave a loud cry. The girl's lashes began to flutter madly. Beneath my hands her pulse began to steady, stronger and faster. Warmth seemed to blossom on her skin. It had barely been thirty seconds. Captain Goode's power was rather astounding.

Her mother rushed forward. "Pippa! Pippa!" She pulled one hand away from me to clutch it fiercely and I frowned, but simply placed both my hands on her other arm. There was no question—the girl was coming to.

"Mama?" The croak came before her eyes opened, but that quickly followed, revealing lovely, lively brown eyes.

"Yes, darling! I'm here!" Her mother climbed on the bed and cradled Lady Pippa to her, almost dislodging the charm. I had to jostle to keep my grip. If the woman would just give me one moment, her daughter would be fully cured.

"What happened?" Lady Pippa sounded stronger with each word.

"You were ill, my darling! We thought you might die but here you are, here you are, my dearest!" The girl gave a whimpering cry at the foreign idea of death and buried her face in her mother's bosom. The charm slid to the side.

"Excuse me, Lady Pippa, but I need you to stay still for just one more moment."

My rather grumpy words and replacement of the charm while actually getting a better hold on the girl seemed to remind the room that there was a reason their daughter was alive and speaking.

"My God." Lord Herrington spoke as though he couldn't stop himself. He turned to Captain Goode. "You were right. It is . . . a miracle."

Lady Atherton was glancing at me speculatively. Her lips thinned but I sensed a shrewdness there.

Lady Pippa was progressing nicely to a full crying fit at this point. Presumably, her body was somewhat shocked to come back to a healthy state and her mind was just as bewildered. However, it was a very . . . vigorous tantrum she was throwing and I felt it safe to let her go.

I got up and gave the maid, who was looking between me and Captain Goode as though we were a witch and a sorcerer, a reassuring smile. That seemed to make things worse as she gasped and crossed herself.

Rollins was more conflicted when he returned to lead us out. His lips twitched into an actual smile as he noted his Lordship's daughter, pink and lively in her mother's arms.

"Thank you ever so much, Rollins. We are so sorry to discomfit you today. You do excellent butlering," I told him.

"It was my pleasure," he said, sounding both sarcastic and sincere. I decided to assume it was the latter.

Lord Herrington, however, was pure gratitude as he met us back in the main foyer. "I don't know how I can possibly repay you," he said. "And the Society."

"I am sure we can find a way," Captain Goode replied. "All we ask for now is your support."

"Of course! Anything! Whatever you need, just say the word."

"Thank you. You'll be hearing from us."

I felt my stomach turn as I watched him vigorously shake Captain Goode's hand. I didn't quite like being responsible for putting this man in debt to the Society when I didn't even know how those debts were to be paid.

"Thank you, Lady Atherton," Captain Goode said when we were back on the drive. "I hope Miss Wyndham will be content to join you on other calls like this."

She smiled at him. "Indeed, Captain. My husband always told me that the Society did such important work. I am sure Miss Wyndham sees the good of helping."

With that, she allowed herself to be handed into a very sleek carriage that looked as though it had been painted only this morning, it gleamed so in the sun.

"For a society that is doing this for the good of England, you do enjoy holding people to favors," I said when I was alone with Captain Goode.

He led me toward the street and responded slowly, kindly. "Men like Lord Herrington and the late Lord Atherton have run this country for centuries while the rest of us relied on their favors."

"So now you get to turn the tables?"

"More that we are invited to join their table," Captain Goode replied. "This is mutually beneficial. Lord Herrington has a seat in the House of Lords and a vast fortune. We may simply ask for him to use his influence if we ever need his help, or perhaps provide funding for our society to grow and do more."

I frowned slightly. "So people without powers, members of London society, they know about the Society?"

"Only a select few, like Lady Atherton. They have to earn their place like anyone else," Captain Goode said. "England is changing. You can feel it. The voting reforms, Mr. Cardwell's improvements, this Society. My brother and I were born with nothing. To be in a place that judges by merit; where anyone can gain respect, advancement, and comfort for good work; where men and women of the highest and lowest birth can work together, it is something I am quite proud to be a part of."

"That sounds . . . rather democratic," I said.

"I was hoping it would sound inviting," Captain Goode said expectantly.

"I don't know," was all I could say. I was running out of logical arguments and relying on the unease in my chest, my anger for Dr. Beck.

A crackle sounded in the wall next to us and Captain Goode gestured to the open portal. "Please, Miss Wyndham, before you write us off forever, let me show you something at the Society. I think it will be of interest to you."

"Unfair," I said as Captain Goode opened a door to reveal a beautiful library. The room seemed to stretch on forever. Bookshelves lined all the walls. Hundreds, thousands of volumes. The air carried that wonderfully comfortable and musty scent of dust, age, and wisdom that only worn books can emit. Mahogany tables and desks were arranged for studying and chairs were grouped more casually around the fireplaces—two that I could see.

"We keep records that go back many years. I wanted you to see who came before you—which role you would be filling."

The shelves seemed to be divided into several sections. There was one large set of shelves with a gold placard declaring it POTENTIALS. As Captain Goode led me by, I quickly sussed out that it was organized by region and chronology.

Another shelf was labeled HISTORY and seemed to be organized by topic. Some volumes focused on historic events, others were biographies of people whose names I didn't recognize, and there were even books on oddly specific objects like jewels and weapons.

Finally, we came to POWERS. It was organized alphabetically by type, it seemed. My eyes searched wildly, not sure what specific words the Society had chosen to assign. Some of the terms were completely new to me. There was the word Captain Goode had said about Emily—*Telekinesis*: "the power to move objects using only your mind," said the subheading. *Intangibility* seemed appropriate for Oliver. *Strength, Portals, Fire,* they all kept catching my eye. But Captain Goode was pulling out a volume for *Healing* and handing it to me.

"Finding a healer has always been one of the Society's highest priorities," he said. "I know you are reluctant, but you would be a most valued member." I thumbed through the fragile book carefully. It reminded me of a peerage book, except this lineage was limited to two names, one of which was mine. There was limited information, simply my date of birth. The other name, Meiko Inoue, had a bit more, noting when she was born (1680), when she joined the Society of Aberrations (1703), when she was married (1706, to Richard Best), when she had a child (1707, Patrick Best), and when she died (1713, beheaded). So, healers could be killed. That was . . . important to learn.

"I will let you read," he said. "When you are done, please come find me at the back garden. I have one more thing to show you."

I nodded, too engrossed in the book to pay him much further attention. I turned the page to see details about Miss Inoue's healing, which seemed similar to mine. She healed herself and others by touch and proximity. The noted times, however, were so much faster than my own. A broken leg could be healed in twenty seconds, her own in ten. A sizable cut in ten seconds, her own in five. And the range of her healing was nearly one hundred feet. If she had improved to this level, could I?

I turned back to the shelves, looking almost unconsciously for the book that would contain information on the power diametrically opposed to mine. But before I could find *Illness* or *Death*, my eyes stopped on another.

Charm.

My heart was racing and I barely noticed that I was turning the pages. Three entries. Two men and one woman had come before Rose, as far as the Society knew. I had to read the words over and over before they penetrated.

"Anyone who spends time in the charmer's company will grow to love them. This may take many forms: romantic, paternal, platonic—but it will only grow stronger the more time spent in their company. They are irresistible, no matter what they do. This is not to say that the charmer can convince others what to do. In fact, it can be quite dangerous and unpredictable." A little farther down, I saw what they meant. A charmer found in Denmark in the late 1600s had been killed by a mob of people—men and women—who wanted his attentions for themselves. A Persian general with troops so loyal that they refused to let him endanger himself by commanding them in battle. An Italian courtesan in the early 1800s was imprisoned in a tower for most of her adult life by her protector.

I felt sick and weary as I slid to the floor, letting my corset dig into my hips uncomfortably. Still, I could not stop turning the pages. My little sister. She hadn't wanted a short, tragic life. She didn't want to conquer the world or bring men and women to their knees. She just wanted to help people. Help people with the power that *I* possessed. I let the book close gently in my lap and looked to the window. The oppressive sky still let in a comforting shaft of light, as though the sun were pushing hard at the clouds' surface, ready to break through.

Rose would want me to help people.

The Society would have me help people.

I sighed again and got up, placing the book back on the shelf, letting my hand linger on it. Rose would be an entry here soon, the small facts of her life listed neatly next to the others. Unfinished.

I left the room, letting the door close on the lives of the people who came before us.

Finding the back garden was easy enough. I could make out two figures on the terrace—Miss Grey and Captain Goode. I pulled my cloak's collar up and pushed open the french doors. The garden was somehow beautiful, in full health and bloom despite the winter. A stone fountain sat in the center, bubbling up water in a steady rhythm, and surrounding it was a verdant, well-maintained lawn, occasionally broken up by low hedges, stone pathways, and brilliant displays of flowers that should not have been in season.

"I feel so invigorated, so thrilled to have helped," Miss Grey was saying. "I have been hoping to do this kind of good for so long."

"I do believe you have found your calling, Miss Grey. I am so pleased—more pleased than I can say to have you here." Captain Goode was smiling awkwardly down at her.

"Hello," I said.

They both turned and Miss Grey's eyebrows shot up. "Evelyn! You *are* here! I almost didn't believe Captain Goode."

"I wouldn't have either," I said, coming to the railing. "You look well."

Miss Grey was pink and pleased and had never looked more lively. "Indeed! Captain Goode's power has given me much more control. I can accurately determine locations and I remember the dreams very clearly now. I was able to bring him information on two people I dreamt of last night." They shared a smile.

"How . . . is this garden here?" I asked, feeling like an intruder in their moment.

"I believe it's that boy," Miss Grey said, pointing to a group of four figures congregating in the garden.

Oliver looked up and gave us a sardonic wave, while two girls and another boy, who all looked to be about Oliver's age, gave us curious looks and returned to their practices. One girl took flight, floating up a few feet into the air and moving in circles. The other lifted her hands and small rocks rose up at her command. And the boy simply walked across the lawn as grass, vines, and flowers grew all around him.

"A moment, ladies," Captain Goode said, before striding down to the gardens and separating the group into two pairs. He made his way back over to us, looking genuinely excited. "They are going to start with a game. It's all in good fun—a simple contest of which team knocks down the other first." He turned to the two teams. "Are you ready?" he shouted.

After four nods, he waved his hand and the game started quickly as the players enacted their plans and anticipated their opponents. Vines burst out of the ground and flailed unpredictably in all directions, while small shields of earth popped out in defense. The flying girl wove and attacked through the chaos, but Oliver kept his teammate protected by grabbing her and rendering the both of them intangible.

I gasped. He had never been able to make another person intangible! "You taught him to do that?" I asked Captain Goode.

"Mr. Myles? Why, he discovered it himself," he replied proudly. "I simply raise their powers. By practicing with these heightened abilities, they teach themselves how to control it best."

"But in one day . . . ," I said. "And how does your influence help control it?"

"They get used to the higher level and learn how to access it by habit. It gets into their bones; lets them see how it feels to use their powers to their fullest extent. It's the same for an archery or fencing expert—they don't even have to think about it, their bodies just understand what to do. They do it by instinct. After a while, Mr. Myles may not even need me. Same for you as well." Was that why Miss Inoue's healing was stronger than mine?

I watched in awe as the game continued at a chaotic pace. Both teams were evenly matched, attacking and counterattacking, doing everything they could to stay on their feet. At some point I lost track of Oliver as he got buried in a mess of bushes, leaving his teammate to deflect attacks from both opponents. The girl who controlled the rocks seemed to be managing it, until they slowly moved to striking from both sides.

She turned and shouted desperately, "Oliver!" The flying girl seized the opportunity and swooped in like a hawk at full speed.

A moment of confusion followed, as she passed right through the earth-moving girl and flew into her plant-covered teammate. They both fell to the ground, eliminated, as Oliver emerged from the ground underneath his teammate, grinning.

"He's a fast learner," Captain Goode said with a nod of approval.

Oliver said something that made the other three laugh and I saw his smile grow. He was happy. In fact, all four of them looked perfectly content, even the two who had lost. It was hard to deny that they were adept with their powers.

"I shall decrease their powers momentarily. The boy with the vines has some trouble controlling his, and we don't want to have him wake up in a tree again," Captain Goode said, chuckling with Miss Grey.

"Can you remove someone's power entirely?" she asked innocently.

"Only when necessary," he said, looking at me to see if I would take issue with yet another revelation.

But with that simple exchange, my world shifted entirely.

"You can take away our powers," I said, the words echoing in my ears, hard to hear over the roaring of my thoughts.

"Yes—but of course I wouldn't do that to you, Miss Wyndham," he said, looking a little alarmed at my reaction.

My thoughts were swirling so fast I could barely keep up with them.

Miss Grey could find people with a new accuracy.

Captain Goode could take away our powers if so desired.

Sebastian Braddock was missing, hating himself for what his power had wrought.

And Rose. She would want me to use my gift.

As each thought landed, a gear whirred into place, locking me into my destiny.

"I'll do it. I will join you."

Captain Goode and Miss Grey looked up at me in surprise and hope.

"Under one condition. You will find Sebastian Braddock and take away his power."

Chapter 6

It took a week for Miss Grey to find him.

A week spent making calls with Lady Atherton at the most exclusive houses. A week spent secretly healing everything from their mild aches to their deadly illnesses. A week spent listening to Lady Atherton sing the praises of the charm I carried. A week watching her win more friends for the Society.

A week spent trying to find the right words to say to Sebastian.

I still didn't have them when a note slipped through a crack in the air, asking me to be in my garden at four in the morning. Anger, anxiety, excitement, and gloom swirled in my stomach for hours, forming too many concoctions. I couldn't simply settle on one feeling because it changed constantly, overwhelming me.

I didn't sleep. What would *he* say?

When the appointed time came, I bunched my bedcovers together and shoved some extra clothing under them, hoping it would be enough to fool the maid who would light the fire shortly.

Satisfied it would do, I awkwardly looped the long plait my maid had braided the evening before around my head, pinning it as much as possible. The question of my dress was another thing. Since I certainly couldn't manage a corset by myself, the only

choice I had was to wear my long night rail under my old traveling coat. Hopefully, it would disguise my shape and therefore the fact that I was in my nightgown if anyone were too curious. That, along with my heaviest, thick-soled boots, and I was ready for Mr. Redburn in my back garden, shivering against the February chill. A cold drizzle was dripping down my neck.

"Where are you, you rude little man," I muttered, hoping to make the devil appear as I called him.

"What a lovely morning it is, wouldn't you agree, Miss Whinehard?"

I whirled around to see a portal in the middle of a thick hedge. Mr. Redburn's arm was held through to me, the rest of him in a room beyond. I frowned, but stepped forward and took a breath as I was yanked into a study at the Society of Aberrations. Warmth immediately hit my cheeks as I took in the room and its early-morning occupants.

Mr. Kent was slumped against the fireplace mantel, looking as if he hadn't had the best sleep. Or, judging by his stained shirt and sloppy necktie, it was likely he had not been to bed at all. "Miss Wyndham, good morning, if we can really call it that." He looked rather seedy, actually.

I gave him a rueful smile as Captain Goode appeared in the doorway holding an oversized book.

"Ah, good, the team is all here," he said. "Miss Wyndham, have you met Miss Chen?"

He gestured to one of several great wingback chairs, the buttery, green leather back hiding the chair's occupant. I moved slightly to see a young woman about my age, legs slung over the chair's arm. Shorter strands of dark hair were slipping from her low chignon. She raised an eyebrow, gave me a sardonic salute, crossed her arms over her chest, and closed her eyes again. Even with her eyes closed, there was something about the set of her mouth that suggested she knew some joke you were not quite in on.

"Miss Chen, Miss Evelyn Wyndham is our new healer. Miss Wyndham, Miss Fei Chen has the ability to break down objects, crumbling or exploding them if she stares at them too long."

"If I close my eyes, it's not because I'm sick of you. Usually," Miss Chen drawled, and I started as I recognized an American accent.

From the corner of my eye, I could see Mr. Kent peering closely at my costume and I pulled my coat up to the neck. "Where did Miss Grey find Mr. Braddock?" I asked Captain Goode.

He motioned us over to a desk, where he set the book down, opened it up to a map of a particular region, and pointed to a small, penciled marking. "Southern Italy. Right here to be exact."

I noticed the map was dotted with a few red markings and a couple of green ones. "What are these?" I asked.

"Travelers like my brother and Mr. Hale can only create portals to places they've seen, so we keep a record of their accessible points. The red marks are Mr. Hale's, the green ones Mr. Redburn's."

Mr. Redburn poked his head in for a glance at the atlas. "Not bad—my closest is about a hundred miles away."

"How . . . long will we be traveling for?" I asked, heart sinking. I hadn't even had tea, let alone packed a nice crumbly cake.

"We're up in the middle of the night to help this princess, and then she complains about it," Mr. Redburn said to his brother before turning to me mockingly. "Don't worry, you'll be back before London's awake."

"Don't mind him," Captain Goode said as his hands fell on my shoulder.

The warmth of the power filled me and I tried to commit the feeling to memory, so I might be able to do it on my own. So I might help Sebastian learn to control his.

Mr. Redburn opened a portal on the wall next to us. Mr. Kent gestured me forward. On the other side, the Italian sky had achieved that slight glow and warmth of predawn. A breeze whipped strands of hair from their pins and I took in a deep breath of thick, almost-warm air that coated my throat. My coat was welcome, but now it was the only layer I needed, instead of being insufficient against London weather.

An "oomph" announced the arrival of Mr. Kent behind me. He shot Mr. Redburn a dirty look while Miss Chen strolled ahead of me, looking as though she had simply stepped through the door between a bedroom and antechamber.

An endless black field sprawled in front of us. As my eyes began to adjust, picking out the stars above, I slowly discerned Mr. Redburn and his method for traversing the hundred miles. Crackles sounded rhythmically every few seconds as portal after portal opened in front of him, revealing breathtaking views of the horizon from treetops. It made sense to me now. Since he could only open portals in places that he'd seen, he was using each portal to give him a view of the next point, effectively doing the traveling for him.

Mr. Kent's low murmur filled my ear. "So. Very exciting, finding Mr. Braddock finally."

"It is," I said, not meeting his gaze. I wasn't very much in the mood to see their small rivalry resumed.

"I've missed him," he said. "Some things you just can't find elsewhere in London society."

I rolled my eyes, expecting the obvious joke. "What did you miss? His moping? His cowardice? His dangerous presence?"

"I was just going to say his noble nature," Mr. Kent said, pretending to look shocked. "I didn't know that was how you really felt about him."

As I sighed, a portal crackled open for a final time and Mr. Redburn stepped into it. Miss Chen followed and Mr. Kent and I trailed behind her, trying not to stumble in the thick grass.

Done mocking Mr. Braddock for the moment, Mr. Kent turned to badger Mr. Redburn. "If you can open a portal wherever you can see, have you ever tried sending someone to the moon?"

"Yes," Mr. Redburn answered, and then frowned. "It didn't work, but if you keep asking me questions—"

"Yes, yes, then you'll make sure it works on me. I know, clever retort."

An orderly copse of trees was laid out at the far end of this field. At one corner, there was a small run-down barn, which seemed to be our destination.

"You sure this bloke isn't going to give us trouble?" Mr. Redburn asked me.

"No, if you simply let me talk to him," I replied.

"That's too bad," Mr. Redburn said as we stopped in front of the barn. "I was hoping for something a bit more fun."

One side was made up of a large door, one that would swing forward to let livestock and machinery enter. Mr. Redburn reached out, tested it, and found it locked. He gave it a loud, pounding knock. "Mr. Braddock!"

No response.

He repeated the process and I added my voice. Still nothing.

Mr. Redburn stepped aside and gestured Miss Chen forward. "Try not to bring the whole barn down."

With those promising words, Miss Chen began to stare hard at the target. Suddenly I heard the metal hinges protesting as the door shook itself apart, falling in great wooden chunks as we all stepped back to avoid the flying splinters. I pulled my coat up over my mouth, bits of wood scratching at my eyes.

"Such a lovely power," Mr. Redburn said wistfully, staring greedily at Miss Chen. "I can't wait to have it again."

She gave him a dark glare as the door fell open. The sky was rapidly turning to day now, bright rays just beginning to rise over the trees.

I stepped through, onto the rough wooden floor of the barn. The sun was slanting through the cracks in the wall, making the dust spin in a tentative, almost dreamy light.

My feet found a creaking floorboard but I still turned at a rustling sound.

Sebastian Braddock was staring at me, his body halfway out a window, his features outlined in the morning dawn.

His hair is longer, was my very silly thought. Of course it was longer. Who would have cut it for him while he had been . . . doing whatever it was that he was doing. His eyes, too, looked different. Darker, so the green was harder to discern. Impossible, but the man seemed to have grown at least another inch or two, broad shoulders even broader under his vest and linen shirt. There was also something slightly feral about his expression—though that could arguably be because we'd just broken down his barn door.

"Sebastian . . . It's Evelyn. Don't worry," I said cautiously. A chill went up my spine as I crossed the floor slowly.

"Evelyn," he breathed, his voice hoarse. He quickly looked out the entrance at the others, anger beginning to etch over the lines of surprise on his face. "You shouldn't be here. I . . ." His voice drifted off as he finished his leap out the window.

"Wait!" I shouted.

I was still too stunned to understand what exactly was going on, but my legs seemed to independently make the decision to go after him. I ran out of the barn and saw him making his way across the field, away from the brilliant dawn, as though he were some kind of demon. I rushed after him, hoping to magically make up for his head start, but Sebastian was too fast and unhampered by skirts, broadening the distance with every step.

He was going to disappear again.

"Sebastian, stop running!" I yelled, out of breath.

"Then stop chasing me!"

"No, you started it!"

"Well, you shouldn't have come!" He continued at that break-neck pace, not even turning as he shouted back to me. Really, I was unequal to the chase.

Until strange things started happening in front of him. Miss Chen's power cracked and exploded the ground into great hunks of grass and dirt, as though something was tunneling up from under the earth. His path blocked, Sebastian veered to the left and I kept pushing, following, beginning to catch up. I would make him explain himself. Explain where he had been and why. Explain why he took off *again* now.

The earth continued to erupt around us on this path, too, dirt flying through the air and the ground emptying out into small holes by Sebastian's feet. He did his best to dodge them, leaping around them to stable ground, but his foot caught, he stumbled, and that was all I needed to seize him from behind.

Tripping over a hole, I brought both of us to the ground with a clumsy tackle. "No!" Sebastian shouted as that familiar and wild sensation from his touch flew through my veins, taking my breath away as if I'd just leaped off a cliff. He struggled against my hold, caught between trying to rise to his feet and trying not to hurt me.

"Just—stop—running—!" He pulled out of my grasp and I began to slap at his legs.

"Let me go," he growled.

"You are so bloody ridiculous," I responded, lunging for his foot. But he yanked himself loose and was running off again.

I should let him go. I should let him run forever, if he wanted to.

"We have a cure!" I bellowed.

He stopped.

"What?" I could barely hear him, but I felt the weight of the one word, what it meant to him. All the hope that was in it.

"We have a cure . . . for your power," I said, trying to catch my breath.

He took a few slow, heavy breaths, turning to see if he'd imagined the words. The wind blew across the fields, his hair flying wildly, his long coat billowing behind him. He stared at me.

"We have a cure," I repeated, not knowing how else to say it.

Somehow, the third time worked. I could see the notion slowly come over his face, deathly white in the pale light. He clenched his fists, his body stiffened, he took a step forward—

And he fell into a hole.

Chapter 7

T HE NEXT THING I knew, the ground opened up below me and I was dropped on the rug in the Society of Aberrations foyer, a foot away from a very confounded Sebastian. Mr. Redburn, Mr. Kent, and Miss Chen followed a moment later, taking a portal straight from the barn.

"It's nice to see you can accomplish something other than complaining about us," Mr. Redburn said, looking down at me dispassionately.

"Hello . . ." Captain Goode was poking his head into the hall.

Mr. Kent lifted me to my feet and away from Sebastian, toward a chair in the corner. "Did he hurt you? Is this far enough to heal?"

"No, yes, I'm fine," I said, trying to turn back.

His hand gripped my arm and his eyes were pointedly on the ceiling. "There—there's also the matter of your coat. . . ."

My cheeks warmed as I realized why my body felt cooler. For heaven's sake, why did this keep happening to me? I spun around and closed my coat tightly around my nightgown. "Thank you, Mr. Kent."

"Oh, I was actually offering to take it for you, but yes, fine, you're welcome."

Sebastian's panicked voice echoed from across the room. "Please don't, I'll hurt you," he said, recoiling from Captain Goode as he tried to help him to his feet.

"Oh Lord, is he always like this?" Mr. Redburn asked.

"Sometimes he's worse," Mr. Kent put in, escorting me back.

Sebastian stood tense, looking ready to run again. "Where are we?"

"Welcome to the Society of Aberrations, Mr. Braddock," Captain Goode said with a smile. "My name is Captain Simon Goode, over there is my brother, Mr. Felix Redburn, and this is Miss Fei Chen. I believe you're already acquainted with Miss Wyndham and Mr. Kent."

Sebastian met my eyes with a sharp look. I knew he would not have forgotten the Society of Aberrations either. "Dr. Beck's society."

"Oh, wonderful, this again," Mr. Redburn said, tossing his coat into one portal, then opening another to pull out a glass of what looked like whiskey.

"The Society is actually a branch of government, and they didn't approve of Dr. Beck's experiments," I explained to Sebastian, coming closer to him. I gave him the answers I had needed to hear in order to trust them. Why Dr. Beck was able to hide his research, why they sent Mr. Hale to watch over them, and why Mr. Hale ran away himself.

"Do you believe them?" Sebastian asked, his face close to mine. He looked so tired. I ached to smooth a hand over his jaw, to try to soothe away some of his pain.

I nodded. "Mr. Kent and I questioned them extensively."

"And you can really take my power away?" he asked Captain Goode.

"Temporarily, at first," Captain Goode replied. "But with time and practice, you should be able to control it on your own."

Sebastian's eyes glowed so bright I couldn't breathe for a moment, watching the way hope transformed his face. "And what is it you want from me?"

"Just help," Captain Goode answered. "There's a purpose to all our powers. Help us help the world."

"My powers aren't exactly suited to that purpose."

"Miss Chen destroys things by looking at them," Captain Goode countered, gesturing at her appreciatively. "Yet she provides us valuable protection."

"Until the day I accidentally stare at the sun for too long," Miss Chen added, shrugging.

Sebastian looked at me one more time and I gave him a nod, smiling involuntarily, trying to tamp down the joy at having him here, having him find some kind of peace.

"Very well," he finally said, and took a deep breath. "If you really think you can remove my power."

"I already have. When you first arrived," Captain Goode said.

Sebastian's eyes widened. He looked at his hands and then to me for confirmation. I grabbed his hand, searching for the sensation that I had begun to think belonged to us. But now there was nothing. Nothing but his warm, bumpy palm beneath mine, thicker with calluses after his strange journey.

He was cured.

Sebastian looked utterly stunned. He squeezed my hand before letting go and I couldn't tell if he was about to burst out into laughter or tears. He nodded firmly, his jaw tight, and offered his hand to Captain Goode. Without hesitation, Captain Goode shook it.

"Thank you," Sebastian managed, his voice a beautiful rasp.

"Does this mean we are done?" Mr. Redburn groaned. "Can I leave now?"

"Oh, for God's sake, give the man his life-changing moment," Mr. Kent snapped at Mr. Redburn. "No one here actually believes you have anything important to do."

"You society types think you're the only ones with important business. I've plenty," Mr. Redburn argued.

"Do you really?"

"No," Mr. Redburn said with a growl.

A portal opened up next to him, through which he was about to throw a punch at Mr. Kent. But Captain Goode seized Mr. Redburn's shoulder. The portal closed, his powers turned off.

"Felix, you *do* have important business," Captain Goode said, vexation in his tone. "The morning orders should have come in. It's time to deliver them."

Mr. Redburn looked very much like a stubborn child as he stormed out. "Fine."

"My apologies," Captain Goode said, scratching his head in embarrassment. "Mr. Braddock, I'm sure you'd like some time to settle back in. Please return on the morning of the eighteenth and I'll remove the power again." I could swear I saw the smallest hesitation before he smiled. "I'll be sure to give you the tour of the building then." He gave a bow and left quickly. Something in his abrupt departure made me nervous, but I couldn't say why.

Quiet fell over the hall. Miss Chen's eyes were darting around and I began to realize it was her way of not breaking down all the objects near us.

"Hmm, I don't like this. I'm usually the one to ruin those nice moments," Mr. Kent said.

Miss Chen coughed and slid forward. "Welcome, Mr. Braddock."

"Thank you, Miss Chen."

She shook his hand briskly and Sebastian stared at the clasped hands warily. But she did not wheeze or grow faint. Instead her eyes darted between all of us and a smirk emerged. "Enjoy this little . . . situation between the three of you," she said with a wave of her hand.

Before we could ask what that meant, she turned on her heel and left the room.

That left us an awkward little trio standing in silence. "Well, this is . . . strange." Mr. Kent seemed to think saying it all out loud would ease the tension, but it did not. "I don't know what Mr. Braddock should do next," he continued. "Walk into the street and touch everyone, I suppose."

The air grew thicker.

Sebastian grimaced slightly. "Ev—"

"Well—"

We spoke as one and I could feel Mr. Kent rolling his eyes at that.

"Mr. Braddock. We must take you to see Mae first. She has been waiting to see you for months," I said firmly.

"I . . . I should, indeed, see Mae. If I am to stay, that is." Sebastian would not meet my eyes, though I felt Mr. Kent's intent gaze.

"Of course you should stay," I said, letting anger come to the forefront of my confused emotions. "Unless you have urgent matters to attend to in that Italian barn?" Because, really, why on earth had he left?

He shook his head. "No."

"What were you even doing there?"

"Nothing."

"Were you on your way somewhere?"

"No."

"When were you planning on returning?"

He didn't even bother with a vague answer. Fine.

"Mr. Kent, will you please ask Mr. Braddock when he was planning on returning?"

Both men looked at me, one with horror and one with delight.

"Why, Miss Wyndham, I wasn't sure you had it in you. Mr. Braddock, when were you planning on returning to London?"

He had to shout the question because Mr. Braddock was, of course, running away again. He made it to the door with his hands over his ears to block out Mr. Kent's power, but it wasn't far enough.

"Never," he said before he could wrench open the door. His steps slowed and I saw his shoulders set. I didn't have to force myself to anger this time. *Never?* He was going to leave his poor fiancée wondering about him *forever?*

He swallowed miserably and threw a dark glance in Mr. Kent's direction. "My power was too dangerous. And I . . . I did not think it a good idea to be back here." As uneasy as he was to be honest around Mr. Kent, I thought I knew what he was really wanting to say. *I did not think you would want me here.* For that would be a very foolish, very Sebastian way to think.

"Mr. Braddock, none of us blame you for what happened," I said, though perhaps it would have been more convincing if I weren't shouting furiously.

"Well, to be fair, I blame him a little," Mr. Kent said.

"Not helpful," I growled.

"I mean, you can't deny he—"

"Kent!" Mr. Redburn's voice echoed across the foyer.

Mr. Kent sighed. "What?"

"New request. You're needed in Parliament."

"Very well, I will stop there on the way home."

"Oh, but this is very important business because you are an important man," Mr. Redburn said with a sneer from the top of the stairs. "You must go *now*."

"Not a good time. I can't just leave when there're matters to discuss and tender looks between—ah!"

A portal opened up below Mr. Kent and he fell through to somewhere outside the Palace of Westminster. Mr. Redburn tipped his hat to us and disappeared through his own portal, whistling a pleasant tune to himself.

"I . . . don't think I want to ask him for a portal," I said. "It's a short walk to Mae's anyway."

Sebastian nodded and opened the front door. Together, we stepped out into the frigid air. At least the drizzle was gone, and the sun was straining through the sky filled with thick, fast-moving clouds. The streets were half empty, only the earliest of workers out. Gleaming carriages winked as they caught the rare sunbeams.

We began wending our way slowly down the streets. I could smell the hay and earth next to me; feel him, uncomfortable and brimming with things he wanted to say. It was a silent quarter mile before he chose to speak words I never thought he would say.

"Mr. Kent is right, you know," Sebastian said quietly, with a misery that sounded as though it had lived in him for all the months he had been gone. "There is a list of at least a hundred things I could have done differently and saved her."

"And I have my own list of things I could have done," I said, trying to bite back the rush of anger. "If I am mad at you, it is only because you ran away and disappeared with no word or warning to anyone. You could have stayed to help. You could have simply informed us you weren't dead."

The words barely hit the air as we turned down an unpopulated lane, but I knew he heard me as he sucked in a sharp breath.

He hid no emotions from me now, eyes unguarded, and I could see the heartache that matched my own.

"Evelyn, please, you have no idea how much I regret that day."

"I think I have some idea."

"I have thought every day about you—your loss. And every day, I only saw how I would make things worse if I were here."

"And I only thought of ways you would have made it better."

I felt angry tears welling up, threatening to spill straight over to sadness. It was a strange feeling, to want to throw something at him and protect him from dangerous flying objects at the same time.

"I took her from you," he said.

"You didn't."

"I brought you nothing but pain and—"

"Don't say that. That's not true."

"But if I hadn't gotten involved, she might still be—"

"Stop. You are a complete and utter—"

"I am. And I don't deserve your forgiveness."

"I forgive you. It's done. There's nothing you can do about it!"

Tears were coming now, hot and miserable down my cheeks, as the months of fear and anger overwhelmed me. Mr. Braddock stopped and moved to hold me, hesitating just before he could touch my face. But I could see how much he wanted to and for some reason that made me cry even harder.

"You have shown me far too much kindness. And then you found me and cured me. It's more than I deserve. You have only to name what I could do to make this better and I would do it."

We stared at each other in the alley for long minutes, vulnerable and open. I did not know what to say to his outpouring of guilt and he could say nothing that would bring my sister back. I stared at his unshaven beard, the redness that rimmed his eyes, the chapped, trembling lips, and ached, for him, for Rose, for Mae, and for me.

Finally I wiped at my eyes and took in a few deep breaths, letting the fact that he was here, in front of me, not off God knows where, be a comfort.

"We should continue on." I began walking again, letting the sun's bit of warmth hit my tear-streaked cheeks. "You are back. You have a cure. You can live a normal life. I just don't want you to let your guilt get in the way of that. I've kept count and you've helped more people than you've hurt, Sebastian Braddock, and you have plenty of time to do more." Casting my eyes toward him, I could see Sebastian looking at his own hands with a combination of wonder and skepticism.

"And you believe the Society is the best place to do it?"

"I think I actually do," I said. It had been only days and we'd already accomplished a great deal. "And I think it's what Rose would have wanted. Joining a society, learning, helping each other and the world."

His gaze fell on me. "That is a convincing point."

As soon as I allowed myself to simply take pleasure in the fact that Sebastian was back in my life and would be working toward the same goal, Mae's town house loomed large. A shutter came down on my faint joy and I felt like I was saying good-bye already. I could sense the eagerness in him as we neared, a charge in his step.

"I cannot believe I shall be able to shake hands without harming anyone."

I nodded but didn't trust myself to say anything till we were ushered into the Lodges' parlor, piano notes coming from the next room. I managed to smile at Cushing, however, who looked overjoyed at seeing Mr. Braddock and rushed to find Miss Lodge, though in a stately, calm, butlery way.

The piano stopped and I could hear a gasp before Miss Lodge rushed in, her eyes finding Sebastian instantly. Her cheeks were tinged in blotches of becoming pink; her whole being seemed to suggest light and wholesome goodness. Then, instead of his usual distant bow, Sebastian opened his arms for a hug and Mae absolutely glowed. As I watched her and Sebastian embrace for a long moment, their first hug in years, I couldn't help but wonder if I was more pleased for them or sad for myself.

Chapter 8

". . . And why are you looking at the mirror like that?"

"I am not looking like anything," I said, glowering at my mother in the reflection.

She simply raised one eyebrow. She was terrifyingly good at it. The perfect arch, the perfect amount of disdain, all while telegraphing that she knows exactly how things are—and you do not.

"I hope you have been more pleasant with Lady Atherton," she said, coming over to the vanity to adjust my hair. She gestured for Lucy to leave us.

Over the past two days, Lady Atherton had continued to keep me extremely busy—not only with our usual morning calls, but with endless shopping for the Little Season. In and out of the modiste's for measurements and fabric selections for walking, day, riding, and evening dresses; the glover's for white kid gloves that would not last one wearing, so thin and soft you could see the outline of fingernails beneath; the shoemaker for encrusted heeled slippers, soft half boots, and gleaming riding boots; not to mention the various accessories she deemed necessary. She had even ordered a rushed dress for tonight's event, delivered to my house only hours before. I felt very much like a doll.

"I have been perfectly civil to Lady Atherton," I finally answered my mother.

Mostly because my annoyance had transferred to Sebastian. He'd promised to call when I left him at Mae's. But two days had passed without a word.

"I am glad to hear it." Mother tugged at my coiffure, loosening the strands slightly so it flattered my face more.

I had simply offered him all he could want in life. Was it so wrong to expect a little gratitude? One measly little call?

"And Lord Atherton? He is very pleasant as well."

She gave me an encouraging look and I resisted the urge to fall asleep at the thought of him. Lord Atherton had joined us on a number of our calls and, to put it simply, he was the greatest bore that had ever existed. He was so starched and cold I suspected he would crack like marble if someone were to knock him off his perfectly polished boots. I settled for a noncommittal "Mm."

My mother looked at me suspiciously. "I believe Lady Atherton encourages the match as much as your father and I do."

"I'm very lucky she favors me," I forced out, suspecting the Society was responsible for that. Lord Atherton and his mother would certainly not be showing any interest otherwise.

Mother frowned. "I do hope you realize that. You cannot afford to be stubborn and wait forever. You must take advantage of the chance."

Right. That was undoubtedly what Sebastian—no, Mr. Braddock—was doing. He was cured. He could finally marry Mae. And there was no reason for me to be angry or concerned or despairing about him for one second longer. Our obligations to each other were over.

"I understand," I said. "I will."

Somehow, that only further incensed Mother. "Our fortunes could shift as suddenly as they have before—"

"Mother," I half-growled. "I am agreeing with you!"

"Yes, far too quickly," she snapped. "I know you, Evelyn. You mustn't treat this lightly."

Well, it seemed I couldn't be disagreeable, nor agreeable. No matter what, we'd find a way to argue.

Mother fixed her own hair in the glass and sighed. "We only want what's best for you. Consider it. Please, truly consider it. He is an earl. You won't find a more comfortable marriage."

She was right.

Not about Lord Atherton, heavens no. I could imagine a more comfortable marriage to a rock. In fact, I could start a list of the thousands of various inanimate objects that would make for more comfortable marriages and I'd probably die before finishing it. But there was only one marriage I could really consider comfortable, the one person I had considered accepting before I lost Rose, before I found my power, before everything changed.

Mr. Kent had declared himself only a few short months ago. Then, he'd respected my wishes, giving me time and space to mourn my sister, to think about my future. But he didn't disappear, either. No, he'd spent months trying to help me, fixing my reputation and searching for me when I'd gone missing. And since he'd found me again, he'd tried to make every moment into exactly what I need.

Maybe it wasn't too late.

Maybe I could still fall in love with Mr. Kent.

"I promise to try tonight," I finally said to my mother.

Maybe something in my face really had changed because that seemed to convince her.

She smiled in relief, adjusted the rose in my hair, and gave me a final cursory examination. "Good."

I bid her good night, feeling the slightest bit of optimism for the evening. Yes, Mr. Braddock may have been marrying Mae, and the man my mother wanted me to marry might be a turnip, but I would throw off this moping. Mr. Kent would surely be supplied with quick wit and ready smiles tonight.

My attempt at good spirits was tested soon enough by Lady Atherton as our carriage rattled by the Thames, a slight muddy stink rising off the river. "I am so glad you decided on the cream silk for the evening, Miss Wyndham," she said.

"Thank you, Lady Atherton." It was an absolutely beautiful gown, a pearly cream that glowed whenever light hit it.

"Such a talented modiste, Mrs. Valant. She hides your figure remarkably well," she added, making me wish to smack her with my overly beaded reticule.

"Very good choice in Mrs. Valant, Mother," Lord Atherton put in, adding nothing whatsoever.

"Indeed, as my dear husband used to say, 'the apparel oft proclaims the man,'" Lady Atherton said.

Ah yes, wise words from the late Earl of Atherton, William Shakespeare.

I smiled stiffly and looked out the window. Under the curtain, I pressed my gloved fingertips to the frosted glass and wrote a two-word plea to the outside world: *Help Me.*

Gaslights passed slowly as we crawled along to Piccadilly. The Winter Exhibition at the Royal Academy may not have been as widely attended as the later summer one, but Lady Atherton had made it clear to my mother that it was not to be missed.

After ten long minutes where Lord Atherton discussed the weather in every possible variation, the shouts, bubbling laughter, and halloos suggested our arrival at the front of Burlington House, and the sight of the grand courtyard and columned facade confirmed it. A rush of three footmen quickly opened the carriage door, handing Lady Atherton down, then me. I watched closely to see if Lord Atherton's knees would even bend as he stepped out of the carriage. They did, barely.

We advanced toward the main building, crossing the open courtyard with cobblestones as smooth and orderly as anywhere in London. Even the horse's offerings seemed artfully composed. Still, the shouts, the smoky light pouring from the hall, and my own preoccupations all converged to give me a tightness across the forehead. I tried to focus on the night, on Mr. Kent, on a happy future.

Without Lord Atherton, of course.

As we entered the brilliant foyer Lady Atherton took time to pose in front of the marble steps, letting the splendidly arranged lights show off our dresses as we slowly made our way to the ladies' retiring room. It was the usual crush as we gladly handed off our fur-trimmed mantles, already warm from the press of bodies. As we worked our way farther into the grand and crowded central hall, I checked furtively around for Catherine or Mr. Kent's familiar faces, but I couldn't see them. Lord Atherton led me and his mother through the crowds, the two of them introducing and reintroducing me to earls and duchesses and barons and marchionesses I had seen during last year's Season but never been quite worthy of their attentions.

Attentions I had now, as Lady and Lord Atherton's guest. I struggled to keep track of the Lord Overstones and the Lady Glasswoods, resorting to creating rhyming songs in my head to tell them apart.

After an interminable flurry of names and repeated small talk,

Lady Atherton finally allowed her son to escort me into the galleries. I took his arm and we joined the thick crowd flowing under the archways and circulating each room, Lord Atherton constantly craning his neck to make sure his mother was always in sight for propriety's sake.

In a moment of weakness, as I longed for Catherine's opinions, I made the grave mistake of soliciting Lord Atherton's. "Are you fond of art?" I asked politely.

"I suppose."

"Do you prefer certain artists? Or styles?"

"Generally the ones that most accurately portray their subjects." Dry as sticks.

"Do you have a favorite?"

"Well, there is a portrait of my mother that hangs in our dining room that really captures—"

I stopped walking. Partly because I didn't want to hear the rest of that, but mostly because a particular favorite of mine happened to catch my eye.

It was a striking painting by Mr. Turner, depicting a small boat of fishermen, caught in the middle of a storm. You could feel the wildness of it, the dark desper—

"Bad weather there, it seems," Lord Atherton observed with perfect seriousness. "Not at all the right time for fishing."

That was it. Time to lie down and quietly die right here. No one who knew what I was enduring would fault me.

I must have actually looked a bit ill because Lord Atherton held out his arm for support.

"Miss Wyndham, are you feeling well?" he asked.

"I . . . I find I am feeling faint, my lord. But I fear I can't make it to the refreshment room," I said, barely caring to disguise my hint.

"Indeed . . . I've heard art can be exhausting for ladies," he said, leading me over to an empty seat in the center of the gallery. "I will fetch you a drink."

He gave the world's stiffest bow and quickly departed, disappearing into the crowd, which gave me the perfect chance to do the same. As soon as he was out of sight, I hastened out of the room and scurried from gallery to gallery, hoping to find my friends. I squeezed through two more packed rooms of British and Dutch oil paintings before turning into a gallery of Mr. Rossetti's, where I was suddenly very thankful Catherine had such a clear, distinctive laugh.

There she was in the corner, most daringly without bustle, and I suspected without corset as well. She was rather enamored with the Aesthetic Dress Style that had been scandalizing London over the past few years. She spoke animatedly at Mr. Kent, who was admirably fitted in his tails, wielding his ever-present cane. His sly, tight-lipped smile seemed sincere as he watched my friend speak with her hands all akimbo.

I could swear that I felt . . . something while I watched him.

Or at the very least, I wanted to.

As they moved to another painting, I realized Mr. Braddock was greeting them, his arm looped around Mae's, and then I was *very* sure I felt something.

This was the first time I had seen Mae out in an evening dress. Her own cream bodice was tightly fitted, gliding elegantly over her corseted figure. A subtle, stylish bustle and an ordered row of tight skirts made her appear deeply impressive. Of course, her easy smile and bright eyes ruined any sense of intimidation, giving an overall picture of a stylish, lively girl as she made the acquaintances of Mr. Kent and Catherine. She and Mr. Braddock looked content together, without the worry of his power or her illness to weigh down on them. They could finally be a normal, happy husband and wife.

I paused, feeling suddenly tall and obtrusive. Of course that had to be when Mr. Braddock's eyes found mine. His arm was no longer entwined with Mae's and he took a quick step toward me, hands fisting in his elegant white gloves. I don't believe he even realized he had moved until a frustrated look overcame his dark features. He brought more attention to himself by stepping back even faster and coughing loudly as he stared in another direction entirely. A slight crease appeared between Mae's brows—her polite, subdued response to Mr. Braddock's erratic behavior.

But Catherine stared at him with her mouth open. "Mr. Braddock? Are you unwell?"

He coughed again, and grimaced. "Very well, thank you, Miss Harding, I was just—"

"Good evening." I saved him from any further fumbling. Three pairs of eyes landed on me and I was rather gratified to see that they all looked pleased. I refused to give the fourth pair another glance.

"Oh, thank goodness, you're here," Catherine said. "Mr. Kent was threatening to write notes to you on some of the paintings, so you'd be able to find us."

"I was going to do it tastefully," Mr. Kent argued. "They would have looked like fluffy, informative clouds."

Mae looked confused and chose to turn us back to less abstract ground. "How are you, Evelyn?" she asked quietly, reaching out for my hand. She gave it a gentle squeeze. I made the attempt at an answering smile.

"Oh, very well. And you? Have you kept Mr. Braddock busy?" I looked at the space just to the left of his ear and smiled brightly.

"I would say so." Mae gave Mr. Braddock a quiet smile and softly touched his wrist. "My parents were very happy to see him.

We had some lovely dinners, a night at the theater, and I was even well enough to go ice skating on the Serpentine!"

Ice skating.

Mr. Braddock was sure to be a graceful skater. Holding Mae's hand, spinning together, cheeks pink and smiles wide—*Stop it! Stop thinking about it. You don't even care.*

My stomach roiled and I laughed loudly to cover. "Ah yes. That—uh, that sounds delightful. Ice skating is always delightful, unless you're falling, then it's not so, uh—"

"*Delightful*, I believe, is the word you're looking for," Mr. Kent supplied.

"Indeed. Thank you."

Mae was staring at me as though I might have fallen and hit my head. "Yes, well, fortunately it seems I remembered the motions well enough. It was perfect."

"I can imagine," I said, still unable to get their charming evening out of my head. "Mr. Kent, we must go someday."

Mr. Kent gave me a wry look. "Of course. I'd been meaning to ask you that question for months, but I thought it would be horribly rude."

I suppressed a smile. "How kind of yo—oh bloody hell."

The words slipped from my lips the moment Lord Atherton and his mother entered the gallery, both looking around through narrowed eyes. Mae blushed and Mr. Braddock cleared his throat, while Mr. Kent just smirked and Catherine rolled her eyes.

"No—I—hm. Catherine, can you please lead us in another direction? I wish to avoid my mother's newest choice for son-in-law."

Despite my strict No Noticing Mr. Braddock policy, I could not miss him whipping his head around to see who I was referring to.

Catherine grinned at the theatrics and gestured to a small gallery a few paces ahead. "Now, these pieces may not be so finely showcased, but I think you will find that the favoritism at the Royal Academy means that some of the true talents are relegated to the back rooms or hung practically near the ceiling, where you'd need a ladder to properly view them. . . ."

Catherine's monologue rapidly turned into a rant as she led Mae and Mr. Braddock toward the underappreciated paintings. I tried to follow but my blasted bustle held me back a moment when the tight crowd converged.

Mr. Kent slowed and took my arm. "Miss Wyndham, you need only say the word and we'll escape."

"What word is that?"

"*Balloon.* I know a fellow who will sell a spacious one for a fair price."

"You have . . . a balloon fellow."

"Yes, hot-air balloons can be very handy," he said, as if this were a perfectly normal gentleman's accessory.

"And we will simply sail away?"

"Fly off, never to return." He smiled and I focused on his brown eyes—his lovely, inviting—and most importantly, *not* ridiculously green—brown eyes. Sailing off with him certainly held a strong appeal. Leaving responsibilities and worries behind—

Leaving Lord Atherton behind, who had found us, somehow. "Miss Wyndham, there you are."

"Balloon," I muttered to Mr. Kent.

"Well, I need a little more warning than that," he whispered back.

Lord Atherton stood stiffly, raising his head as if to show off the length of his neck. "I daresay that running off without a chaperone is not something my mother would approve of."

"Oh I'm sorry, my lord, I thought I saw your mother in here,"

I said with all the sincerity I could muster. "But then I found my dear friend instead. May I introduce you to Mr. Nicholas Kent?"

"Good evening, Mr. Kent," Lord Atherton said with a bow, unable to act impolitely. His hair was particularly springy tonight and I resisted the urge to see how much shorter he would be if I pressed it down.

A slow smile crossed Mr. Kent's face. "Lord Atherton. A pleasure to meet you. I have so many questions I've wanted to ask you—"

But Lord Atherton was saved as Mr. Kent's question was interrupted by a loud cough. At the end of the hall, Mae was doubled over, wheezing, as Mr. Braddock backed away, eyes wide and face white. All of a sudden the room seemed to slow and I felt sure that we were back at the night I first met him, at the ball at Bramhurst, when an eager girl tried to grab him. How much things had changed since then.

But Mae's distress and his distraught face were the same.

Without worrying about what Lord Atherton would say, I rushed over to Mae as fast as I could, taking horrible, mincing steps in the blasted slippers Lady Atherton had insisted upon. Finally, though, I was able to pull Mae into my arms, trying to touch as much skin as was possible while simply seeming a concerned friend. I grasped under the lace at her wrists until I had her hands fully in mine. Mr. Braddock had backed away against a wall, as far from the others as possible. Catherine and Mr. Kent were close on my heels. They hovered slightly, my usually well-humored friends' faces uncommonly serious as Mae recovered. Her breath came back and her pulse steadied under my fingers.

"Catherine, dear, can you help me bring Mae to the ladies' room?" I asked.

She nodded, and we helped Mae up and led her slowly back through the room.

"Miss Wyndham!" Lord Atherton looked shocked as I ignored him at the entry to the gallery, continuing to focus only on Mae. Finally he sneered and stalked off.

There was nothing special about the retiring rooms, really. It was more of an excuse to keep contact with her, to wash away Mr. Braddock's effects. What had gone wrong? It had only been two and a half days. He was supposed to have until tomorrow morning. I would need to see if the odd sensation when Mr. Braddock and I touched had returned.

Mae continued to take shaky breaths and as we walked, she tried to talk between them. "The first—the first time I return to society and I—I fall ill again. How do I keep letting this happen?"

"Mae, you felt ill for a moment; there is nothing to be alarmed about. It happens to all of us. I nearly fell unconscious ten minutes ago listening to Lord Atherton talk about the weather."

"And just when he comes back, too," she said, letting a strain of misery color her usual cheer.

"You need a good rest. I promise you, you will feel perfectly normal in the morning."

She didn't say anything until we set her down on a plush settee in the retiring room, but I knew she was still blaming herself.

"I'll be right back," I reassured Mae. "I am going to have your carriage called and get you something cool to drink. Catherine, will you wait here with her?"

Catherine looked at me oddly, wondering why I wasn't the one staying, but didn't argue. "Of course."

I made my way back to the gallery where I'd left Mr. Braddock and Mr. Kent, standing quite apart.

"Is she all right?" Mr. Braddock asked, hurrying forward. His hair was in disarray and lines of distress feathered out from his eyes.

"She's perfectly fine," I said. "She's more worried that her illness came back than anything else. But I held her hands and walked her slowly. It should have staved anything off."

Mr. Braddock ran his hand through his hair, a gesture he had clearly done many times since we left minutes before. "Thank you."

"It was nothing. Now, take off your glove," I said. "We need to see if your power has come back."

He nodded miserably and removed his glove in jerky motions. I reached for his hand, stumbling slightly at the impropriety. If anyone were to notice. . . . But Mr. Kent stepped in front of us to block us from the crowd. After all, this was no tender touch. I was simply trying to solve this mystery.

And my suspicion was correct. I gasped as I felt the answering thrum in my blood. Faint, but there. I looked up to meet his eyes, the dark green swirling with pain and anger. He roughly slid his hand away and I felt unconscionably bereft.

"Captain Goode said three days, didn't he?" I asked them.

Mr. Braddock nodded heavily, ruined at the notion of hurting Mae. "Yes. I was going to report to him tomorrow morning, but I should never have trusted this to last."

"Perhaps they didn't realize quite how potent your power is," Mr. Kent said, eyes harder than I would have liked.

"Or he lied," I said, a twisting in my stomach. Were they so desperate to recruit me that they'd say anything?

Mr. Kent looked uneasy. "I'm sure he just miscalculated. Mr. Braddock can just see him every day to be sure."

"Until he lies again to get us to do something else for him," I said. To what end, I could not be sure. But my suspicions began to form like a sculpture taking shape.

"Mr. Kent is right," Mr. Braddock said.

Both Mr. Kent and I spoke at the same time. "Really?"

"Yes," Mr. Braddock muttered, clearly compelled by Mr. Kent. He shook his head and sighed. "I have no other option. Perhaps they were just wrong about the time frame. I won't risk it again, but I do want to believe they have good intentions." He gave me a slight smile. "I even found our old friends Arthur and William—they are working for the Society, too, collecting information at the Park Club. And they've seen no reason to distrust them."

"That is good. We will just have to ask Captain Goode," I announced.

The gentlemen nodded, too. It *was* possible that Captain Goode simply did not understand how fast Mr. Braddock's power would return.

"Excuse me." Lady Atherton's high voice cut through the tension between us. "Miss Wyndham, it is time to take our leave."

I had no chance to say good-bye before she started escorting me away, a barely concealed vexation in her movements.

"This simply will not do. You cannot be running away from your chaperone in public." Her voice was an affronted hiss.

"A friend had a fainting spell," I said. "I was trying to help her."

"And somehow found yourself speaking intimately with two unmarried men."

"They are . . . friends," I said weakly.

"I simply hope you understand the situation: The most important members of London society are here and we introduced you to them." She continued, "Think of my son—your behavior is embarrassing him."

Frankly, I was surprised he felt any emotions at all. "My lady, I am grateful for the introductions, but I don't need—"

"We are doing more than that for you, Miss Wyndham. We

are raising your position in London society, but you must meet a higher standard of decorum. An earl requires more in marriage than a girl who can heal. She must also have manners."

With that alarming announcement, we reached the retiring room. I did not notice Lord Atherton silently waiting outside when we emerged with our cloaks. I'd believed him to be an inanimate piece of art.

As the Athertons drove me home in stony silence, I glanced at them, suddenly wishing I had Mr. Kent's power. Was Lady Atherton the one making a match between me and her son? Or was it the Society? Was this supposed to be a reward for me by elevating my position? Or was this a reward for them by putting a healer in their home?

Stewing in these uncomfortable questions, I grew suddenly tired. I was tired of rewriting my opinion of the Society. I was tired of wondering what Rose would wish me to do. I was tired of constantly wondering if I had made the right choice, if I even had a choice, or if I was being manipulated at every turn.

I closed my eyes and leaned back against the stiff brocade of the seat. Tomorrow. Tomorrow I would go to Captain Goode for answers. I would decide once and for all if they were on our side or not.

Chapter 9

AFTER THE DISASTROUS night at the Royal Academy, Mother was at her most fawning when Lady Atherton called the next morning to take me on our healing visits. Mother managed to both apologize for my actions and send me many discreet and indiscreet warnings for obedient behavior today, all at the same time.

We had only one frail matron to visit before Lady Atherton told me I was to be dropped off at the Society of Aberrations for another mission. She seemed as glad to be rid of me as I was of her—but not as glad as I was to speak to Captain Goode. He owed me answers. Owed Mr. Braddock answers.

"I need to speak with you," I said, stomach swirling as he ushered me into his office. "It's about Mr. Braddock—"

But before I could even finish he was shaking his head regretfully. "Ah yes, yes—Mr. Braddock came to me last night."

"He did?" I asked rather stupidly. Of course he had—he would want his power removed as soon as possible.

"Yes, I was very sad to hear that his friend Miss Lodge had to be uncomfortable in his presence. I hear you helped her recover. He was very grateful for that." Captain Goode sighed, absently riffling papers on his desk, looking weary as he continued. "We thought we knew the timing, but alas, we are still learning."

"You really thought he would have three full days?"

Captain Goode grimaced. "I did. We've never had anyone with Mr. Braddock's power before, I'm afraid. In such cases, I find the closest analogue for guidance, but I made the mistake of looking to Miss Chen's power when I really should have looked to yours. According to the records in the library, healing has a gradual return. I will continue to research, but I suspect there is a difference between powers that are constantly active—like yours and Mr. Braddock's—and ones that must be activated, like Miss Chen's or Mr. Myles's."

He gave a heavy sigh before continuing. "In this case a weaker state seemed to emerge after forty-eight hours. I will, of course, remove his power daily now, just to be sure. As long as we don't need him at full power for a mission."

I nodded slowly. "I . . . Well, that does make sense," I muttered. And it did. But I still didn't feel perfectly comfortable. I could think of a hundred reasons they would lie. Maybe this was a subtle experiment to test his powers, or a way of making Mr. Braddock doubt his control, or even an attempt to make the Society look fallible and human. But these fears only felt legitimate in my head. Spoken aloud, they would sound like the sort of paranoid over-thinking that would get someone locked in an asylum.

Captain Goode stood and gestured to the door. "Let me enhance your abilities before we find Mr. Redburn. I believe everyone else has already gathered."

I let the strange warmth run through me, washing away the chill that there was something here I still didn't trust.

"For God's sake, where did they go?"

From the moment we stepped into the dusty Bombay alley, Mr. Redburn searched the sunny streets and grumbled as we made our way to the main thoroughfare, where Miss Chen, Mr. Kent, and Mr. Braddock weren't the hardest people to find. All we had to do was follow the curious gazes of the sea of Indians to the only foreigners on the street. Granted, Mr. Kent was also making somewhat of a spectacle of himself, tasting an unfamiliar pastry and attempting to get its name and ingredients from the poor vendor. Mr. Braddock wore a pained expression, trying to divert Mr. Kent, and Miss Chen seemed to be pretending she had no connection to either of them.

"Please, what is this delicious gift?" Mr. Kent asked, almost moaning as he ate.

The vendor responded in what I could only guess was Hindi, which rendered Mr. Kent's power all but useless for the situation. Mr. Kent let out a heavy sigh, searching for someone to translate, when his eyes landed on us.

"Miss Wyndham, you must try this. It will render all other food dull by comparison."

"I'm not sure I want to ruin the act of eating for myself quite yet."

"A small price to pay for the smug sense of superiority you—"

"Are you quite finished?" Mr. Redburn interrupted.

Mr. Kent made a show of nibbling even slower. "Might I recommend that you don't request someone's expertise and then complain about their process?"

"My usual tracker is with a different group now. You are the only adequate alternative."

"Ah, the only adequate alternative. I dream of a wife who will use such a term of endearment one day."

"Really, one might assume that you were married already, and to Mr. Redburn," I said, tired of their bickering already, well aware that we were collecting more and more interest by the second.

"Who are we looking for?" Mr. Braddock asked, turning us

back to the topic at hand. His eyes looked tired and he had lost some of the ease that came when he thought his power under control. I wanted to hit Captain Goode.

Mr. Redburn unfolded a sheet of paper to reveal a remarkably detailed sketch of a young Indian woman. "Miss Radhika Rao. We think she's gonna be reluctant, thus why we brought you all. Your . . . persuasion could be necessary." He bared his teeth in a not-grin at Mr. Kent and Mr. Braddock.

"What does she do?" I asked.

"She has influence over the weather. You can imagine the things she can do," Mr. Redburn said, leading the way down the road. He looked back at us, as serious as I had yet seen him. "She's about as dangerous as he is." He pointed a thumb at Mr. Braddock.

Even Mr. Kent was shocked into silence by that. At least until we found ourselves knocking at a door for several minutes, without any response.

"Looks like your information is wrong," Mr. Kent said. "Let's go back to the fellow with the delicious food."

"Should I break the door down?" Miss Chen asked in her usual tone, the one that straddled the line between boredom and sarcasm.

Mr. Redburn sighed and shoved his face into his hands. The rest of us waited uneasily while he groaned out his impatience.

"No, we're going to the marketplace," he finally said, lifting his head and he began striding purposefully down the street.

I may not have liked the man, but he had a very good sense of direction. The crowds grew larger and the roads narrower as we neared the marketplace. The strong scents of spice floated through the air. Bright, colorful garments and strange fruits filled the stalls around us. I couldn't help but marvel at the chaos. At the ways life could be so similar on the other side of the world and astoundingly different at once. It was not unlike the markets in Covent Garden that Rose and I had begged Mother to let us see during my Season last year. Rose had been presented with gifts from no less than three vendors.

The sky was clear and I could feel myself baking under such a hot sun as we wove through the crowd. Mr. Braddock kept to my side, letting me neutralize his power but saying nothing. I opened my mouth several times, wanting to order him to stop blaming himself for things that were beyond his control, wanting to apologize for my role in his distress, and knowing I should simply stay out of it.

I settled for uncomfortable silence.

When we finally made it to our destination, the girl had already noticed our inconspicuous group. She matched the drawing perfectly—a young woman in her twenties, with a lovely set of bangles on her arm and a pink garb that swooped over her black hair and around her red bodice and gold-trimmed skirt like she was wrapped in a sunset. She stared skeptically as we approached her rice stall.

Mr. Redburn took the lead, glancing down at his paper then back up at her, eyes narrowed. "Hello. Do you know who we are?"

She didn't answer his question for a few seconds. "No. What do you want?" she finally asked coolly. I noticed, however, that her bare arms were tensed.

"We know you have a power . . . and we have ones as well," Mr. Redburn said. Looking around to see if anyone was paying us any mind, he picked up a handful of rice, opened a tiny portal about the size of his palm, and threw it through. The next second, rice rained into the woman's empty hand.

If she was surprised, she didn't show it in the least. "What do you want?" she repeated, falling into shadow. The sun ducked behind clouds that I could swear had not been there a moment before.

"We want you to join us—" Mr. Redburn said, ready to give her the Society's usual speech. "We can give you everything you need—"

"No," she interrupted, the clouds thick above us now.

Mr. Redburn frowned. "You haven't heard what we have to offer—"

"You Englishmen are all the same," she said, anger simmering under her every word. "When you first learn of us, you treat us like goddesses. You revere us, humbly ask for blessings, and weep with joy when you're bestowed the smallest token. Until you want more. Until you decide that we were put on the earth to serve you, to fulfill your every request, to raise you up higher than the rest. Then, any mistake you make becomes our fault. Any deficiency you have is due to our cruel selfishness. Any pain you suffer means we're to blame. And in the end, the best we can hope for is to not be punished for knowing you."

I felt a shiver run through me and that was when I realized it was getting colder. A strange fog began rolling in to surround us. A soft rumble came from the sky and I could see some of the shopkeepers eying it warily and packing up their wares.

Mr. Redburn's limited patience had been reached. He leaned forward and hissed as the sky rumbled again. "Look here, missy, we know what you've done."

A crack of lightning split the sky. Mr. Kent hastily pushed Mr. Redburn aside and tried a different approach. "I'm terribly sorry, my acquaintance here hardly knows how to talk to people. Please, let's start again and allow me to introduce myself. My name is Nicholas Kent, and accompanying me is the lovely Miss Wyndham, the frowning Mr. Braddock, the eternally calm Miss Chen, and the . . . Well, that's Mr. Redburn. How are you?"

"Irritated," she replied and another crack of bright light twisted across the sky.

"A perfectly natural response to Mr. Redburn. Now, Miss Rao, I understand what you're thinking right now. You don't trust us. When I discovered my power, I didn't trust anyone. I still barely trust anyone, for that matter. Most people are terrible. But when Mr. Redburn here came to me, I joined because he said I could help my family. Do you have a family?"

"No."

"Well, isn't that inconvenient," Mr. Kent said, giving me an exasperated look. "Let's—let me ask you this. Is there anything we can say that could convince you to trust us?"

"No."

"Is there anything we can do to make you more likely to join us?"

"No."

"Is there anything we could do that would make you like us more?"

"Yes."

"What is it?"

"You can leave."

Mr. Kent nodded slowly in defeat. "I . . . see. Well then, it seems that's that. If you're ever passing by in London, please be sure to call," he said, handing her his card, which she didn't take.

He set it down on her table between the spices and rice, tipped his hat, and turned back to us. The clouds began to part, the fog dissipate. "Well, that is unfortunate," he said to us, clapping his hands together.

"We don't leave without her," Mr. Redburn said slowly to Mr. Kent, as though he were a child.

"What?" I began, but Mr. Redburn continued over me.

"Braddock, I'm going to open a portal to a locked room underneath her. Then I'll send you in and you simply have to put her to sleep. How long does that take? Ten seconds? Chen, stand by in case she finds a way to run."

Miss Chen gave him an icy salute as my heart began to pound and my skin felt clammy. Could he be serious? Mr. Redburn snapped his fingers under Mr. Braddock's face in impatience. "Braddock? How long?"

"I don't . . . understand what you're suggesting," Mr. Braddock finally said, beginning to back away.

Mr. Redburn sighed. "We aren't here to ask her to return to London with us if it suits her fancy. We have orders to bring her back."

"Against her wishes?" Mr. Braddock asked, his lip curling back in distaste, his eyes pinched.

"Do you have any idea how many men have died because of her? Do you understand how dangerous she is—the things she has done?" Mr. Redburn growled.

"Like what?" asked Mr. Kent mildly.

"Like killing people!"

But before Mr. Kent could ask Mr. Redburn to elaborate further, he turned to Miss Rao.

"Remember, girl, you could have just come with us pleasantly." With that, the crackle of one of Mr. Redburn's portals opening sounded under Miss Rao's feet.

Only she didn't fall in.

A massive gust of wind blew apart her stall and threw us all in different directions. I hit the ground hard, landing on my back, rice raining over me. Above us, lightning struck a stone tower, sending scattered rubble across the nearby rooftops and down to the market. I dove for cover under a stone balcony I prayed was strong enough. Thunder roared and heavy showers of rain and rubble came down all at once above me.

"*Argh!*" I screamed as the balcony itself collapsed, threatening to crush me until it shattered into a million pieces in midair, the flying debris striking my temple.

"Evelyn!" I heard Mr. Braddock call out, voice full of terror, but I was temporarily stunned and unable to locate him.

"Up," Miss Chen said, pulling me to my feet with a wiry strength. "You're all right."

"You fool, she can heal!" Mr. Redburn was yelling. As the dust settled around us and my healing took effect, I could see Mr. Braddock clambering over the rocks toward me, Mr. Kent behind him, both men determined to see to me.

"Oh, for Christ's sake, follow *her!*" Mr. Redburn snarled and threw a portal at Mr. Braddock's feet. He and Mr. Kent fell through it, one after another. I looked around wildly as a shout brought my attention to the growing fog and crowds of panicked people. I caught a glimpse of Miss Rao staring at us as the chaos tumbled around her. A great clap of thunder sounded as Mr. Braddock and Mr. Kent appeared in front of her, both men looking disoriented as she turned and ran into the fog.

"Go!" Mr. Redburn yelled. The two men began to reluctantly run after Miss Rao upon seeing me on my feet.

"Come on." Miss Chen grabbed my hand and we scrambled over the debris from the nearby stalls to follow.

Another hand seized mine. "We're taking a different route," Mr. Redburn said grimly.

A portal crackled open in front of us, a window of clarity in the fog. He pulled Miss Chen and me through and we found ourselves on top of a nearby rooftop, looking over the city. Mr. Redburn scanned the foggy streets for a sign of the chase. Another portal crackled open and we continued moving from building to building, searching.

"There," Mr. Redburn finally said after three more roofs, pointing at Miss Rao's bright figure running nimbly down a drab, narrow street.

He opened another portal and we followed him through, appearing on the street in her path. She looked at us impassively but kept running.

"Miss Chen, do it," Mr. Redburn said curtly.

Miss Chen concentrated on the road in front of Miss Rao, and jagged cracks appeared, crawling across the street in front of us, effectively creating a barrier of impassable gaps. Unable to continue forward, Miss Rao turned to find Mr. Braddock and Mr. Kent on her other side.

Both men looked unsure how to proceed, but Mr. Braddock cautiously made his way toward Miss Rao with slow, deliberate steps, hands held passively out in front of him.

"I promise, we don't want to hurt you," he said, low and calm.

"Then why are you chasing me?" Miss Rao asked, wind and rain curling around her, a dangerous whip that she could unleash at any moment.

Mr. Braddock took a step closer to the maelstrom, but was careful not to get close enough to hurt her. "We want to help you control your power. I don't think you want to be a danger to yourself and the people around you. I know I don't wish to, which is why I am working to control my power, too. We can do this together." Faint hope beat in my chest watching Mr. Braddock in his element, helping people, lending his strength to someone who couldn't bear to ask for it.

The rain was barely a light drizzle. The fog seemed to be clearing. But the air felt thick with something. The hair on my arms seemed to rise in small pinpricks of rough skin.

And then Mr. Kent was running straight at Mr. Braddock, his

mouth set and eyes wild. A stunning white light filled my vision and a booming roar of thunder filled the air as Miss Rao unleashed a lash of lightning, striking Mr. Kent after he knocked Mr. Braddock out of harm's way.

My mouth could barely form words as the dust around them settled. Miss Rao had disappeared into the retreating fog. I ran forward to see Mr. Braddock rising to his feet, dusty and unharmed. On the other side lay Mr. Kent's crumpled body, unmoving, smoke rising from his smoldering jacket.

I was by his side in an instant, seizing the closest part of his body and then as much of him as I could grasp as Mr. Braddock stumbled away, letting me use my healing. I could feel Mr. Kent's tattered clothing, his bubbling skin on his back, but most of all, his heart, beating no less tenaciously than I'd expect from him. His eyes, however, remained closed and I could feel no breath leaving his nose and mouth.

"Go," I heard Mr. Redburn say behind me as he and the others disappeared into another portal to find Miss Rao.

"Wait—" Mr. Braddock was saying, his voice desperate, but the portal closed. The sky above rumbled again and the wind around us seemed to surge stronger, whistling across the silent street.

"Come on then, you stupid man, you're all right. Get up," I said brusquely, angry at the tears that were forming. Surely it was not too late. It was simply an injury. A terrible injury. But what if he did *not* wake? No. No, that was an unthinkable thought.

"Ah . . ." Mr. Kent stirred in my arms, rasping and coughing. "This is just how I imagined heaven might be."

"Stop, Mr. Kent," I said, laughing in relief. "Need I remind you that you were just struck by lightning? Is this any time to be flirting?"

His warm eyes fluttered open. "Any time is the time to flirt with you," he murmured. A slow smile. "To be honest, I'm feeling better than when I started the day. That enhanced power of yours is . . . impressive."

It was hard to argue that. I stood up to survey him. His worst burns had become barely visible discolorations and the skin on his back was smooth. I felt pure joy rush through me as the enormity of the moment finally dawned on me. He was not dead.

He shook a lock of hair from his face as he climbed to his knees and looked up at me solemnly, his face truly handsome in this surreal moment. "Miss Wyndham, I feel this is an opportune moment to remind you that what I said as we rushed off to Dr. Beck's house still stands." The wind grew stronger around us, blowing dust all over the street. More lightning struck nearby and thunder roared, but not as loud as the thump of blood beating fast in my ears.

He slowly raised himself to standing, looking every bit the elegant young buck, and still somehow every inch a man to be reckoned with. "I know I should not take such liberties with an unmarried woman. . . ."

"Especially when you've alluded to your indecent past."

Mr. Kent nodded soberly. "I have. Before I met you, I went to brothels, gambling halls, scandalous music halls, all sorts of indecent places."

"And let me guess, ever since you met me, you've changed?"

He shook his head. "No, I just want to do these indecent things with you."

With that, he leaned forward slowly, giving me time to back away if I wished to. But I didn't.

When his lips touched mine they were soft and cool and I hesitantly pressed mine back. I could feel him smile at my response as he reached one hand to my cheek, shivers running down my spine as his fingers continued to move, grazing the fine hair at the nape of my neck. His mouth was no longer smiling as he pulled me tighter, urgent, and I felt his tongue tease between my lips, along with a little shock of electric charge.

At that I pulled back suddenly, breath coming all in a rush. I was trembling, flushed with confusion, wanting to turn away and never think of this again, another part of me wanting to see if there was any more to be learned between us. I swayed slightly, his arm still warm against my waist.

"Evelyn," he said throatily, his brown eyes drowsy and warm, chest rising quickly. "I have been wanting to do that for ages." I was suddenly aware of details I had never noticed before, like a freckle directly in the center of his dimple when he flashed his half smile, and the tiny pinpricks of stubble that had stroked my cheek.

"Mr. Kent."

I whirled around to see Mr. Braddock, covered in dirt and blood. His eyes were dark and angry, voice a raw growl. My heart dropped and suddenly I felt overwhelmed with the flood of emotions I had felt in the last hour.

"Mr. Braddock." Mr. Kent nodded at him curtly.

The two men stared at each other like asinine stallions.

"Thank you for saving my life," Mr. Braddock said stonily, his eyes unbearably sad. "I will not forget it."

"And I will send you daily reminders to make sure," Mr. Kent replied.

"Too bad, I had my money on Mr. Braddock," Miss Chen said, her arms crossed lazily. She shook her head at me ruefully. "Last time I bet on anyone's romantic prospects."

Next to her, Mr. Redburn stepped out of a portal, dusting off his jacket.

"What happened? Did she get away?" I asked, ignoring Miss Chen's commentary.

"No, we caught her," he said, looking all too pleased with himself. "Pulled her into a portal when she was distracted. She'll be fine."

"And what happens next?" I asked. "Will she remain locked away against her wishes?"

He rolled his eyes. "My brother'll speak to her—make sure she does the right thing. He has a way with people."

I could feel the same unease from before curling through my body. "And what is that way?"

Mr. Redburn shrugged his shoulders. "I don't know, feeding her a great deal of candy."

Mr. Kent's hand was on my back, failing to be soothing. In fact, it was rather irritating. "She will be all right, Miss Wyndham."

"Do you think this is really helping people?" I asked Miss Chen.

She opened her eyes, looking as cool as always. But I felt sure that she was actually deeply uncomfortable. "Depends if you're asking an Englishman or an Indian."

A portal back to London crackled open and Mr. Redburn sighed. "Are we done here?" he asked.

"No, we're not done," I told him. "Where did she go?"

"That's none of your concern."

"I'm making it my concern," I said, and turned to Mr. Kent. "Can you ask him?"

"Kent, don't you speak a word," Mr. Redburn warned him with a growl.

Mr. Kent looked at Mr. Redburn. And looked at me. And back at Mr. Redburn. "Where did you—"

Mr. Redburn threw a portal below Mr. Kent and he disappeared before he could finish the question. Then he did the same with

Mr. Braddock and Miss Chen, leaving the two of us alone. "Before you start whining about them, too, I sent them all home. Now let's get something settled, Miss Wyndham."

He fussily smoothed his queue as he stepped forward, making me stumble back. "You ask too many questions. Your job? To do as we tell you to do." His hand snaked out to grab my wrist and keep me close. We were on a deserted street and my friends were gone. I could sense myself beginning to panic but I forced myself to concentrate on Mr. Redburn, staying slack in his grasp.

"In return, you keep your pretty new house and we make sure your family is safe. If you get too mouthy? Well. I don't think you will like the consequences. So next time, you do what I say. You don't sic one of your little lapdog boys on me or begin to challenge me. Is that clear?"

He sneered as I stared back at him, trying to comprehend the threat. Before I could say anything, a hole opened below me and I fell back into my garden.

The comforting scent of wet earth rose around me. I took a deep breath as I clambered to my feet, trying to calm the fury and powerlessness roiling through my body.

I didn't know whether it was Mr. Redburn who was the dangerous one, or if it was Miss Rao, or if it was the whole blasted Society. But nothing about that mission felt right.

Chapter 10

WELL. I COULDN'T shiver in the garden all day. At least my mother did not know I was here and would think I was still out with Lady Atherton. I shuffled around the side of the house, ducking beneath the many windows. As soon as I made it around the corner I rushed to the street to call a hack.

I needed to know who Miss Rao was.

I needed to know why we had to capture her.

I needed to know where this information was coming from.

I needed answers.

The Society of Aberrations' footman had none. When he let me in, he did not know of any new arrivals, of anyone named Radhika Rao, or of any sudden changes in the weather. I told him I could find the library myself, but instead went up to the living quarters, putting my ear up to various doors. None of the maids I passed had any notion of a young Indian woman arriving.

I couldn't barge into every room, but I did have a friend who could help.

Oliver was in the gardens, training hard with the flying girl, dodging a flurry of attacking vines from the boy who could control plants. When he saw me hovering by the entrance, he let the

vines pass through him and headed over, leaving the other two to train on their own.

"Miss." He nodded at me.

"Hello, Oliver, are you well?" He gave me a shrug that conveyed nothing.

"Bit bored—wish I could be on missions." He crossed his arms and raised a brow.

A dart of fear hurtled through me. "There will be plenty of time for that . . . later . . . ," I said vaguely.

He rolled his eyes. "That's what *everyone* says."

"Actually, you might be very helpful to me," I said, hoping to flatter him into assisting me. "This morning we found a new recruit. An Indian woman, Miss Radhika Rao. Have you seen her?"

Oliver frowned and shook his head. "No one new today. There was a woman who could sing you to sleep that they brought yesterday. And I spied on Captain Goode's tour the day before."

"You—never mind. She should have come an hour ago, but none of the house staff have seen her."

"Maybe they took her to the recovery room. If anyone gets sick or hurt that is where they would be sent. And then you'd probably be sent for, actually."

"Where is it?"

"I'll show you."

He waved good-bye to his training partners and led me upstairs to a room that looked like a small ward in a hospital. There were ten beds lined up against the walls. All of them were unoccupied.

"I suppose I should just speak with Captain Goode," I sighed, feeling more nervous than I probably needed to.

"He isn't here," Oliver said. "He raised our powers and told us to train just before he left."

Wonderful. More hindrances.

"But his office is there," Oliver suggested with a smirk, leading the way.

Captain Goode's office. Tempting. Oliver was halfway down the hall and I followed, not sure if I should be encouraging this behavior.

"Oliver, I don't want to make you do something that might lead to trouble."

He shrugged. "I already did."

"You *what?*"

"I snuck into his office the second day I was here. I don't like not knowing everything. Didn't trust 'em."

"Then why did you join them?"

"Easier to sneak around from the inside." He looked at me calmly, as though it were all very obvious.

I stared at him. Oliver was even more skeptical than I had thought. "Did you find anything suspicious?" I asked.

He shook his head. "Not the first time, but I didn't get to look at everything. But I was planning on checking again."

"Do you do this a lot?" I asked, suspicion beginning to build in my mind.

"Yes," he said plainly. "Don't tend to trust people."

I stopped cold. "Does that mean you went through my things? And Miss Grey's?"

"Yup," he said easily. "Did you give those letters to Mr. Braddock? You had a lot of unfinished ones—"

"All right, no more of that," I said hastily, herding him in front of me.

Soon we found ourselves in a hallway of offices for the higher-ranking Society members, Captain Goode's at the very end. Oliver poked his head inside the locked room to check if it was empty, while I peeked around the corner to make certain no one would surprise us. The area clear, Oliver took my hand and I clenched it tightly.

The rational part of me knew that he was capable of pulling another person with him. But the irrational part of me conjured up a distinct image of our bodies stuck halfway through the wall for Captain Goode to find.

Thankfully, with a small shudder, we were through. The office was rather efficient and boring. The walls were covered with a mundane, peeling yellow wallpaper with simple, ugly landscapes. A small shelf of books with ordinary subjects—politics, history, religion. A glass cabinet displayed some of Captain Goode's awards for service in the army, along with a family photograph where Mr. Redburn smiled like he actually found something entertaining.

Captain Goode's desk was another matter entirely. Some drawers were locked, but Oliver was able to overcome that tight security with ease, sliding his hand in and pulling out stacks of files. He went to the office entrance and poked his head out to keep watch, while I sorted through the papers and folders. Many of them were intricate details of Society members and some were names I recognized from my healing rounds with Lady Atherton. Those files listed all their business ventures, investments, offices held—essentially everything the Society would need to know when it came to calling in their favors.

Mr. Braddock's name caught my eye next. Just underneath were files on Mr. Kent, Miss Grey, Oliver, Emily, and me. With a chill running down my spine, I opened mine to find a handwritten record of my activities. I flipped through the pages, my eyes moving too rapidly to fully process each sentence. There was a list of all my friends and family, information about my father's financial situation, a report on my sister's death, a log of my activities and the people I've healed since joining the Society, observations of my powers, and unnecessary notes that I was stubborn and argumentative.

I felt sick. While it wasn't surprising to see all these notes, it was dreadfully uncomfortable to hold them and feel the weight of all the information they had on me. But I forced myself to close the file and stay on task. I needed to find out what they had done with Miss Rao. I set aside the named files and searched through the ones labeled by month and year.

The February 1883 file was filled with a number of short, handwritten letters. Orders, I realized as I skimmed through them. Orders from the anonymous head of the Society to Captain Goode. I sifted through lists of the families I had visited with Lady Atherton. Names of politicians and the questions Mr. Kent was to ask them. The address of a building Miss Chen was to destroy. Similarly destructive and sometimes constructive orders for a number of names I didn't recognize—other powered people under the Society's employ.

Then I found the recruitment orders. For Miss Grey, Oliver, and myself. For Miss Tolman, who could sing you to sleep. For Miss Lewis, the girl who could fly. They all gave brief instructions for how to persuade us—from appealing to our desire to control our powers to gifts of wealth.

My hand trembled as I read the note on Mr. Braddock's recruitment. The head called Mr. Braddock dangerous, claimed he had killed many people in the past, and questioned whether he had completely reformed. He ordered Captain Goode to turn off his power and tell Mr. Braddock to return to the Society a day *after* it came back. Mr. Braddock's reaction would help them determine whether he could be trusted with the power. And if he truly wished to control it, then his need for the Society would only be strengthened.

So I had been right to suspect them. The head blatantly lied to Captain Goode so he would lie to us. All part of a manipulative plan to make Mr. Braddock feel more dependent on the Society.

My blood was boiling as I got to Miss Rao's and read the words: *A danger to the British realm. Antagonizes and murders innocents. Recruit or capture at all costs.*

Suddenly, Oliver's hand grabbed my arm. "He's coming!"

In a panic, I threw the files back together and Oliver slipped them back into drawers. By the time we finished, we heard a key rattle in the door. As the lock clicked, Oliver seized my hand and pulled me straight down through the floor.

We landed hard on an assortment of wooden chips and shavings in one of the training rooms. The strange flooring was quickly explained as I looked around to see an assortment of split and shattered logs—and Miss Chen.

"Dammit!" She cried out. A loud crack and crash sent another log to bits, and I coughed as wood dust hit my mouth. Oliver was already on his feet and helped me, too.

She was at the other end of the room, curled over, her face against her legs, breath coming in harshly drawn gasps.

"I . . . Sorry to interrupt, Miss Chen," I said, feeling the urge to babble and wondering if my cheeks were as red as they felt. "We did not mean to startle you. Oliver was just showing me what he'd learned with his power and it worked rather too well."

She ignored me as her breath slowed and just when I thought we should leave her in peace, she finally spoke. "By all means, interrupt me when my power is at its highest." Her voice was shaking a little, but she still managed to be sarcastic. "Do you also run into burning buildings for fun—you probably do, actually. Never mind."

"We surprised you," I said quickly. "I am sorry."

"You don't understand." Slowly she pulled herself upright, running her hands over the pieces of hair that had fallen from her braid. "I was practicing raising and lowering my power. It was extremely high when you came in. I could very easily have killed you." She still wouldn't look at us.

But I wasn't able to contain myself. "You can truly do that?" I asked.

"Kill you?" she muttered, then relented, tossing her gaze to the ceiling. "I'm getting better. Still mostly terrible."

"But to have *any* control . . ." My thoughts were racing to Mr. Braddock, already imagining the alternatives to depending on the Society.

"It is not easy. But when you have a power like this one, I promise you'd want to turn if off sometimes too. Raising it higher is part of the practice." She risked a quick look at me and I nodded, thinking about how constantly she had to divert her attentions so things did not fall apart.

She glanced up at the ceiling to Captain Goode's office. "I'd be careful barging into rooms, Miss Wyndham." Her voice was soft and cool but something in it made me freeze to the spot.

"What do you—" But she didn't have patience for my weak evasions.

"I snuck around at first, too. I didn't like what I found. But I liked what they did when they found out even less." She split another log and I covered my mouth with my sleeve.

"What did they do?"

She was quiet for a long moment. She turned to me and I saw only a flash of fear and anger burning in her eyes before she slid them away again.

"Go. Be less foolish." But it didn't feel like a rebuke as much as the best piece of advice she could give.

"Please, tell—"

"Go." Another log shattered, faster and more explosively than the last. Then the split pieces broke up, over and over till the log was simply a pile of dust.

I glanced at Oliver. "Let's go," I said.

I gathered my skirts and tiptoed around and over the split pieces of wood. When he reached the exit, he peeked his head through the wall and out into the hallway to make certain it was empty. I turned back again and saw Miss Chén covering her face with one shaking hand, but Oliver was slipping me out of the room and she disappeared from view. We were quiet for a long moment as we walked back to the foyer.

"Thank you for your help today, Oliver."

"Sneaking's always fun." He grinned up at me and waggled his brows.

"Can you pretend I simply wished to speak to you?" I asked him quietly.

Oliver rolled his eyes impatiently. "I'm not dense."

He began slipping through the wall but I called him back.

"Please be careful. They aren't being honest with us." I could tell that he wished to roll his eyes again, but instead he nodded.

I began walking briskly for the exit. I didn't want to spend any more time asking after Miss Rao and alerting people in the Society. Even though Captain Goode had passed Mr. Kent's tests, he was faithfully following orders from someone who wanted him to lie to Mr. Braddock. They wanted Mr. Braddock's power to fail him and hurt someone. They wanted Mr. Braddock to feel like he needed the Society. They wanted all of us to feel that way. I was right not to trust them that very first day.

I left the Society and decided to walk to Miss Grey's. It was not far and I found that I needed the relief of stomping along the street, shouldering by pedestrians. Chaperones be damned.

Miss Grey made a pretty picture in her small, comfortably appointed drawing room. She was composing a letter as her maid ushered me inside.

"Evelyn!" She smiled brightly but it immediately faltered as she noticed my furious expression. It fell further when the maid left and I removed my cloak and revealed a dusty, slightly blood-stained dress underneath.

"What's happened?" she gasped.

"What happens to the powered people after you locate them?" I asked.

She took my hands and led me to a chair, not looking to see if I was ruining it with my dirty dress. "Tell me what happened— are you all right?"

"I'm fine, I'm unhurt. I just—I need to know. Where do they go?" I knew I was being frustratingly unclear, but I couldn't seem to make my mind work properly, too riled up after our trip to India and the letters I had found in Captain Goode's office.

Miss Grey slowly stepped back, her eyes full of concern as she took a seat across from me. "Well, dear, they join the Society. As we did. And they either contribute when their power is helpful, or, if they can't quite control it—or are young and unstable—they train."

"I know that's what Captain Goode has said. But are you certain? Have you seen or dreamt about the people again after you located them?"

Miss Grey looked so perplexed I had to review what I said to see if it was so absurd. Or perhaps it was that I couldn't keep the acid from my voice. "I haven't kept track. . . . I have been focusing my dreams outside of England lately. There's Miss Tolman. She's learning to control her singing power better."

"And besides her? Anyone else?"

She agitatedly brushed back a red strand of hair. "Evelyn, what are you truly asking me? I thought you were happy working with the Society."

"I was trying to be, but I just returned from a recruitment mission for a woman in India."

"Miss Rao," Miss Grey said. "Yes. They sent you?"

I nodded. "Along with Mr. Kent, Mr. Braddock, Miss Chen, and Mr. Redburn. When we asked her to join us, she refused. Then, Mr. Redburn insisted that she had killed people before and that our orders were to bring her back no matter what."

Miss Grey stood then, looking a bit nervous. "Captain Goode has said the Society recruits dangerous Aberrations for this very reason—in case they are a danger to themselves or any other people."

"But she wasn't dangerous until we attacked her! Mr. Redburn tried to force her into one of his portals and only then did she start a massive storm to defend herself. I don't believe Mr. Redburn was telling the truth at all." I started to feel sick, thinking of all the people with powers who might be hurt by the Society, by people like Miss Grey, who believed they were doing good.

By people like me.

Miss Grey nodded slowly. "Did Mr. Kent ask her if she had actually hurt people?"

"He never had the chance. But you're the one who found her. Did you ever dream of her hurting anyone?"

"She certainly has the potential to," Miss Grey said. But it came out slightly mechanically and I could almost see her mind working, looking for explanations. "And the Society has other sources of information. . . ."

I repeated the question.

She shook her head with a sigh, looking pale and worried. "No. From what I saw, she was living a quiet, simple life."

"And we just ruined that," I said.

I had ruined someone's entire life. I leaped to my feet, pacing, trying to escape my own guilt.

"Now they are keeping her God knows where, and for how long? Until she agrees to help the Society like we are? Make London a warm, sunny place?"

"We can ask Captain Goode about it," Miss Grey suggested, trying for a smile.

"No!" I almost yelled. "He lied to Mr. Braddock about how long he could turn off his power."

"He said he made a mistake. He was very apologetic about it." She turned her chin up slightly and I wondered if her fondness for Captain Goode was clouding her judgment.

"The recruitment order he received said to lie to Mr. Braddock. They wanted his power to wear off so he felt more indebted."

"And how are you determining all of this?"

"By sneaking into his office with Oliver and seeing it all. They have records on all of us and that's how they manipulate us into joining."

"Evelyn!" she admonished, but then went silent for a moment. "He lied?" she asked, a little bit of distress creeping into her face.

I knew why she wanted so desperately for the Society to be good. After dreaming of powered people and believing herself mad, after months of torture in an asylum, she now located people easily with Captain Goode's assistance, with so much less strain and effort. Indeed, she looked far healthier than she ever had. Her hair was shining and her eyes had no shadows to dull their brightness. And she finally had a purpose, believing she was doing good by finding and helping new recruits all over the world.

And here I was, bringing it all crashing down.

"I'm sorry," I said, sinking back down into the seat she offered me at the beginning. "Captain Goode might just be following orders because he trusts the head. But you know me."

Miss Grey smiled sadly. "You always questioned everything I tried to teach you. Rose was a far more polite student."

The mention of Rose settled us both into silence, as it usually did. If she were here, I felt sure she'd want to check on Miss Rao, make certain she was well. She never forgot to inquire after our patients in the days after we treated them. She would never leave someone in distress.

"I'll try to dream of Miss Rao," Miss Grey finally said. "To see where she is and if she's well."

"Thank you," I said. "It would ease my mind to know."

I could see in her eyes that she was really hoping this was all a misunderstanding, that the Society was everything they professed. But I found myself almost hoping for the opposite, that they would just come out and tell us they were evil. Then at least I wouldn't have to do all this anxious wondering and waiting.

"Evelyn, you're brooding," Catherine said.

"Don't you dare say that."

"It's true."

"Even so. Only a terrible friend would say such a thing."

"It's the only thing to say that will get you to stop. You have no further information. Wait until you hear from Miss Grey."

It had been three days since India, and I was getting restless. I had strongly considered storming . . . somewhere. The Society perhaps. Again. That was what I might have done in the past. But no good had ever come from my angry impulses during my search for Rose.

Instead, Catherine and I were sitting in my morning-room window seat, drinking cup after cup of tea, snug as we read the papers and watched the world pass by, cold rain streaming down the glass to obscure the picture. The weather outside was gray and wintry. I couldn't help but wonder if that was the normal London weather, or if it was Miss Rao's doing. If she wasn't in the Society, where was she?

"And what am I supposed to do until then?" I asked. Irritably.

"You could open your present," she said brightly, pulling a slim, exotic-looking box from her reticule.

"Catherine! You didn't need to get me anything," I chastised. I tried to put on an appreciative smile, knowing that unless her present contained information on Miss Rao, I would not be easily distracted.

I lifted the top and found a small, gold-tipped metal fan folded up in the pretty, velvet-lined case. Gently, I took it by its weighted handle and opened it. An elegant gold thread created an intricate pattern on expensive black silk.

"Thank you, this is lovely, truly." It was. I smiled brightly, thinking of the next time I could use it.

"I appreciate you pretending to like the silly fan part, but here's the real fun," she said, clicking a latch on the handle. With a soft scrape, something emerged from within. A gleaming dagger.

"Goodness, Catherine, you . . . this is . . . You simply could not have gotten me anything more perfect. Where on earth did you find this?"

"Paris. The shop owner received it with the rest of an old estate. Something about it made me think of you."

"It's wonderful," I breathed. Though there was no sun to be seen, the dagger caught every bit of light in the room, glinting.

Catherine grinned back, making the freckles on the apples of her cheeks crowd together. "Perhaps you can use it to fend off your many suitors."

"Ha," I said lightly, releasing the lever to let the dagger click back into place. It was once again an ordinary fan. I decided then and there to never leave home without it.

"Mr. Kent stopped by yesterday," Catherine said innocently, sipping at her tea.

"Hmm," I said, hoping if I seemed bored enough I could avoid the topic altogether.

"He told me about India."

Blast.

"I don't know what you mean," I said evenly.

"Evelyn. He kissed you!"

"He might have," I said.

Catherine kicked at my feet.

"Fine," I said, putting my cup down on the tray near us and turning to her. After all, perhaps she could help me sort out my complicated feelings.

"You do like him, yes?" Catherine asked, her clear eyes unwavering.

"I . . . I do. Of course I do."

"But you hesitate?"

I did hesitate and, infuriatingly, I knew exactly why. Sebastian

Braddock. There was no use denying it. Engaged he might be. Elusive and ridiculous and constantly shouldering more responsibility than was truly his to bear—and yet, whenever I tried to decide what Mr. Kent's kiss meant, Mr. Braddock would barge into my thoughts.

"Oh dear, you're brooding even more, somehow."

"It's just that I do not think it fair, necessarily. Mr. Kent seems so sure of his feelings for me. Whereas I'm more . . . muddled." I looked out the window again, feeling uncomfortable meeting Catherine's eyes.

"And, well, when he kissed you?" Catherine coughed slightly.

I felt my cheeks burn. "It was . . . nice."

"Nice?"

"Yes. Nice."

Catherine narrowed her eyes at me.

"It was nice! It just wasn't like . . ." *Ah.* I had not meant to continue that thought. Catherine pounced on my slip.

"Like what?"

"Like nothing."

"Evelyn. Like what?"

"Nothing!"

"Evelyn Margaret Wyndham, like *what*? Or are you going to force me to say it for you?"

I stared at her, startled. "Say what?"

"That I suspect you have been kissing that Mr. Braddock." She put down her empty teacup and crossed her arms, raising her eyebrows knowingly at me.

I gaped at her. "How did you know?"

"Ha!" She was giggling uncontrollably, her face split with a true smile. "I had no idea. I was just trying out a wild guess."

I hit her with one of the cushions and climbed out of the nook, hot and feeling the need to move. "It wasn't a real kiss. . . . It was complicated."

"I was under the impression that he and Miss Lodge were well acquainted." Catherine wasn't laughing anymore.

"More than acquainted. They are engaged. Secretly," I said shortly. For a moment I felt sure she judged me. "I did not know that when he—well, when . . . when we kissed." She nodded solemnly.

"You believe me?" I asked, feeling guilty even though there wasn't reason to.

"Of course," she said staunchly. "But you have feelings for him, don't you?"

I didn't answer for a moment.

"I . . . I don't . . . Well, of course I have feelings, I have feelings about lots of things," I said stubbornly.

"Hmm." Catherine picked up the paper and pulled out the Agony Column she had been trying to distract me with earlier. "Are they something like this? 'Oh! Feel your lips upon me still, soft and fleeting. Come back to me, oh darling! Do not use me so. . . .'"

But Catherine couldn't finish, quite overcome with giggles as I whacked her with the pillow.

"I shall never tell you anything again," I said, snatching the paper from her hands and smoothing it with my own.

I would read that particular entry later.

"I did not see you together for long, dear, but it did strike me that there was something between you."

I looked up to see her cleaning her spectacles on her skirts, avoiding my eyes.

"I—there is nothing, Catherine. Really. He is a distraction, nothing more."

And wasn't that true? Thinking of him did nothing productive: It solved no mysteries surrounding the Society of Aberrations, and it only tangled my thoughts as I tried to practically contemplate proposals and almost proposals.

Besides, there was nothing to ponder. Mr. Braddock was to be married to someone who was not me. And I had received a perfectly nice kiss from a charming, delightful man who happened to be one of my best friends. I was lucky, really.

"You're doing it again," Catherine said lightly.

But there came a knock at my door—a maid delivering a letter. All thoughts of Mr. Braddock and Mr. Kent flew out of my head.

Miss Grey had dreamt of Miss Rao. She had been taken to the Society of Aberrations after all. And locked in a prison hidden deep below.

Chapter II

T HE HARD PART about sneaking out of my house and into a prison for powered people should have lain mostly with the prison part. But no, the trouble began with my mother.

I had hoped to appease her by continuing my pleasant behavior, but every attempt I made only roused her suspicions further. My smiles were met with narrowed eyes. My compliments for Lord Atherton's wit and Lady Atherton's shrewdness were received with vague grunts of agreement. My wish to embroider with Mother after dinner was answered with an audible gasp as if I had shouted the vilest curse.

Perhaps embroidery was going a bit too far.

Stubbornly, we both sat in the small parlor, embroidering for far longer than either of us wished. I needed her to sleep, so I might sneak out without fear of being caught and questioned, while she needed to understand what exactly was wrong with me.

"Are you feeling well?" she asked, after a half hour of tense needlepoint.

"Yes, I am feeling perfectly well," I said. "How are you?"

She didn't respond. A half hour later, she eyed me suspiciously as she stabbed at her square. "I can't recall the last time you wanted to do this."

"Lady Atherton recently reminded me of the value," I said calmly.

Another half hour passed. "Evelyn, what are you planning?"

I could feel her eyes on me, but I dared not look up. "I am planning to finish this flower and go to bed, so I might wake up at a reasonable hour."

She set her work down with a tired sigh and rose to her feet, giving up at last. She rang for her maid and spoke softly with her. Before leaving the room, Mother had one more accusing glare to give me. "Good night. If you happen to have need of something, I've asked Pretton to watch for you."

It wasn't hard to find her meaning there, concealed in the thoughtful gesture. After she retired to her room, I took the long way back to my bedroom and confirmed it with a quick peek into the servant's hall. Mother had asked our poor butler to keep an eye on the exits. What did she think? That I was going to sneak out at midnight and set someone free from prison?

It almost made me miss the freedom in Lady Kent's home.

Fortunately, freedom was still quite accessible when one can self-defenestrate without fear of injury. After Lucy helped me undress for bed, I immediately redressed for escape, finding a good use for one of my fifty new tea gowns, crept down to a first-floor parlor and promptly jumped out the window. One sprained and quickly healed ankle later, I snuck around the back garden and took a hansom to the public house near the Society.

I was late. Rushing inside, I immediately saw Mr. Kent flirting rather obviously with the barmaid. But he turned as soon as I walked in, grinning as his eyes found me.

"Is Oliver not here?" I asked him, a little out of breath.

"No, it seems I am the only man you can count on, Miss Wyndham."

I couldn't help but smile back at him.

"While we wait," he continued, "we could discuss something very pleasant. A certain moment we shared just a mere three days ago." Mr. Kent was leaning toward me now and the barmaid sulked off.

But Oliver appeared through the wall at that moment, looking at us both suspiciously.

"Hi," he said flatly. "I know I'm late but they kept us while a girl who can turn people into pigs practiced turning us into pigs and I was stuck as a pig for a really long time and I really didn't like it."

"Oh dear," I said. We stared at each other. "I'm glad you are no longer a pig." He nodded in appreciation. "No one suspects that you left?"

"No, they think we are all resting. After being pigs and all." He seemed extremely affronted at having been a pig. I felt guiltier and guiltier for drawing him into this plan.

"You know you don't need to do this—you are sure you want to?"

He nodded impatiently.

"Mr. Kent, can you check?"

"Oliver, are you sure about this?" Mr. Kent had been giving me a significant look since Oliver's interruptions but he turned toward him now.

"I said I am!" Oliver confirmed, very exasperated. "It's fun. They have too many rules."

And with the indisputable logic of a stubborn young man, we crossed behind a pillar. I took Oliver's hand first and Mr. Kent grasped the other. Oliver took a deep breath, and pulled us down through the floor. For a second, I felt like I was walking on air, walking through air, and was air itself, until I felt wet dirt below me. We were in the cellar a few floors down. "Good work," Mr. Kent whispered.

We walked west, heading farther down the street, now one building from the Society. At the next wall, Oliver pulled us through confidently. I could still feel the dirt but it didn't seem to touch me, as though we were weightless, drifting by. With a gasp, we arrived in a storeroom cellar.

Miss Grey had said the jail was about forty paces west from the northwest corner wall we passed through. Quietly, I counted my way over in the dark and stopped at the nondescript spot.

"Straight down another floor," I whispered to Oliver.

"This reminds me of that lovely kiss we shared," Mr. Kent said as he handed me a lantern. "That feeling of weightlessness."

I ignored him, of course. Oliver snorted at us in disgust but took our hands again to plunge downward this time, sinking, floating down as if we were in water. I tried to ignore the complete darkness and trust in Miss Grey's directions and Oliver's control. My feet finally found the ground, gently, as Oliver let go.

"You are getting better," I whispered.

"I know," he whispered back, arrogant, but amusingly so. "Someday I'm gonna slide right into the Queen's palace. Steal a cup of tea. Try on her crown."

"Miss Wyndham," began Mr. Kent, "you don't seem to be appreciating that this atmospheric location is the ideal place to discuss our lips and the way they once touched."

"You are mistaken; this is assuredly not the time," I hissed in annoyance.

I turned to dig out a box of matches and lit the lantern to be sure we'd actually dropped into the right place. It was a simple corridor of gray stone walls, a low earthen ceiling, and iron-barred doors. Nothing unexpected, except for the fact that it was somehow much colder inside than out. Frost and icicles had formed around the walls and ceiling.

"This is . . . a strange prison," Mr. Kent said cautiously.

Holding the lantern before me, I led the way down the corridor, hearing the occasional crack and crunch of ice under our feet. Our breath was visible, each one curling like smoke before disappearing. I cautiously peered through the first door and nodded at Mr. Kent. A thin, sallow-looking man lay on the floor, turning and flipping his hand in the air as though he were playing with an invisible ball.

"Hello, sir," Mr. Kent said quietly.

The man looked up and smiled, revealing toothless gums. "Hello, guv."

"Why are you in this prison, sir?" Mr. Kent asked.

"Killed quite a lot of people."

"Indeed? That is a good reason for prison," Mr. Kent said drily, and seemed ready to turn away, but I was thinking of Mr. Braddock, who would give anything not to have hurt people.

"Ask him if he did it on purpose," I whispered.

"Now, you killed plenty of people, I understand, but was it on purpose?"

"Oh, to be sure."

"Did you . . . enjoy it?"

"Yes, deeply pleasurable. Just biding my time before I can do it again."

Mr. Kent frowned and looked to me. I had no further questions. "I see, we will keep that in mind. Excuse us a moment."

With that, we quickly walked to the next door, hoping this person was here for smaller crimes.

"Like to eat the ones I kill," a pretty young girl said.

"No one ever notices me," rasped an older lady at the third door. "Until I cut their skin into the loveliest ribbons."

"Do you want me to tell you what you taste like?" The first

girl was at her door, watching our slow progress. We did our best to ignore her giggles. Oliver was looking more and more pale, but set his jaw tightly.

"What a lovely set of people," Mr. Kent said lightly.

"We should find Miss Rao," I said, trying to keep my worries from overwhelming me. I couldn't help but wonder what she might have done. Was the recruitment order true? Was she like these remorseless souls?

We passed a few more cells before finding her. She was sleeping, sitting up against the wall, her unbound hair hiding most of her and the darkness doing the rest.

"Miss Rao?" I said quietly.

She barely moved. "You."

Mr. Kent cleared his throat. "We are sorry to see you in this state, Miss Rao. Pardon me for this question, but I need to ask, why are you in here?"

"Because my winds can sink ships. Or my rains can flood villages. Or my lightning can destroy cities," she said. "You want my power since you British have taken everything else."

I stepped toward the cell. "They told us you killed many people."

"That is a lie."

"How many people have you killed?" Mr. Kent asked.

"None," came her quick answer. "I just wanted you out of my country and instead you've imprisoned me in yours."

I let out a heavy breath. "Have they hurt you?"

"You keep speaking as if you aren't responsible for this." She rose to her feet and walked toward the door, into the lantern light. Her hair fell back, revealing bruises and half-healed cuts covering her face. There was dried blood from a crack in her lip and one eye was swollen shut. "You can keep me here in the cold. You can keep removing my power. You can keep hurting me. I will never help you."

I gritted my teeth and forced my knuckles to relax. While Miss Grey's note had sounded unpleasant, seeing Miss Rao's injuries sent shudders through my body. Even if we didn't know it at the time, we were responsible for this pain.

"I'm . . . sorry," I said simply. "We will get you ou—"

Something metal clattered down the hall. Footsteps. A faint glow was growing brighter from around the corner.

"Oliver," I hissed, putting out the lantern. "Bring us in there. Quickly."

His hands grabbed mine and Mr. Kent's and pulled us inside with Miss Rao.

"Why do you hide from them?" she asked.

"We made a mistake," I whispered back, taking her hand. She made to pull away. "Please, it will heal you. We are so sorry for—"

Our breaths held, we listened as the crunching footsteps grew louder and louder. There was a brief pause at every cell.

Miss Rao's hand was cold in mine and I squeezed harder, hoping my power could heal any damage this icy cell had done. As the guard came near, I released her hand and Oliver silently guided Mr. Kent and me to the cell wall. The lantern light and footsteps came ever closer, the temperature dropping. When the guard seemed to be just outside the cell, Oliver's hand tightened around mine and he slipped the three of us through the wall into the next cell. All I caught was a glimpse of dark hair, glowing blue in the chilly light. In the darkness we waited, not daring to breathe, letting the footsteps fade away.

"If you let me out, I can cause searing pain to anyone you wish," a voice hissed. "It does not leave a mark."

Oliver's hand trembled and I would have screamed had I not lost complete control of my voice.

Mr. Kent found his faster. "Thank you for the offer, but I can just invite them to my mother's dinner parties. Mr. Myles, if you will."

Oliver pulled us back into Miss Rao's cell, shaking his head. "Maybe being a pig wasn't so bad after all." I let out a sigh of relief, but chills still crept up my spine.

Miss Rao fixed me with a suspicious glare. The bruises and cuts that had marred her face seemed to be fully healed. "You are no longer with them. Why?"

I held her gaze as steadily as I could. "We made a mistake. I do not believe you deserve to be here. They lied to us."

"Who?" she asked, fury in her eyes. "Who is in charge of this?"

"I don't know. It's kept very secret," I said.

"Then we will ask," she said.

Before I could explain that we couldn't simply ask, I saw the flash of a small blade as Miss Rao swept past us, clenched a bar on the door, and began carving at a rusty end that already bore marks from her knife.

"Uh . . . did . . . we interrupt your escape?" Mr. Kent asked.

A few heavy strokes and the bar snapped off.

"Yes," she said and squeezed through the gap. "But you may help."

By the time Oliver brought Mr. Kent and me to the icy hallway, she was already making her way down to another cell.

At the sight of Miss Rao's freedom, the other prisoners seemed to grow restless.

"Let us out, too!" one whispered.

"She's not even been here for a week!" the cannibalistic girl complained.

"Be quiet or we won't be able to get any of you," I hissed back.

"Mr. Kent, there must be others like Miss Rao, people who don't deserve to be here."

"I don't know how much time we have to question everyone," he replied, frowning.

"Question this man," Miss Rao said, pointing at a cell a little farther down. "He is always yelling that the head of the Society is a man with no power."

Mr. Kent, Oliver, and I gaped at her. I hurried down the hall and peered in to see a bearded man with wild eyes pressing his face against the bars.

"Is that true? Does the head of the Society of Aberrations not have any kind of ability?" Mr. Kent asked the man.

"It's true, he doesn't," he replied in a deep rasp. "And I won't say another word until you let me out."

"Hmm. Are you one of those sorts of people who enjoys hurting others?"

"Yes," the man said, looking confused by his answer.

Mr. Kent grinned. "Ah, a complicated moral dilemma you present, sir. Either I release you into the world for the information, or leave you here and never know. Blast it. I wish I could simply ask you: Who is the head of the Society of Aberrations?"

"The Duke of Fosberry," the man said with a scowl.

Mr. Kent looked pensive for a moment but my heart was leaping. A name! We had a name! "Huh. How exactly did you come by this information?" Mr. Kent did not look nearly thrilled enough.

"I was his guard."

"A guard? As in, for his person?"

"Yes."

"And how long have you been down here?"

"Ten years," the man snarled. "All right, you got what you wanted—now let me out."

"I don't believe I did," Mr. Kent said. "The current Duke of Fosberry is eight years old. I assume you were the guard for his late father. Did he ever tell you who would succeed him as head?"

Blast.

"No, damn you," the bodyguard growled. And then he said a word that shocked even me as he stuffed his fingers in his ears.

But Mr. Kent just raised his voice. "Do you know how the head is appointed?"

I looked around nervously at the prisoners. We were drawing more of them to their doors as Mr. Kent spoke louder and louder, and they were begging for us to let them out, their yelling and clanging echoing down the hallway.

"No," the bodyguard said, raising his voice. "No more questions unless you let me out!"

"Who was his predecessor?"

"The Earl of Hartwell!" he yelled at the top of his lungs in a frenzy, pulling hard at the iron bars, jamming his face up against the small opening, his spit flying in tiny flecks. "You lying, cheating scum! Guard! Guard!"

He couldn't hold back the answers, but he could get us caught. A heavy door cracked open. Clattering footsteps and freezing winds preceded the glowing guard.

"Help!" the cannibalistic girl joined in, shaking her bars. "They are escaping!"

"Go!" I shouted.

"They'll keep you down here with me and you can ask all the questions you want!" the bodyguard shouted after us.

We hurried down the corridor, but I found it hard to keep my balance. The ground grew slick with ice, the air was getting colder, and then a biting cold blast struck my legs from behind.

"Miss Wyndham!" Mr. Kent shouted.

The cold ground hit me hard and kept me there. I couldn't get back up. My feet were frozen—rather literally—to the ground.

"Go, Oliver, take them first!"

Thankfully, Oliver and Miss Rao listened to me. Only Mr. Kent disobeyed, sliding to the ground next to me, trying to pull my feet from the ice that seemed to be growing around them, making me gasp as the cold seeped through my boots, my stockings, prickling against my skin.

The slide of nimble feet on ice came louder. I twisted around to see the dainty guard ambling forward, intent on me, while Mr. Kent tried in vain to chip away at the ice on my feet with the edge of his cane.

Up close I could see her hair was somewhere between brown and black, shining in the strange light that surrounded her. Her skin gleamed; a pattern of snowflakes tattooed her neck, hands, and everything not covered by the thin dress she wore. She smiled, seeming to feel no discomfort.

"That was a mild blast." Her voice was low and rich. She gave a short whistle, her frosted breath thick in the air. "If you call the boy back now, that will be all the punishment you get."

"I'm sorry," I said flippantly. "I don't really feel like it."

Her eyes lit with a blue fire and she let out a laugh that sent shards of ice flying. "Oh, you will, you'll feel like doing whatever we say once they find out what you have done."

Mr. Kent dropped his cane, giving up on my feet and reaching into his jacket. He pulled his pistol out, but the guard didn't need to draw her own weapon. She exhaled a quick concentrated burst of freezing air that hit Mr. Kent's hand before he could even aim, encasing his hand and gun in ice.

"That your answer then?" she asked. "Fine."

And then she started to inhale, drawing in a great gust of air.

"Wait! What are your thirty favorite foods?" Mr. Kent asked.

His question forced her to cut her breath off and answer. "Shepherd's pie, roast turkey, ice cream . . ."

Mr. Kent leaned down and smashed the block of ice that was his arm against the mound at my feet. This seemed to do the trick, shattering both and letting him pull me up. One boot remained stuck in the ice, but we wrenched my foot free and scrambled away. A heavy dread was beginning to replace the surge of panic that had run through me till now. Mr. Kent pulled me toward the end of the tunnel as the guard chased us, still listing her favorites.

". . . beef stew, tarts, bacon . . ."

I stumbled, the cold making me numb. I felt like I was running at the bottom of the ocean, unable to push forward.

". . . fish soup—ha!" The guard finished her list with a shout of victory I could barely register before my whole body sang with pain. Cold sank into my bones, my muscles grinding to a halt, my skin stinging fiercely, a scream lost in my throat.

"Oi!" I heard, then a scrawny but strong hand had my elbow. I was being pulled up and through the dirt, feeling nothing but the cold that seemed to burrow deep into my bones. Behind me I could hear a frustrated roar from the guard but she was too slow, too late and up, up we went till we reached a dark alleyway outside the Society. Back, again, on solid ground.

The pain still held me in its grip and I fell to the ground, unable to stand. Mr. Kent reached out to touch my cheek and I yelped, the warmth burning as much as the cold. I could see him asking me something, looking a little desperate. I stared vacantly for a moment, letting my vision settle, letting my body heal itself and my shivers dissipate. I gasped and it seemed immeasurably warmer than the guard's freeze. I had never been so pleased to smell the sooty London air.

"Please, Evelyn, are you all right?" Mr. Kent was asking me. Behind him, Miss Rao's face was lifted up, her eyes moving rapidly as she scanned the skies.

"I am, I am," I said, coming back to myself slowly. "We must go. They will look for us."

I slowly regained the ability to walk as the four of us hurried silently through the claustrophobic alleyways, barely lit by moonlight. Oliver slipped us through fences and dead-end walls. He seemed to know exactly where to go.

After we were some blocks away, I stopped him, thinking about the guard's warning.

"Thank you, Oliver," I said urgently. "We can manage from here."

"I'll get you home," he insisted, his eyes bright with success.

I felt sick. What if they punished him for this? "We can do that from here. You must get back to bed before they check on you."

He hesitated for a moment, then turned to slip away. I could swear I caught a glimpse of hurt in his eyes. "Fine."

"Oliver," I called, trying to tamp down my fears. "You did wonderfully tonight. I can't wait to see all the amazing things you do."

That got me a quick grin before he slipped through a wall, back toward the Society.

I turned to Miss Rao. "You are welcome to come with me, if you would like, though I may have to find some story for an unexpected guest."

Miss Rao was already backing away, her glare saying not to follow. "I prefer to do things alone."

"Well, take my card at least." I pulled one from the sleeve and handed it to her.

She reluctantly took it from me, fog curling around us. "I do not see the reason. I am not going to return."

"We can help each other. I'm certain there are others who don't deserve to be there."

"I am not fixing your mistakes for you."

"I am not asking that, but . . . your powers are incredible."

"I know."

I hesitated. "I do not think they will give up."

She nodded, looking into the night sky. "Neither will I."

She hurried away then, padding through the street in thin slippers, not even seeming to notice the biting cold. She disappeared into the dark.

"Perhaps I should have asked if she planned to take revenge on the eight-year-old," Mr. Kent said, breaking the moment of tension that had begun to build.

I sighed. "I just wish we could have done more."

"We'll figure out who the head is and go back," Mr. Kent said. "This was the right idea, Miss Wyndham. We know some of their secrets now. And we got the chance to finally go ice skating."

And it was true. But as I tried to fall asleep that night, the various warnings and clues from the guard began repeating in my head.

It was only the next morning, when I awoke to a chilling message, that I realized we should never have entered the prison.

Chapter 12

I FLEW UP THE stairs to Catherine's room, every beat of my heart telling me how stupid, stupid, stupid I had been. Catherine was white as a sheet as she lay in bed, her maid tending to her.

I rushed over, stripping off my gloves, reaching for her left hand. "Is she conscious?"

"W-what?" The maid was distraught and close to tears.

Catherine's injuries sent an uncontrollable shudder through me. Her limbs had been broken and twisted into unnatural angles. Her right foot was a limp, horribly boneless thing, hanging at the ankle. Her left leg was broken higher up, the cracked bone poking through the skin. Her right arm was broken at the forearm in the same awful way. Dear God, what had happened to her?

"Evelyn?" Catherine moaned.

But thank heavens, she was alive. That was all that mattered.

"I'm here," I said. She would recover. That was the only thing to hold on to now.

"Please, go check to see if the doctor has arrived," I told the maid, taking the cloth from her gently. "I am a nurse. I can stay with her."

"I—yes, of course, miss," she said with a nod, and left the room, taking deep breaths and hurried steps.

As soon as the door closed, I threw the cloth aside. I put my other hand on Catherine's head, hoping that would get rid of her pain quicker. Her bones shifted into place slowly, infuriatingly slowly. The silence in the room was overwhelming, pressing against me until the smallest sound of her breathing, which seemed to be slow and steady, was all I could focus on. It took a few minutes for the bones to reknit themselves and her wounds to fade back into her skin, now a healthy pink. I could feel desperate tears ready to fall now that the danger had passed.

"I'm sorry," I whispered.

"Yes, how dare you save my life," she said softly, sleepily.

"Does anything still hurt?"

She slowly pushed herself up on her bed, looking almost healthy and normal, save for her torn nightgown. "I . . . don't think so."

"Can you tell me what happened?" I asked.

She shook her head and two dots of anger warmed her cheeks. "I don't understand it. One moment I was crossing the room to write a letter and the next I couldn't move, my body was frozen. Then my bones just . . . broke. I was on the floor, feeling immediate pain all over. Like my body had been dipped in hot candle wax. It felt deliberate. I thought I saw someone in my balcony window, but it happened so fast."

Catherine's anger and fear bubbled over till a few tears squeezed out. She shook her head resolutely. "And then Mary found me and I begged her to get you. I knew I had some broken bones, but I didn't know how serious it was."

"Are you sure it doesn't hurt now?" I asked.

"I'm sure," she insisted.

Deciding to risk it then, I hugged her tightly, pulling her back down to the bed. "I'm so sorry," I said again.

"If I understood how it was your fault, I could accept your apology," she said, her voice muffled against my shoulder.

"I suspect this was the Society's punishment directed at me." There could be no question. There was no other reason to hurt my friend. The prison guard had threatened as much last night. "For helping the woman in the prison escape. Or the information we discovered."

Catherine straightened back up at that. "What information?"

"Mr. Kent questioned a bodyguard to the former head of the Society. He told us that the heads don't have powers and that the last two were the Duke of Fosberry and the Earl of Hartwell. But we don't know who the current one is or how he is chosen or—why am I telling you this? Catherine. No—do not even ask—stop it—I see your research face."

But she was already lost to me, pensively staring out her window. "Fosberry and Hartwell . . . I know the names. They were political men. I'm certain I can find a connection if there is one to be had. . . ."

I held her down in bed as she tried to get up. "Catherine, you must rest. You almost died."

"But I didn't, thanks to your healing," she said, tentatively stretching her limbs, wiggling her toes. "And now I can help you."

"No, what we need to do now is keep you safe from another attack."

Catherine patted my arm and leaned her head against mine. "They could have done worse. I think they've already made their point."

And that was when we heard the commotion from downstairs. A thudding of boots on the stairs and a chorus of shouting voices. Catherine and I sat up and I slid off the bed, ready to stop anyone who attempted to hurt her again.

But when the door banged open, it was a very irate and very familiar man.

And Mary, trying to dissuade him. "Miss Harding's been badly hurt, sir!" she said.

"So have others!" Mr. Kent said. Then he noticed the grisly scene. And the rips in Catherine's stockings and dress. "My God! Miss Harding, what happened?"

"An attack, it seems," Catherine answered. "I'm fine. It looks worse than it is. Evelyn helped me. Mary, please go downstairs and wait for the doctor. He won't be needed." Mary was staring at Catherine and me in utter shock, but she closed the door behind her.

Mr. Kent strode to the bed and grabbed our friend's hand.

"Who else has been hurt?" I asked.

"Laura," Mr. Kent answered, out of breath. "Tuffins sent me a message saying there was an accident but I—I don't know now—"

I jumped to my feet immediately. "How bad is it?"

"I don't know. I don't know," he said, dazed. He turned and headed for the door. "I shouldn't have left her alone."

I faltered. "Catherine, I—"

"Go," she interrupted, climbing out of her bed. "I will be right behind you."

As we threaded our way through the streets in the hansom, for once it was me reassuring Mr. Kent. The fact that this was just a warning from the Society, that I could heal Laura and she would be as healthy as before, helped him feel better about his sister. But as calm and optimistic as I forced myself to sound, I couldn't help the roiling in my stomach, the horror at how badly things could have gone.

Miss Chen had been right.

When we finally arrived at the Kents's house, we were greeted at the door by an exhausted Tuffins. "Miss Wyndham," he said, with the barest of smiles. "Please, come in. It has been too long."

"How is Laura?" I asked cautiously.

"She is resting in her room," Tuffins replied gravely. "We gave her some laudanum to help with the wait for the doctor. She was in a great deal of pain. We believe she hurt herself at the top of the stairs and took a tumble."

And that was enough for Mr. Kent to bound up two floors in seconds. Tuffins and I tried to keep up, but then we crossed in front of the wrong door on the landing.

"You!" a sharp voice called out. "Your presence here is unwelcome," Lady Kent hissed as she emerged from the drawing room. She leaned heavily on the doorframe, wincing as she shifted weight from her bad knees.

"I came to help your daughter," I said. I tried to keep a firm voice, but it was hard to forget the humiliation I endured the last time I was here.

And it seemed Lady Kent had a keen memory of it, too. "Tuffins, please show Miss Wyndham out."

But nothing happened. Lady Kent stared at Tuffins, perplexed. I followed her gaze to find him continuing toward the next flight of stairs, pretending not to have heard her. "This way, Miss Wyndham," he said.

"*Tuffins!*" Lady Kent shouted. "Did you not hear me?"

"I'm afraid I'm having a bit of trouble with that, my lady," Tuffins replied.

Lady Kent looked absolutely furious. She did not have to leave the doorway for her threat to be loud and strong: "Well, perhaps another steward might be able to hear!"

I stopped. I was too sick with worry over my friends, too

furious at her pigheaded thinking that I was some kind of deviant sullying her home.

Enough. I marched back to Lady Kent. She froze, confused, but as soon as I seized her free hand, she shouted, "Miss Wyndham! I insist that you leave!"

She tried to yank her hand from mine but I held tight.

"Lady Kent, I know you hate me. I know you delighted in throwing me out of your house last year based on scurrilous rumors and trumped-up scandals. So I am giving you two presents today: The first is a shocking new story to tell about the wicked Evelyn Wyndham. The second is that you are currently being healed by my magical healing power. Yes, I have one. No, I really don't think that rumor will stick, but please feel free to try it out on the ton."

I let go of her hand. She stared at me, uncomprehending for a long moment. I turned and headed back up the stairs to Tuffins. "Be sure to tell them my monstrous final words to you—they will be outraged, I'm sure: *I truly hope you feel better.*"

With that, I marched up behind Tuffins, who led the way to Laura's bedroom.

Inside, I found Mr. Kent watching over Laura's sleeping form, already looking as if he'd been there for hours. He was in his shirtsleeves, eyes burning with a dull anger. I hurried over to the bed and found what had seized Mr. Kent's attention. Among other injuries, a small dagger was lodged in Laura's leg. This was no simple tumble—it was a deliberate attack.

Mr. Kent became my shadow, peeking over my shoulder and anxiously raking through his hair as I took Laura's injured leg and slid the blade out in one quick motion. I wrapped a cloth around the wound, checked her breathing, and smoothed fine strands of hair away from her forehead, too restless myself to wait patiently for even thirty seconds.

She was so still. Laura was simply not Laura if she was not bouncing around, desperately in love with someone. It was unnatural to see her like this.

As I watched her bones heal, the bleeding slow, and the bruises fade away, I let out a heavy sigh of relief. Within a minute, she looked like she might on any normal morning before rising from bed.

I removed my hand, but I felt a warmth envelop it. Mr. Kent guided my hand back to Laura's. "Please," he said. "A little while longer. Just to make sure she is completely healed."

She already was, but I did it anyway to ease his mind.

"I'm sorry for this. For asking you to come to the prison," I said, my voice hoarse.

"No, it was the right thing to do," Mr. Kent said. "I just don't believe I can keep doing the right thing if this is what happens."

"So you will just do whatever the Society asks?"

He looked up at me, his hand still on mine. "I would do terrible things for the ones I love, Miss Wyndham."

I felt my body go tense at the thought. "We—we'll have to ask Laura when she wakes up, to find out what happened," I said, trying to pretend that I didn't find our closeness very strange. "But . . . Where has Emily been?"

There was a knock at the door and Tuffins entered carrying a tray of supplies. "In case you needed something," he explained. One day, I'd have to find out if he had some sort of mind-reading power.

"I actually do . . . ," I said, letting go of Laura's and Mr. Kent's hands. "Do you know where I might find Miss Kane?"

A strange look crossed Tuffins's face before he nodded. "She is . . . on the roof."

"The roof," I echoed slowly.

"It would probably be best if I . . . showed you."

I glanced back at Mr. Kent, but it didn't look like he was ready to leave his sister's side anytime soon.

"I will be right back," I told him.

He barely looked up as I left the room.

Back in the hallway, Tuffins started to lead me up toward the fourth floor.

This staircase was a disaster. Paintings were in disarray, shards of wood littered the rug, and half the wall hangings were no longer living up to their name.

"This is where Miss Kent had her accident," Tuffins said. "I did not mention it before, but when I found her at the bottom of the stairs, she was . . . Well, she was floating."

"How . . . strange."

"Hmm," Tuffins replied, completely straight-faced.

Well, that might explain the destruction. And why her injuries weren't worse. Emily must have managed to catch her before she hit the bottom.

We reached the fourth-floor landing. Tuffins knocked on the wall, cleared his throat, and looked upward at a broken skylight. "Miss Kane, Miss Wyndham to see you."

"Go away!" came a shout.

"Thank you, Tuffins," I said.

He bowed and proceeded back downstairs, betraying no sense of curiosity as to how young girls were floating or breaking through skylights.

"Emily?" I called up to her. "Is everything all right?"

She sniffled. "No."

"Tell me what's wrong."

Hesitation. Then she finally spoke. "They hurt Laura."

"I know, but she's not hurt any longer," I said. "I healed her."

Emily's head poked out over the skylight, her eyes red and raw. "Good. But they still hurt her."

"Did you see who did it?" I asked.

"It was the ghosts! They made the knife fly!"

"There are no ghosts. Are you certain you didn't see a person do it?"

"No, you lied about curing me! There are still ghosts and they are angry! They will hurt her again and next time they won't catch her!"

I sighed, my neck beginning to hurt as I strained to look up at her. "Will you come down?"

"No, they'll hurt you, too."

"There are no ghosts!"

"Yes there are!"

"But you must have seen what happened. Laura was floating when Tuffins found her," I said. "Someone made her fall and you caught her."

She looked at me uncertainly. "The ghosts do what they want."

"No, you didn't want her to fall and you made sure she didn't," I said firmly.

My eye caught a hatch door to the roof on the ceiling. I stepped up onto a chair and pulled on the cord. With a squeak, a ladder slid down. I started climbing.

"No, don't come up! They will get angry again," she said.

"No, Emily. You are going to get angry," I said. "And you are going to take control of your power."

I unlatched the hatch and pushed it up and open. The morning light was bright and the street noises were loud, but the moment I climbed out, the roof tiles seized my attention. They were vibrating and rattling. Emily cowered in fear against the chimney.

"Please, they don't want you to come closer," she said. "I—I don't think the ghosts want me to have friends. They will hurt all of you."

I felt an anger rising inside me, her words reminding me what the Society had done to Catherine and Laura.

"I won't come closer," I reassured her, taking cautious steps toward the back of the house. "But I need to talk to you about ghosts. Do you see them?"

"Yes!" she exclaimed immediately.

I fixed her with a hard stare. "Do they look like people?"

She didn't meet my eye, looking around guiltily. "No."

"What do they look like?"

"But I feel them," she said softly.

I nodded, taking a tiny step forward. "I know you do. But do you remember when we first got to London, there were people in a room. People with all kinds of strange abilities. You remember that I can heal people who are hurt, right?"

She nodded quickly. "Yes, Laura told me about it."

"Good. And her brother, Mr. Kent, has he ever asked you a question?"

She furrowed her brow. "I . . . yes. I didn't like it."

"Because you answered him, right?"

"Yes. And I told him I thought Lady Kent was a goblin lady." She huffed. "She isn't nice to Laura."

I stifled a grin. "No, no she isn't. But do you see how we all have things we can do that go beyond a regular person's abilities?"

Emily was staring off the roof. "My mama said it was ghosts."

Oh no. The poor girl. "What did she do?" I asked softly, taking another step toward her that she didn't seem to notice.

"They called a priest. Mama and Papa were scared." She sounded so far away.

"Where did you live? In Ireland?"

"The farm. I miss it." She was sinking against the chimney now, her small frame shaking slightly.

"And when did you go to the asylum?" I tried again.

"My sixteenth birthday," she whispered.

"Oh, Emily, I'm so sorry." I knelt on the roof and began edging closer. "Miss Grey's parents put her in there, too. Mine would have if they had found out about my healing, I'm sure. But it isn't evil. You don't have to hurt anyone. And it's not ghosts."

She looked at me, peering through her long lashes, tears streaming down her face as she finally admitted in a choked voice, "If it's not ghosts, then it's me. I'm the one who did the bad things."

I had to force myself not to rush to her. "It's not your fault. You did not mean to." I tried to make sure I didn't sound too fierce, but I was thinking about Mr. Braddock, about Miss Chen, about everyone who didn't understand what their power was and only saw it do terrible things when it first appeared.

"I didn't want to hurt Laura," she said, pleading at me. "I swear it."

"You didn't, I promise," I said instantly. "It was another person with a power. I think you saved her life." I smiled at her and could swear she looked the slightest bit hopeful.

"You can control your powers. I believe in you," I said resolutely. "You will do so much good with them. Laura's will not be the only life you save."

I scrambled to my feet and walked to the edge of the roof, looking until I was positioned correctly.

"Be careful!" Emily was staring with her hands outstretched and I gave her a reassuring smile.

"You can do this. You have the power. You control it."

"Miss Wyndham!"

"Now, catch me." With that, I stepped backward off the roof and Emily gave a shout.

"No! Stop!"

I did. In midair, just before I landed on Laura's bedroom balcony. The roof tiles stopped rattling. Emily poked her head over the edge and gasped. "Oh!"

I laughed. "Can you set me down?"

I felt my body lightly drop the remaining foot to the balcony. I'd chosen the spot to jump because it wouldn't have been deadly if she hadn't caught me, but this was more pleasant all the same.

Mr. Kent flung open the balcony door, eyes wide. "Miss Wyndham, what on earth—are you—"

"I'm fine," I said as Emily gave a little laugh and sailed down next to me. "Did you know that Emily has an extraordinary power that has nothing to do with ghosts?"

Chapter 13

T HE SOCIETY of Aberrations was evil.

After two days of waiting, dreading further attacks upon my family and friends, that was the only thing I could be sure of. My friends were safe, now, but if I crossed the Aberrations again I wasn't at all sure Catherine or Laura would survive. Or I could find myself in prison, my powers being siphoned off regularly by Captain Goode.

And he was directed to do so by someone who did not even have a power. Presumably, a lord of some stature. Presumably, someone I had even been introduced to, or at the least had seen at a ball or function.

I was pacing wildly, as I had for the past hour. I let Lucy help me undress as much as was necessary and then dismissed her. I had brushed my hair over and over, trying to determine what we should do, when the slip of paper fell into my lap. The note demanded my presence in the gardens in five minutes for another Aberrations mission. I wanted desperately to rip the note into a million pieces, ignore the Society forever, and tell them I was done.

But I couldn't. I couldn't risk Catherine or anyone I loved again. The long-familiar pang at the thought of Rose came again

as I slowly dressed, hating the Society with every inch of my being. I slid Catherine's fan up the sleeve of my dress, its weight comforting.

Ten minutes later I entered the chilly garden and was ferociously unhappy about it.

Mr. Redburn looked as thrilled as I was. "You're late," he huffed, snatching my arm, yanking me through a portal and into the Society of Aberrations. Captain Goode was waiting and put his hand to my shoulder immediately. I resisted the urge to slap it away.

"Congratulations. Hurting young women to retaliate against me—how very big of you," I snarled at them, fighting the warmth of Captain Goode's power. I would stay strong. Stoic.

"Miss Wyndham," Captain Goode began, looking grave and tired. "I can exp—"

"She gets no explanations, Simon," his brother snapped. "Now let's go."

With that, I was unceremoniously dropped through a portal and onto a city street. It was night and the air was wet and cold. I looked around, my side smarting.

"Miss Wyndham. A pleasant New York welcome from Mr. Redburn, I see." Mr. Kent was helping me to my feet, a bite lacing his lighthearted comment.

"She'll be fine," Mr. Redburn said, appearing on the street next to Miss Chen, who wore her usual look of indifference. "It's her friends who have to worry."

"Then you admit it." I went cold. "You caused those accidents."

Mr. Redburn snorted. "I wish I could have caused them. I love those assignments. The Society sent others, lucky bastards. Well, at least I have tonight."

Mr. Kent was barely able to keep his composure. He seemed

to be holding hundreds of angry questions at bay. "What is happening tonight?" he asked.

"We're retrieving a very misguided man who betrayed the Society and ran away," Mr. Redburn said with a smile, not even minding the forced revelation. "He's right this way."

"I'm not going anywhere with you," I said.

"Yes, you are," he said, walking away. A portal opened beside him. It seemed to lead back to London—directly to Catherine's house.

"So you're just going to keep subtly threatening us if we don't do everything you say?"

"Believe me, if we were trying to be subtle, you would know it."

"Actually, that would negate the very meaning of subtle—" Mr. Kent said before he disappeared into a portal below him.

Three seconds later, another portal opened up, depositing him and a rush of mud on the street beside Mr. Redburn as he marched back to us.

"This is as explicit a threat as I can make," Mr. Redburn said to me. "Follow the Society's orders, or I will visit your friend, take her to the tallest, most jagged-edged mountain I can find, and throw her off. Now, for the last time, we are going this way." Mr. Redburn headed down the dim, empty street.

Mr. Kent attempted to wipe his suit clean as he climbed to his feet. "I will murder that man," he said evenly, sounding so sure I was surprised Mr. Redburn didn't fall dead on the spot. He glanced back at me and stalked off after Mr. Redburn.

"I suggest you follow," Miss Chen said, seizing my arm. "You're lucky your friends are still alive."

Every step toward Mr. Redburn boiled my blood hotter. "Did— why do you say that?" I whispered to her.

"They killed one of my brothers the last time I refused them.

They don't have any qualms about that," she muttered back. I turned to see that her eyes weren't just calm and cool. They were banked fire. They were a glass ready to crack at any moment.

"My God. They are monsters." I felt a fury clawing its way out of my mouth, but I forced it back down, trying to find a rational solution. "What if we all refuse?" I suggested. "Then there'd be no one to carry out their threats."

"There's always someone who breaks," she said.

"Like us right now," I said bitterly. "We have no idea what Mr. Redburn is going to ask us to do to this man."

"We don't have a choice at the moment," Mr. Kent said, squeezing out the mud from his sleeves. "Until we know how to keep everyone safe, we have to work with them."

"And how long have you been trying to figure that out, Miss Chen?" I asked, glancing at her sideways.

"Almost a year," she answered.

No one had anything to say to that. I wondered where Mr. Braddock was, wishing for a look from him, a word, an answer that would tell me exactly what we needed to do. That we had to do what was right and not give in to their threats, no matter how personal they were. I worried he was on a mission of his own. He had the most difficult position of all. Anything he'd be forced to do would hurt someone. It was an impossible choice for him to make.

Soon, we caught up to Mr. Redburn, finding him looking up at a five-story building.

"All right, children, we're going in. Third floor. Stay close, this one can open portals to anywhere, too. You might recognize him."

Mr. Redburn's portal led into the middle of a narrow room, where three strangers sat in front of a fire. A young girl with black hair in braids, an older woman who looked like the girl's mother, and a white-haired man, presumably the man we were looking for. My heart was thrumming so quickly I felt sick.

Mr. Redburn spoke again. "You should have known we would find you, Hale. I'm sick of wearing your power. There's a prison full of new ones I've been waiting to steal."

I felt my breath leave me. This couldn't be him. He looked completely different from the last time I'd seen him. Unless he'd . . .

The girl with the black hair leaped up and cried out something unintelligible. She would have run toward us if Mr. Hale hadn't grabbed her around the waist and dropped her through a portal that appeared below her with a crackle. Before Mr. Hale could follow, Mr. Redburn reached into a portal of his own that opened across the room. He seized Mr. Hale from behind, but the mother, spryer than she looked, struck Mr. Redburn, shoved her companion into the hole, and dove in after him.

Mr. Redburn rose to his feet just in time to see their portal close. Then he turned to us angrily. "Yes, by all means, stand around like idiots. Don't grab them or anything."

A large crack opened below all four of us, dropping us into a sweltering forest. The mud squelched below my feet as I managed to land properly, but Mr. Redburn was already off and running. I lifted my skirts and followed the rest of the group, running through brush and bugs and hot thick air. Through the trees I could see Mr. Hale and his group stepping through another portal into a city and all of a sudden, Mr. Redburn had thrown open his own portal into our path.

A horse whinnied and a carriage almost knocked me down as I emerged in the middle of a busy street, somewhere that seemed to be the Orient. Mr. Kent grabbed my hand and pulled me along so we would not get left behind—as much as I didn't want to help the Society I also didn't want to get stuck anywhere, never able to find my way home. We chased after our targets into a narrow alley that ended at a wooden door that was slammed shut before Mr. Redburn could reach it. He rammed against it hard, but it wouldn't budge.

"Chen!" he yelled, slamming against it again as Miss Chen reached him. This time it shattered into a million pieces and he made it into the building as another portal on the wall closed.

Mr. Redburn opened his own portal again, leading to a glaringly white tundra. I almost slipped on the ice as the cold air struck me harder than a physical blow. About twenty feet ahead of us, Mr. Hale and his companions were racing to enter another portal, when Mr. Redburn opened a second one right in Mr. Hale's path.

I heard a crackle next to me and turned to find Mr. Hale accidentally transported back to us. Mr. Redburn met him with a hard punch on the nose that knocked him off balance. So off balance, in fact, that he stumbled backward and fell.

But he didn't hit the ice. He fell into his own portal, which sent him crashing down onto Mr. Redburn's back. As Mr. Hale brought him to the hard ground, he continued to pound at Mr. Redburn's head while opening another hole that crashed them both down over Mr. Kent. In a matter of seconds, Mr. Hale created a pile of bodies as if he'd employed this strategy against difficult odds before. I didn't know where to run as he landed on Miss Chen.

The pile disappeared again, but I wasn't hit. I waited in the cold silence for a moment until a portal deposited Mr. Redburn, Mr. Kent, and Miss Chen, along with a few gallons of water.

"What in God's name just happened?" Mr. Kent sputtered out.

"He tried to pile us on each other and get away," Mr. Redburn said, getting to his knees. "But falling in water ruins that."

He opened a portal on the ground between us, providing an

expansive view of our surroundings from the sky. Mr. Redburn searched for Mr. Hale's family, finding they'd run farther away and Mr. Hale was opening another portal to escape.

"I'm tired of this. Just grab his family when I say so," Mr. Redburn said. "He won't run if we have them."

Mr. Redburn's new portal opened up on a wet farm filled with a number of astonished workers, some staring down the field at Mr. Hale's group and some at us. I splashed through the mud a few steps, trying to keep up, but Mr. Hale was looking over his shoulder at us, already running into another portal. And then I heard a crackle below us as Mr. Redburn tried to head them off.

My stomach lurched and my scream caught in my throat as our next destination seemed to be miles up in the sky. I fell with only a brief, horrifying second to panic and wonder if this sort of fall would kill me.

And then I hit a surface, hard. I scrambled up, finding the stars and the moon closer than I'd expected. We were on a quiet rooftop, surrounded by a city crowded with buildings, pointed domes, and towers that seemed to be reaching out to the sky for help. The distinct *click* of a gun broke the silence.

Mr. Hale was standing above Mr. Redburn aiming a pistol at his head. He pulled the trigger without hesitation, a faint crackle sounded, and the gunshot rang out. But Mr. Redburn didn't fall.

Mr. Hale did. He hit the ground and cried out, blood staining his left leg. Mr. Redburn had opened a tiny portal in front of Mr. Hale's gun at the last second and sent the shot into Mr. Hale's own leg. The gun broke into pieces a moment later as Miss Chen climbed to her feet.

"Grab the girl, Kent!" Mr. Redburn shouted, before he opened a portal next to him and seized the mother at the other end of the rooftop. He held a knife to her throat and looked pleased to find Mr. Kent holding the young girl in place by her shoulders. She tried to yell something, to me it seemed, but the words were muffled, as if there were a hand over her mouth. And that was when I noticed she didn't even have a mouth.

Mr. Redburn seemed to make the same observation. "Is that . . . your daughter, Hale?" he asked, mildly amused. "Does she have an ability, or rather—is it an inability to speak?"

The girl gave a muffled moan again and looked at me pleadingly. She tried to wriggle out of Mr. Kent's hold to no avail. He looked utterly distressed and a chill ran down my spine. I reached under my sleeve and pulled the dagger fan loose.

Mr. Hale rocked back and forth, groaning in pain. "Don't hurt her, please."

"Why, that depends on you. The Society was very generous to you and your mother, despite your many crimes. And we told you what would happen if you tried to run."

"What did you do?" Mr. Hale wailed.

"Oh, she's well enough—she simply doesn't have a home anymore. I thought you wouldn't care. After all, you left her there. But you should concentrate on these two now, as you consider this invitation I am extending to you." Mr. Redburn tightened the knife at the older woman's throat. "If you want them to retain their . . . good health, shall we say, you'll return to us and put your powers to good use."

"Of course I will, I promise, please," Mr. Hale begged. It really did sound like him now. The fear that he had for the Society when we last saw him, it was still there.

"Kent, make sure he is making honest promises," Mr. Redburn said.

Mr. Kent frowned bitterly but did as Mr. Redburn asked.

"Mr. Hale, do you truly intend to rejoin the Society of Aberrations?"

"Yes, y-yes of course," Mr. Hale said, looking almost relieved by his answer. He didn't take his eyes off the girl in Mr. Kent's grasp.

"Well, isn't this delightful," Mr. Redburn said. "Now, Mr. Kent, you have your own gun, yes? Shoot the girl."

"What?" Mr. Kent's face was leached of color.

"Do it," Mr. Redburn said, and a trickle of blood ran down from the old woman's neck. She was ignoring it, however, eyes wide and alarmed as she, too, focused on the young girl.

Mr. Hale twisted around to see what was happening. "No—I will join, I told you—"

Mr. Redburn interrupted. "I understand what you told me. You'll join. But what good is that if you don't believe our threats? You'll simply run away again. Mr. Kent is going to shoot her, you're going to watch and hate it, then you'll be more careful with your wife and future children."

"No!" Mr. Hale reached out in desperation toward the girl and a faint crackle sounded below her, but nothing opened. He collapsed in pain.

"Always looking for an escape. Fool." Mr. Redburn turned to Mr. Kent. "Do it. Or do you want me to have a nice little chat with that talkative little sister of yours?"

Mr. Kent looked at me, pleading. "Ev—"

But I did not let him finish. I rushed over to the girl, seized her hand, and pulled her away, Mr. Kent letting go easily. I slid the latch out on the fan and released the blade, holding it out in front of me. There was a satisfying gasp from at least one person.

"No. We won't do this." Even as I said it, I was wondering how quickly I could get to Catherine, how we would keep our friends safe. But we couldn't do this. We couldn't torture and kill people out of fear.

Mr. Redburn flashed to anger before settling on smug amusement. "Fine. I'll tell Miss Harding you said good-bye." He looked at Mr. Hale. "I guess your wife will have to do."

I lurched forward, a scream in my throat, but before I could reach him with the dagger fan, and before he could cut too deep, the knife cracked into a hundred pieces, raining to the ground. Miss Chen. Her hand outstretched, she looked as stunned as I was to see what she had done. Before any of us could move to help her further, the old woman used surprising strength to break free, spinning around, grabbing Mr. Redburn's face, and pressing it in the strangest, most chillingly familiar manner.

He managed to shove her away, but something was wrong. He stopped, his eyes widened, his hands frantically moved to his throat and then his face, which he felt at first, and then started clawing desperately at his skin.

"What's happening?" I asked.

No response. Mr. Redburn opened a portal and landed right by my feet in a heap. As he looked up at me, I found my answer. Skin was pulled over his nostrils, and his lips were fused into one.

He couldn't breathe.

"Don't help him," the woman rasped at me, clutching her bleeding throat.

Mr. Redburn crawled closer, slower, looking up at me in desperation.

"He's going to die," I said, skin goose-pimpling with anxiety.

"It's the . . . only way," she said.

"The only way to do what?"

No response from either the woman or Mr. Redburn. He'd fallen unconscious.

"To do what?" I asked her again. When she didn't respond I cursed and knelt down to take his hand, the act warring within me. "I'm going to need a better answer than that. Even for him. Mr. Kent!"

"This is the only way to do what?" Mr. Kent asked her.

The woman looked at the girl next to me. "To protect Miss Wyndham's sister."

A nasally, tart, familiar French accent.

I dropped Mr. Redburn's hand.

A groan came from Mr. Hale's direction. He climbed to his knees and opened a portal below Mr. Redburn.

There was only time to see him fall into the ocean before it closed.

Chapter 14

MISS WYNDHAM'S SISTER, the woman had said.

It was the heat. The heat was making me feel very confounded. The oppressive heat had me convinced this woman had been talking about Rose. That my sister was here looking nothing like she ever had. Snub nose, freckles, dark hair, no mouth. At the very least, I remembered Rose had a mouth.

And yet.

The older woman staggered to us, pressing against her cut with one hand and moved her other over the girl's absent mouth with a distinct painterly motion. A motion that reminded me of Camille, the woman who had disguised me as a man last year, who had betrayed me to Dr. Beck.

"Dearest? Are you all right?" she asked.

The girl didn't respond. Except to shrink away from the woman's grasp as soon as her mouth returned, and grab at me with a strangled yell. She wrapped her arms around me and buried her face in my dress.

"Ev," she said with a sob, peering up at me. "Y-you found me." That voice. Those blue eyes. It was impossible.

"Ev, please, it's me, Rose, it's—" The girl's sobs cut off.

I could hear Miss Chen beginning to ask what was happening

while Mr. Kent shushed her, but I couldn't move. I didn't know how I remained conscious or how my legs were still working or what legs even were, for that matter.

"No." I shook my head stiffly in the girl's grip.

My heart was aching and I didn't—I *wouldn't*—believe her. I couldn't believe her and find it to be another awful lie, another awful dream. I tried to pull away, pry her off, the world moving too quickly and hope rushing up faster than I could tamp it down. This couldn't really be her.

"No," I croaked out, stumbling back. "Please, please, this is a horrible trick."

"It isn't," she said, shaking her head madly. "It isn't."

"You aren't here—Rose is gone."

"Ev, you have to believe me—this woman, Camille, she just made me look this way, I swear—I swear it on—on Pegasus, our pony that died when you were nine and I made you give him a proper funeral and you didn't laugh when I asked you if he was going to the Pony Elysian Fields."

There was a moment of soft quiet. I dared not move, dared not believe it could be true, worried she might turn to sand or shatter like glass. But she was there with me, still holding tight, still going, trying to catch her breath between sobs.

"Ev, please, your—your favorite part of any ball—the only part you like—is the cake. And the last time we were together— we were going to convince Mother to give us more freedom, and—and—"

I was sagging against the roof's edged wall, hope and pain lancing me from either side.

Her voice lowered so there was no chance of anyone overhearing. "And you love Lord Byron." She began hiccup-laughing through her tears. "You will mock him forever, but I once found a dogeared, underlined, worn volume under your bed and will never tell a soul, I promise."

I had nothing left. I broke. I was on the ground without quite knowing how I got there, desperately holding Rose with me. Her hands felt like Rose's. She smelled like Rose—like home and Bramhurst. I decided I didn't mind if it was a trick. It would be worth it for this small moment in time to feel her arms around me, hear that voice that I had loved as long as I could remember. Whether it was magic or the devil himself, I would worship it for the rest of my days.

Infuriating tears filled my eyes, blurring my vision when all I wanted was to see her face. My choking sobs made it impossible to say anything I wanted to say to her.

I did, however, find the words I needed to say to Camille. "Turn her back. Now."

Camille's throat was dripping blood at a steadier stream—perhaps Mr. Redburn had managed to cut deeper than I thought. "Turn her back or I will see just how long it takes you to bleed out," I growled, and looked at Mr. Hale clutching his leg on the ground. "Him, too."

With a pained snarl Camille marched forward and ran her hand over Rose's face. As Rose appeared before me it was all I could do not to cry out.

"Rose," I whispered, and she pulled away from Camille, back into my arms.

"This was reckless, *ma cherie*," Camille said gently to Rose, her face softening. I hesitated to heal Camille, knowing I might regret it, wanting to let her suffer a little longer. But finally I reached out and grabbed her arm with more strength than I needed to. The cut at her throat slowly closed.

Mr. Kent interjected, looking from Rose to Camille and

Mr. Hale. "This is a trick," he snapped. "Are you Evelyn Wyndham's sister?"

"Y-yes," Rose said, her perfect nose scrunched slightly, a wrinkle appearing between her brows. My heart stuttered at seeing the gesture I thought gone forever.

"I thought Miss Wyndham's sister was dead," Miss Chen said loudly, looking at us suspiciously.

"We all did." Mr. Kent began pacing. There was tension in his body like I'd never seen. He'd almost hurt her on Mr. Redburn's orders.

"Were you dead?" he asked.

"I—no, no, of course not."

"Then how—how are you here?"

"It was them," Rose answered, chancing a fearful glance at Mr. Hale and Camille. "They—they took me."

Mr. Kent turned his attention upon Mr. Hale. "Is this truly Rosamund Wyndham?"

Mr. Hale, still injured, groaned in pain as he was forced to answer. "It . . . it is."

"How did you manage to take her?"

"When she was being held by Dr. Beck—I, ah, I found someone ill at a hospital, hired Miss Camille to disguise her as Miss Rosamund, and switched them."

Mr. Kent stopped pacing. "That is . . . absurdity—if you were planning that, why did you even come to us for help?"

"We needed you to distract Dr. Beck and Claude."

My tears were drying, mostly because my anger had taken their place. "You used us and made me believe my sister was *dead*—"

"It was all to protect Miss Rosamund from the Society," Mr. Hale said, wincing in pain. "It's the only way they would stop. If they think you're dead."

He clutched his leg, a puddle of blood under him. "Please, Miss Wyndham, I—I need help, too."

I struggled to care. With Captain Goode's enhancement, my presence was helping him slowly. That was already more than he deserved. "You'll survive," I said.

"If he dies, you'll be stuck here," Camille snapped, her hands on her hips.

"And where exactly is here?" Mr. Kent asked Mr. Hale.

"Cairo. Egypt," Mr. Hale groaned.

"That's not . . . *too* far. We'll manage."

I looked at Rose, who was shaking her head miserably. "They will never give up. It's something about me. I don't understand it at all." She glanced at Camille and Mr. Hale, shuddering. "They seemed compelled to keep me locked up these past three months. They say it's to protect me. And that girl they made up to look like me . . . she is dead and her family doesn't know. It's my fault. There's something terribly wrong. They said something about a power, but I don't know what it is." Rose spoke helplessly and looked bereft, her small frame bowed.

"I know what it is," I said, grabbing her hands. "And it's not your fault. You simply have the power to make others care for you greatly. But you cannot control their actions. And there is nothing—nothing the matter with you."

She looked up at me, so familiar, but the uncertainty and fear reflected there was new. Another stab of anger hit me as she tried to respond. "I—I don't know. I just, I want to go home, Ev."

"Of course." I smothered her, my voice cracking as the enormity overwhelmed me again. "We're together now. I will get you home, Rose."

"No, you won't," Mr. Hale said, looking up at Rose the way a protective dog might regard his beloved master. "It's not safe."

"We will keep her disguised and tell only my mother and father," I said firmly.

Camille stepped forward. "As careless as ever, Miss Wyndham," she said, turning her cat eyes to me, and I wondered how I had not known it was her from the outset. "The Society is always watching."

"You've seen firsthand what they do," Mr. Hale said. "They will find out about her and they will use you against each other. The only way is for us to keep her hidden and moving."

I clutched Rose's hand, prepared to never let go again. "You're mad if you think I will ever let her out of my sight," I snapped.

"Then you will come with us." Mr. Hale offered me a sick, desperate smile. "Miss Camille can disguise you and leave behind bodies for the Society to find."

Beside me Rose shook even more. I pulled her closer.

"How many of your problems do you solve with fake dead bodies?" Mr. Kent asked.

"Perhaps three out of every four," Camille answered.

"We all love Miss Rosamund," Mr. Hale continued. "We can protect her together."

I gaped at him. That book in the Society library was right. Rose's charm power really did create dangerous fanatics. "You are delusional. My sister and I will never go anywhere with either of you."

A crackle rent the air next to me and I felt Rose's body flinch at the sound. Mr. Hale's desperate hand lunged out from the portal and caught me at the ankle, hard.

"*No!*" I yelled, wrenching myself back from his grip.

He managed to hold on for only a second before Miss Chen made the roof erupt between us and Mr. Kent helped pull Rose and me away.

But it was long enough. Mr. Hale stood back up, his leg mostly healed. Camille came to flank him, the two of them looking ready for battle.

"We aren't leaving without her," Mr. Hale said. "We can keep her safe."

A thin crack in the roof formed a line between Rose's captors and us, threatening to crumble their corner. "You did a fine job of keeping her safe this time, Hale," Miss Chen said, lashing out at him. "She would have been killed if anyone else had been sent to retrieve you. It was *you* they wanted, not Miss Wyndham's sister. You almost got her killed."

He winced, but did not back down. "It is still better than waiting in London for them to find us."

But I could feel us running out of time, running out of arguments, and they were running out of patience. Rose didn't want anything to do with Mr. Hale and Camille, but I did not trust us to win a fight against them, not with their years of experience. And not without risk to Rose.

I had to make the decision.

"We won't just be waiting in London," I said. "Running from the Society of Aberrations is no more realistic than us working for them for the rest of our lives. We must stop the head of the Society. If you truly love my sister and you truly wish to see her safe, then you must help me."

That had Camille's interest. "You know who it is?"

"We will," I said. "We know that he does not have a power. A fact that I am certain Captain Goode will not be happy to know. We can surely get him on our side."

"Except that we just killed his brother," Mr. Hale hissed.

"How long did you know Mr. Redburn when you were with the Society?" I asked.

"Long enough," he said shortly.

"Camille, do you remember his appearance?" I demanded.

"A man like that is rather difficult to forget," she said with a sneer.

"Then, you're going to disguise Mr. Hale as Mr. Redburn," I announced.

Realization spread across everyone's faces at once.

But Mr. Hale shook his head. "No."

"When it's done, you'll get to solve that problem by faking his death and disguising another body," Mr. Kent said. "Why would you refuse that?"

"It's—it's too great a risk," Mr. Hale said. "Captain Goode will suspect something sooner or later. It's his brother, after all."

"And he knows his brother is always in a hurry to be off," I said. "You can avoid him."

"Only until I must go to get my power enhanced," Mr. Hale said.

"Why? What happens then?" I asked.

"He can feel the difference between our powers when he enhances them," Miss Chen answered grimly. "He'll know it's not his brother."

My skin felt like it was tightening around me. "Then give me three days," I said desperately. "That's it. Rose will stay with my friend Catherine while we find a way for her to come home for good."

"But, Ev, Mother and Father . . ." Rose was looking up at me, panicked.

"It will be only a few days, dearest. The Society seems to be everywhere—I don't think we can risk you staying in the same house as me. They would find out."

"Please, I . . . I can't," she said, clutching at me, her eyes flickering to her captors. "I need to be home."

"Impossible," Mr. Hale said, crossing his arms.

"I will be there as much as I can," I said to her, ignoring him. "Catherine will be with you at all times." Rose closed her eyes and another tear leaked out. It broke my heart and I pulled her to me, mumbling into her hair. "I promise, three days and everything will be fine. Better than fine."

"I never liked the plan to keep running," Camille announced. "But I will be staying with Miss Rosamund at this . . . this person's house. I will keep her safe. And you will get rid of this head person."

Mr. Hale nodded. "If anyone—anyone attempts to hurt her—"

"You will not touch her for three days," I hissed. "Mr. Kent, can you make certain of that?"

He nodded. "You two, do you swear to follow Miss Wyndham's plan and leave Miss Rosamund be for the next three days?"

"Yes," they both answered.

"Do you promise to protect Miss Rosamund in the home of Miss Wyndham's choosing?"

"Yes."

"And do you have any idea how horrible you are?"

"No."

"Right. Well, when this is all over, we should sit down and have a talk," Mr. Kent said, then turned to me. "I believe that covers it."

"Almost," I said.

There was still the matter of him. And Miss Chen. They'd both felt forced to continue working for the Society in order to protect their loved ones, and now I'd put them in an impossible spot.

"I know you both have your families to consider and you've already helped me more than I can thank you for. You don't have to be involved anymore—I can continue with Mr. Hale and Camille," I said, catching Miss Chen's eye.

"And me," Mr. Kent said.

"You have your sister's safety to think about," I argued.

"And we now have your sister's as well," he said. "I am helping. You won't change my mind."

I truly did not deserve him.

Or Miss Chen, who was glaring speculatively at Mr. Hale. "I'll help. But first he has to move my family back to America. The Society can come after me as much as they please, but I'll be damned if I see anyone else I love hurt."

Mr. Hale nodded.

Miss Chen threw back her shoulders, her confident smile back in place, her chin held high. "Good. There's a lot that I've had my eye on to destroy."

With everyone on the roof in agreement, Camille returned her hands to Rose's nervous face, and my sister once again became the dark-haired girl who had been a stranger twenty minutes ago. I squeezed her hand hard and the unfamiliar face smiled up at me tremulously.

"You're here," I whispered.

"I know. Ev, please don't let them take me again."

"Never."

She sighed and leaned her head against mine. It felt like we were alone in the world, the two of us against everything. A breeze was drifting in, slowly shifting away the heat. I could feel the tears cooling against my face. Even with three days to perform an impossible task, I still felt free enough to take my first unencumbered breath in months.

Rose was well.

Rose was here.

Rose was alive.

Anything was possible.

Chapter 15

IT WAS DARK, just past the time when drunkards stumbled home and still two hours before servants would rise to begin their day. Thus, Catherine was naturally alarmed when I woke her up from her sound sleep and comfortable bed.

"Did you know that you snore in the most ghastly manner?" I asked.

"*Evemph!*" I assumed it was my name she was attempting to scream, but I had my hand over her mouth to stifle the sound.

"Indeed, it's me, and all is well, so I need you not to yell," I said, slowly removing my hand.

"I never yell—what on earth is happening?" Her hand was fumbling on her bedside table and I reached to give her spectacles to her. I had lit the gas sconce on her bedroom wall on my way in, and I watched Catherine's eyes adjust to the light and find my eyes.

And then, the nervous, dark-haired, snub-nosed girl behind me.

"Catherine, I'm sorry I keep surprising you with unbelievable stories, but . . . I—uh, have another one."

Approximately forty minutes later, Catherine was staring at Rose with wonder. She had interrogated us thoroughly, marching around the bedroom, wrap flying, speaking in a harsh whisper.

"So not only is your sister alive, well, and going to stay here for a spell, but her captors are also insisting that they stay?"

"Captor," I said, hoping that might make it better. "Only Camille. She's disguising Mr. Hale as Mr. Redburn, so he will play that part and stay elsewhere. I am so sorry. I will do whatever I can to make it up to you."

"Don't be silly. I'd be annoyed if you didn't involve me," she said, still pacing. "But you trust them?"

Rose shook her head fearfully and I sighed, the long night catching up with me. "For now. Mr. Kent made certain of that. I don't think we have a choice. It was the only way to keep them from running again. At least for a few days. And," I said, turning to Rose, "if they dared to take you again, I promise I would find you. Miss Grey, our old governess, can find anyone in the world."

Rose did not look entirely pleased as she said, "So many people with these strange powers . . ."

Catherine removed her spectacles to rub at her temples. I hesitated before speaking again. "Camille said she'd like to sleep wherever was closest to Rose. I thought maybe a connecting room—"

Catherine was already waving her hand in agreement. "Mine is the only room with a connecting chamber. This Camille woman can sleep in that room. Rose may sleep in here and I will be perfectly comfortable in one of the guest chambers."

"Rose, are you all right with this?" I asked, reaching for her hand, unable to stop checking to be sure she was made of substance and not a mirage.

She hesitated, looking lost. "I . . . I wish she did not have to be here. I just want to go back to our old life, impossible as it is."

"For now," I agreed. "But once we deal with the Society, you will be home and with Mother and Father, who will be overjoyed. It's only three days, I swear it."

Rose frowned, but nodded. "All right. Three days. I'll try. Though I hate to put you out, Miss Harding," she said.

"It is no bother at all. Though, I don't believe any of the other rooms are ready, and I do not think I am likely to sleep anymore tonight. I may simply sit here," Catherine said, nodding at her window seat. "If that does not discomfit you?"

"Oh, no, please stay! I mean—whatever you find more comfortable." Rose yawned and blushed. "I . . . I find I am quite exhausted."

"Please, you must rest." Catherine gestured to the bed, and Rose, without even undressing, fell beneath the sheets.

"Thank you, you're very kind," she mumbled. Her eyes flickered open and closed, then found mine, and she gave me a tired smile. "Will you stay? For a moment?"

"Of course," I said, hurrying to the bed. I grabbed her hand and swiped back a piece of hair that was falling into her face. "You are safe now," I whispered.

Her eyes were already closing. Her breath went soft and easy as she drifted into an immediate slumber. I wondered if she had truly slept in the months she had been missing.

Catherine curled up on her window seat and stared out the window. Slowly, after some long minutes, I slid my hand from Rose and watched as she cocooned herself in the sheets.

"Catherine," I whispered, going to her. "Thank you. Are you truly comfortable with this?"

"Truly," she said with a firm nod. She kept her eyes on mine, still alert despite the late hour. "I can't tell you how much I regretted being away when all of this started. I could have been here to help you and your sister. To help you with your parents and your new power. Instead, I abandoned you and wandered about the Continent."

I loved and hated her for thinking that. "There was no way you could have known."

"I know, but irrational wishes are the best ones. And in a way, this one's even come true." She gave me a soft, true smile. "I'm so very glad for the both of you, Evelyn. And I simply plan to do everything in my power to help this time."

I hugged her tightly. "Thank you." The clock struck four behind her. "Oh, I must go—it wouldn't do to be missing or give anyone a reason to suspect something is amiss here," I said grimly. "Just . . . please be here when she wakes up. She might be frightened."

"Of course," Catherine said.

I gave Rose one last look. I watched her eyelids twitch with life and her chest rise and fall with every breath. It was everything I'd wished I'd seen that horrible night months ago. And now that she was here in front of me, I had to leave her.

I crept down to the kitchens, where I had left Camille and Mr. Hale, and found myself staring at Camille and Mr. Redburn. The resemblance was uncanny, from the dark hair and little mustache, to the mismatched clothing. But it was different, somehow. As though another artist had tried to recreate the same painting.

"Mr. Hale, you know where the Society is headquartered, I believe. Mr. Redburn seems to skulk around the hallways until he gets the morning's instructions from his brother. Please report to Captain Goode in the morning. Say as little as possible. And can you sneer?"

He did, completing the portrait. Perfect.

"Catherine has agreed to let you sleep in the connecting chamber," I said sternly to Camille. "Rose is safe, content and sleeping. You will do nothing but be alert to any danger."

They gave me slow nods.

"Mr. Hale, if you could help me home? I live in Belgrave Square," I said.

He opened a portal showing the dark neighborhood from above. I pointed to my garden and he opened a new one in the hedges. I started forward, but I was stopped by Camille's voice. "We will do it your way, Miss Wyndham. For now. But if you cannot find a way to keep that girl safe, we will take matters into our own hands."

I stiffened. "Three days, Camille." I turned to meet her eyes, suddenly feeling that she could see all my insecurities and doubts. "You will give me my three days to ensure that she will be safe."

Camille barely nodded. One could hardly call it that. Then she turned and headed to the servant stairs, and I turned back to the portal.

That one step away from Rose was the longest, hardest step I had ever taken. Even though I knew that *not* being home would cause more questions and complications, it was all I could do not to run back and never leave her side.

But by the time I snuck in through the garden, I felt as though I had been hit by a wall of weariness, to the point that I began to wonder a little deliriously if someone with the power to put people to sleep had brushed by me.

I slipped off my boots to carry them and softly padded up the front stairs. I would be less likely to encounter any servants who would be waking soon. The grand house echoed more forbiddingly than ever, but I couldn't help smiling. Somehow, we would find a way to deal with the Society of Aberrations. And then Rose would be here, filling the rooms with her smiles, mending my parents' broken hearts.

I quietly opened my bedroom door, finding the brass knob in the dark. But as soon as I closed it behind me, I tensed. There was someone in here.

My blood was singing, singeing my skin as it prickled, immediately dotting my skin with gooseflesh. I felt for the handle of my fan and pulled it from my sleeve, not bothering to be quiet. The person had surely heard me enter. I lifted the small latch to release the blade with a quiet but threatening *snick* that filled the room. I tensed, knowing if the intruder was going to attack it would be now.

"Ev—"

I launched the dagger toward the voice.

"Ah!" A man hissed quietly and something heavy fell to the floor. I cautiously moved forward.

"I warn you, sir, I am more than skilled in deadly combat," I said, hoping that was something someone more than skilled in deadly combat might say.

The figure, however, had the audacity to snort and cough back a laugh. And all of a sudden I knew exactly who it was in my bedroom.

"Sebastian Braddock, what on *earth* are you doing here!" I only remembered to lower my voice halfway through the sentence.

"You have extraordinary luck," he said, his voice thick with pain. *Oh no.* I stepped forward, my eyes almost adjusted to the dimness. The object that had fallen seemed to be not an object at all: Sebastian was a hulking figure on the floor near my bed. As I crept closer I could see that my knife had indeed found its target and lodged itself snugly in his waist.

"This serves you right," I said, suddenly overwhelmed with rage. How dare he be here? How dare he get himself injured when I couldn't help him? How dare his eyes find mine so easily, the only bright thing in the twisting dark?

Except the knife. That still glinted wickedly. I knelt down to see that I had extraordinary luck, the thin little blade in almost to the hilt.

"I was worried. . . ."

"Hold still," I said. "We need to get you to a proper doctor, that's too much blood." I was thinking quickly, trying to be sure my voice betrayed no hint of concern and simply sounded irritated. "If I stay with you, it should not hurt them at all to sew you right up."

"Ev—"

"Only you, Sebastian! Only you would get a mortal injury in a lady's bedroom!" I snapped. What if he didn't live? What would Mae say if he died in my bedroom? I began tugging him up roughly but he groaned and grabbed my hand with his usual crushing strength.

"Sebastian, we need to go!"

"No—"

"Stop arguing with me!"

"Evelyn! You can heal me!" he finally managed, panting heavily as I pulled him halfway to his feet. His hand was clammy in my own and I wondered how much blood he had already lost.

I spoke slowly. "Sebastian, our powers don't work like that. They cancel each other out. Oh goodness, did you hit your head as well?"

I immediately lowered him back down to the floor and began running my fingers through his hair, looking for a protrusion.

"I—ah, Ev. . . ." He took a deep breath and looked up at me with wild, guilty eyes before I finally realized how inappropriate the position we were in was. He was leaning against the side of my bed and I was draped over his shoulder, my bosom rather shoved against his neck and my hands still fingering the silky strands without his permission.

"Um," I said, finding it nearly impossible to move, despite the impropriety. His breath was coming quickly, hot on my neck, and

I could feel the familiar thrum of my blood answering his. Finally I regained sense and pulled back as he began saying something, but my head was spinning, trying to come up with some plan. What could I do? He had some terrible head injury that made him unable to remember how our powers worked, and my dagger was still lodged in his abdomen. What if I hit some vital organ? I knew nothing about fixing those. And if we were discovered here together—

". . . just need to touch me."

I looked down at him in shock as he began pulling up his shirt with shaking fingers.

"Sebastian!" I closed my mouth on a gasp as a sliver of bare skin was slowly revealed. It was only then that I realized the filtered moonlight was turning the room a silvery gray. I could see him far too well.

And the blood he was quickly losing.

"No, no, no," I murmured. "Oh Lord, what do I do?"

"Evelyn! I've been trying to tell you—Captain Goode lowered my power today. Off completely. You should be able to heal me." His speech was slurred but perfectly lucid.

I stared down at him.

I was a prize fool. It had been a long day.

I placed one hand against his shirt next to the knife and swiftly pulled it out with the other, biting down hard on my lip as he groaned harshly. I lifted the edges of his shirt and pressed down over the wound with both hands.

"I thought you'd be able to tell," he mumbled, eyes closed.

"Knowing your every thought must be someone else's power," I retorted, but it was halfhearted. I had become very, very aware of my hand on his bare skin. How long ago was it that I had attempted to heal him and was unable to do so?

"The . . . sensation," he said quietly, "the one between us. I thought you would notice it missing."

"I . . . I was thinking about other things," I said pathetically. The absurd truth was that with or without his power, Sebastian had found his way under my skin and I was as fully aware of him as ever. That lemony leather scent was filling the air and my skin was prickling. I had to order my breathing back under my control as I tried not to think about his skin, warm and . . . so much of it beneath my hands.

"Why are you here?" I asked, trying to focus again on my anger. How dare he sneak into my bedroom?

"I came to speak with you about the Society," he said, sounding stronger than before. I peeked through my fingers and saw the wound was almost healed. Still, just to be absolutely, completely, thoroughly certain, I didn't move my hands away.

"They sent me on another mission today and I . . . I wanted to tell you about it." He looked a bit guilty.

"And that necessitated you sneaking into my bedroom?"

"I didn't exactly want to leave my card and call on you with Lord Atherton present!"

Good. If Sebastian was giving in to his exasperation with me, surely he was healed.

He sighed. "I waited outside and when I saw no sign of you, I was concerned."

"How did you get in?"

He glowered at me and blushed in the early light. "It's—it's unimportant."

"Sebastian."

"Hmm?"

"Please, please tell me you didn't scale the walls and climb in through my window."

He glared harder.

"If you don't wish me to think of you as some kind of tragic Gothic figure, you really must stop acting like one."

"I am not—" He stopped and irritably brushed a hand through his hair. "The point is, why weren't you here?"

"I was on a mission."

"Oh."

"How long have you been here?" I slowly took my hands away from him, feeling the lack of his touch keenly.

"Um, well, not all that long."

I waited, watching as he darted his eyes around the room. They flickered to me and away again, but it was enough to send another rush of heat to my cheeks.

"Just . . . a few hours. Since midnight."

Finally our eyes held each other.

Don't kiss him.

"I was worried," he said, slowly pulling himself off the bed frame, leaning forward. His face was so close to mine in the quiet morning. My heart faltered once before catching a new rhythm, faster than before. Sebastian's dark hair had never looked so careless and my fingers itched to return to the inky strands. His eyes were the softest mossy green, and I was sure that all his usual awkward reserve had melted in this strange dawn. When I realized that his eyes were glued to my lips, I instinctively parted them, sucking in a fast breath.

Don't you dare kiss him, Evelyn.

He was so close I could have counted the strands of gold that gleamed in the green of his eyes. I could have shifted forward one breath and his lips would be on mine. I was dizzy, lost in the world that existed here between us. But just as he leaned in, the barest second before I'd find the relief I'd craved in his kiss, I let the outside world rush in, and with it all the myriad reasons we should not touch again.

"Rose is alive," I breathed.

No matter how quietly, how gently I had said it, Sebastian reacted as though I had slapped him.

He pulled back. There was no warmth in those eyes now. They'd turned cold, a summer grass hit with early frost.

"I'm sorry, there is no simple way to tell you, but I was on a mission to recover Mr. Hale. He and Camille took Rose during that horrible fire, while we were fighting Dr. Beck and Claude. Mr. Hale used one of his portals to take Rose and replace her with a sickly woman Camille disguised as my sister. You didn't kill her. In fact, you didn't really kill anyone. The woman they disguised was close to death already."

Sebastian had gone statue-still, not breathing at all.

"She's alive. She's with Catherine right now."

He still didn't move.

"She's alive, Sebastian."

I began to wonder if he could die by holding his breath this long. I reached out and grabbed his hand, shaking it a little. His eyes were still blank and dark, but he finally spoke. "I don't . . ."

"She's alive."

He seemed to suddenly remember how to breathe. In and out, never taking his eyes from me. We sat in the growing light. I heard a nearby door quietly click closed. A maid would be here any moment.

Slowly his hand curled over mine and gently squeezed. "You're sure it's not a lie?" His voice sounded raw and tender like a wound.

I shook my head. "She told me things only she could know. Mr. Kent questioned her, and Camille and Mr. Hale were there. They took her in some harebrained attempt to keep her safe. Rose's power seems to make them care greatly about her safety but little about what she actually wants," I said bitterly.

While Sebastian did not exactly smile, the creases in his forehead disappeared some. "She's alive."

"She is."

He reached out to brush a piece of hair behind my ear and we both caught our breath. I was in the same warm space as before; the only thing existing in it was him.

The door began to slowly creak open.

I was on my feet, rushing to it.

"No! Please!" I said, and the person stopped. I coughed, then peeked around the edge of the door to see an alarmed young maid, who must have been the one to light the fire in my bedroom every morning.

"That is, good morning! I am not feeling well and would not like to be disturbed for at least three more hours."

"Oh, miss, my apologies. Shall I not light the—"

"No, no, thank you."

I shut the door quickly. Sebastian was already standing and shrugging on his coat, which had been draped over my vanity chair.

"I should go," he whispered.

"Yes." I did not want him to leave but I certainly could not suggest he stay. I searched for some excuse. "But what did you want to tell me about the mission?"

He bit his lip. "Nothing compared to your news."

"You waited for hours."

"Well, it was just—the mission they sent me on earlier today. We stopped a man who could control fire—he was part of a group that planned to bomb a number of buildings."

I gaped at him. "You could have been killed."

"So could hundreds of others. I saw the plans in his room,"

Sebastian said. "I just . . . I think we truly did some good. Captain Goode had good reasons for India, too. And now this news that they found your sister . . ." He let out a heavy sigh of relief. "I . . . wanted to thank you. For not giving up on me. For finding a place where we can finally help people."

I nodded mechanically, not knowing where to start, or whether I even should.

"It—it makes me feel like there is a reason. For me." A smile began to curl at his lips and my heart clenched slightly. Sebastian didn't know anything about the prison or the threats to our loved ones. If I told him, he'd be torn between horrible decisions. He'd have even more pain, more deaths on his conscience. He'd have to choose helping us over Mae's safety.

"Me too," I finally said with a smile. "Oh, Mr. Braddock? Please keep Rose a secret. I am still trying to find the best way to . . . bring her back."

"Of course," he said. "And please, call on me. I'd like to help."

As I watched Sebastian quietly sneak out my window, I decided exactly when I would call him for help: never.

I had to keep him as far away from this as possible. There was a distinct difference to Sebastian's kindness. It wasn't a selfish sort, like mine or Mr. Kent's, which favored the people we liked. His was all-encompassing, without reservation, a kindness that made me want to be better and find a way to make the Society the place he believed it was and wanted it to be. I would give that to him, to Rose, to all of us.

Chapter 16

A FEW RESTLESS HOURS later I was eating breakfast with my parents, holding back yawns. My mother was absolutely beside herself as she dealt with the final preparations for the ball, constantly calling for one servant or another as new details occurred to her. Not only was her whirling planning giving me a headache, but sitting across from her and Father, knowing Rose was alive, was a new kind of torture. There was not enough tea in the world to make it bearable.

By the time I made it back up to my bedroom and dressed for my morning calls with Lady Atherton, I was quite ready to return to my bed. But that was not possible.

As I was finishing my hair, Mr. Hale appeared in the corner, looking terribly uncomfortable as Mr. Redburn.

"Did he suspect anything?" I asked immediately, worried we'd failed already.

"No. I was rude and vulgar and that seemed to do the trick. I told him Mr. Hale had escaped and he wrote it down in his little book."

"Good. Then this visit is because . . . ?"

"Another recruitment team has just returned and all three need a healer."

My mind immediately went to Sebastian, wondering if he could have left my room and gone straight on another mission.

"Lady Atherton—"

"She already has a note that you won't be ready till later."

Good. I went to the door and rang the maid's bell. I would pretend to be unwell and undisturbed for the morning. I would have to sneak back in somehow, but that was a worry for later.

Mr. Hale spirited us to the Society foyer and disappeared again to deliver orders to other members. A maid came forward, curtsied, and asked if I would follow her. Upstairs we climbed, and down a corridor we walked until we stopped at the recovery room Oliver had shown me a week earlier. Only Oliver wasn't leading me. He was waiting for me, confined to a bed.

His body was covered in bruises and bandages and blood and burns. He was still awake, grimacing in pain, Captain Goode standing over him with a young-looking nurse.

"Oh, good, Miss Wyndham, if you could start with—" Captain Goode was gesturing to another bed but I rushed to Oliver, trying to find a part of his body that hadn't been hurt. I pressed my hand gently to a spot on his dirt-covered cheek; he opened his mouth to speak and a trickle of blood dripped out. Oh God. A small gasp escaped me and I placed my other hand on his shoulder.

Captain Goode was muttering something about the other patients that I ignored, focusing entirely on Oliver. Finally the man must have given up, for I felt his hand on my shoulder and a rush of power. In seconds, Oliver's injuries disappeared and his painful winces lessened. "I woulda . . . been . . . fine," he said stubbornly. But I had never seen him look quite so young.

"Miss Wyndham," Captain Goode said irritably, making me look up. There were two other occupied beds in the room: Oliver's classmates. The flying girl was asleep in one, her legs set at a strange angle. The plant boy was in the bed next to her, also sleeping off his injuries, covered in a series of bruises. I slid into the space between their beds, setting an arm on each of them to restore them back to health.

"How long have they been unconscious?" I asked Captain Goode, trying to keep the fury out of my voice.

A sweet voice came from the corner of the room. "Just a half hour. I sang them to sleep. They were in pain." An older woman rose from her seat, gesturing to Oliver. "Mr. Myles refused it, though."

Oliver was already climbing out of bed, unwinding the bloody bandages off his body. "I didn't need to be sung to like a baby," he said.

"I see," I said, barely keeping from snapping at him in my anxiety. "What happened?"

Captain Goode stepped in with an explanation. "A mission did not go exactly according—"

"Oliver, what happened?" I interrupted.

Oliver glared at Captain Goode for a moment before answering. "This one sent us to get the weather woman. The tracker found her at the docks."

I spun around and glared daggers at Captain Goode. "They are still training!"

"And the prisoner needed to be retrieved," Captain Goode replied, seeming to be as angry as I was. "It wouldn't have been necessary if she was never set free in the first place."

"No, this wouldn't have been necessary if you hadn't imprisoned her in the first place," I growled back. "And to send children?"

"Not. Children." Oliver glared at me now.

Captain Goode spoke through clenched teeth. "I had my orders."

"Oliver, what happened?"

"Well, they had us go with this guy who can find people by touching objects. So he made us run all over till he got on the girl's trail. But when we found her"—Oliver looked straight at Captain Goode—"they made Eliza fly after her." He nodded at the girl in the other bed, whose leg was now straight and even. "And then he told Eliza to get George up in the air, too, and he tried to grab her with a vine."

"And what did Miss Rao do then?" I asked.

"Her winds pushed my friends into a building. I was able to catch 'em as they were falling, but when I was solid, the lightning came . . . and that's all I remember. I think the tracker man brought help." He turned his back on us and stalked over to his friends on the beds, both of whom were now sleeping peacefully. He reached out a hand tentatively to Eliza but pulled it back, settling for leaning on the wall between Eliza's and Peter's beds.

I turned back to Captain Goode. "Congratulations. These children could have died. On a poorly planned mission. To bring in Miss Rao, who was just trying to protect herself."

"I understand the complexity of the situation, Miss Wyndham. But that does not excuse the fact that she is dangerous and we have direct orders to bring her in."

"Orders?" I all but yelled. "Right, let's discuss your orders."

"Perhaps it would be better to discuss this outside . . . ," Captain Goode suggested, smiling nervously at the older woman with the angelic voice.

I let out a heavy breath that surprisingly wasn't composed of flames. "Fine. Oliver, if they try to send you on any other foolish missions, you are always welcome at my house."

He nodded to me and looked back at Eliza, his jaw set. I kept my rage in check for the sake of the recovering patients and followed Captain Goode out of the room.

"You're going to keep following these orders?" I asked. "Even though you don't know who the head is?"

"As I explained when you joined, it's the foundation of the Society," he said, walking me down to his office. "There is a system. There are rules. Do you abandon all of London society when you disagree with a single rule?"

"I've been known to do that."

Captain Goode shook his head in disappointment. "It's always the upper class that can't take orders. They have to be the ones in charge. I'd thought you'd be different, given the respect you show Miss Grey and Mr. Myles."

"It has nothing to do with that. How do you know this system isn't simply an excuse?" I asked. "You know how powerful we are. The potential of what we can do. Have you not considered that this is a way of controlling us? A way of some lords holding on to their power and using us for their own gain?"

"I've considered that since the day I joined. I was in the army for twelve years. They sent me to India during the mutiny, to serve under the command of lords and gentlemen who purchased their commissions and made terrible, selfish decisions that got many soldiers and friends killed. I know what that looks like. The signs when some pompous duke is trying to profit or earn recognition without regard for anyone else. I've been here for years and received difficult orders myself, but I've always come to realize their value later. There's been nothing to suggest the head has any other motives beyond the stability of our country and our community of powered people."

"But he does not have a power at all!" I insisted. "There's no proof of that."

Captain Goode begrudgingly opened his office door to me. "Of course he does. I've received orders in ways that are impossible for anyone else to deliver."

"He has a bodyguard working for him to do that. A man in that prison told us," I said.

"Prisoners will say anything to get out."

"Not when they are questioned by Mr. Kent."

Captain Goode hesitated and frowned at that. "The prisoner you spoke to was misinformed. Or mad. Mr. Kent's power does not reveal the absolute truth, only what the person believes. And I gather if you talked to some of the other prisoners down there, you are aware of the horrible things a person can convince themselves is right."

"Such as when you hurt my friends and threaten to do worse if I don't follow orders?"

Captain Goode sighed and shook his head. "In an ideal world, you would have the same faith in the Society as I do and there would be no punishments. But I understand that's not possible. It took me some time to believe, too. You've been here for less than a month. I have been here for ten years. I promise you will start to see how our powers come together."

Or I'd simply get better at lying to myself. Captain Goode was too afraid to admit there was something wrong—he'd invested too much already. He was not a bad person, he just needed to accept that he'd misplaced his faith, that he was being manipulated.

I kept pushing. "And if Miss Grey can't find the head in her dreams? If I can prove to you the head is lying about who he is, what would you do then?"

"I would receive an order to punish you for even attempting to discover his identity!" Captain Goode said, nearly exploding. He took a deep breath. "This is still the government. It would be treason. So please, do not do it, and don't employ Miss Grey in your schemes, either. She is happy here. I am trying to help you, Miss Wyndham, but I can do only so much."

I scoffed. And people liked to say *I* was stubborn. This man refused to even entertain the possibility that this was anything less than a grand plan. I didn't know what else to do, how else to argue, how to win him over.

"Very well," I finally said, giving up on changing his mind. "I will give it some time. I have no other choice, it seems."

"I'm sorry it has been . . . unpleasant lately," Captain Goode said. "But as I said on the first day, I am certain there is a bright future ahead of us if we work together. Give us some time. I know you won't regret it." I nodded, knowing I would do no such thing.

He gestured me out of the office, wishing me a good afternoon and thanking me for my work. I wondered how he would feel about this bright future if he knew about his brother's fate.

When I found the footman by the exit and asked him to fetch me a hansom, he anxiously asked if I wouldn't be taking Lady Atherton's coach.

"It is waiting to take you back home," he said. "Shall I fetch you in?"

"I—yes, thank you," I said, curious as to why she would be here.

Curiosity immediately dissipated when I was helped up into the carriage and found not only Lady Atherton, but Lord Atherton as well. "You are quite tardy. We were to arrive precisely at ten thirty."

Ah yes. So lovely to see Lady Atherton again.

"My mother thinks I am in bed and unwell," I said.

"You will have to say that she simply missed your leaving to meet our carriage earlier. We need to attend the final fitting for your ball gown."

I sighed and settled in for a waste of the morning. Lord Atherton cleared his throat and proceeded to offer up only the most banal conversational topics, delivered with all the apathy he could muster.

"This is peculiar weather."

"That is a new building, I believe."

"I have not seen that soap advertisement before."

"This is a smooth road."

"Your ball fast approaches."

Finally, the modiste came into view. And just as I was about to follow his mother out of the coach to the shop, Lord Atherton coughed loudly. "Miss Wyndham. You know our parents hope for a match." I nodded slowly, wondering if I could launch myself out over him.

He looked several inches above my head. "I will have a great many responsibilities coming to me in my life. I have a duty to the British realm."

I stilled, that absurd word repeating in my head. I thought back to the tour of the Society, my tour with Oliver of Captain Goode's office. I thought back to the orders I had read.

"I carry a legacy and I insist on putting my time and energy toward that. You would be a useful part of that legacy."

He sniffed once, allowing his romantic declaration to sink in. "We will speak further at the ball."

As he handed me down from the carriage, I realized this waste of a morning had taught me two very important things.

One, Lord Atherton would be proposing to me at my ball.

Two, the head of the Society of Aberrations would be proposing to me at my ball.

Chapter 17

CATHERINE TRIED TO point out that it was possible he was talking about something else entirely; she had a list of suspects that could be connected to the former heads.'

Mr. Kent said half of London would be a suspect if a boring personality was our criterion.

Miss Chen was not following the connection between the weather obsession and the Society's need to capture Miss Rao.

But I knew it was Lord Atherton.

Mr. Hale and Camille were restless. They wanted to know what my nonexistent plan was to keep Rose safe.

Unfortunately, I'd wasted my morning failing to convince Captain Goode to join us and wasted an afternoon writing feverish notes that failed to convince my friends of Lord Atherton's involvement in the Society.

I was beginning to panic. I had to make them understand so we could come up with a plan. I needed to get everyone together in one place. And it had to be in the middle of the night without fear of discovery.

Though when I'd asked Mr. Hale to bring us somewhere remote and private, I hadn't come close to imagining something like this. The Arabian Desert stretched out for miles in every

direction, golden-orange sand dunes shimmering in the rising sun. I was fairly certain that if he happened to forget about us here, we'd be wandering back home forever.

"This is . . . warm," Rose said diplomatically as she stepped out of Mr. Hale's portal.

Catherine followed, squinting, adjusting her eyes to the brightness. "At least we know no one will be spying on us here." I was reluctant to involve Rose and Catherine at all, but Mr. Hale and Camille were not about to leave her behind . . . and it made me more comfortable as well to keep her in my sight as much as possible.

"I wouldn't put it past the Society to have someone buried under the sand here waiting for us," Miss Chen muttered.

Still, there was a hint of smile on her face as she nodded to me. Mr. Hale had removed her family from London, through a portal and back to her home in America. They were beyond the Society's reach, for now, and Miss Chen would be joining them.

As soon as she had her revenge.

"Is it really you?" Miss Grey was running through a portal, grabbing Rose's hands and pulling her into an embrace. "I thought . . ."

Rose nodded and began explaining everything in broken pieces. I had been able to send Miss Grey only the briefest of letters before now.

Another portal crackled open. "Good God, where are we, the sun?" Mr. Kent shouted.

"No," our whole group answered in unison.

He shot me an apologetic look. "That one was meant to be rhetorical."

I found myself nervous as I scanned the group. Everyone was here, waiting for me to start. Mr. Hale and Camille were flanking a nervous Rose and a protective Catherine. Miss Chen was lounging on the sand, as comfortable as ever. Miss Grey was still staring at Rose in wonder and Mr. Kent was smirking, per usual.

I cleared my throat. "Thank you, everyone, for coming. I have asked you here to see if you will help me find the head of the Society of Aberrations."

Silence. To most, this was not a surprise. But Miss Grey went pale and began to wring her hands.

"They claim to be a part of the government, but then they lie to us about our missions and justify horrible acts by claiming it's for the sake of the country. We cannot continue working for an organization that punishes us by hurting or even killing the ones we love. We don't know their motivations or intentions and neither does Captain Goode—he is simply following orders from a head who has no powers. And I believe I know who that is."

Catherine sighed.

"The Earl of Atherton," I said firmly.

"Or," said Catherine, "it could be one of these men." She reached into her purse and pulled out a sheaf of paper.

"Mr. Kent and Evelyn learned that two previous heads had been the Earl of Hartwell and the Duke of Fosberry. I knew the names were familiar, but then I found that both men held the same position: They were each appointed as the Under Secretary of the Home Office."

"You suspect a link between the Home Office and the Society?" Miss Grey asked.

"I do." Catherine nodded vigorously, sending her spectacles sliding down her face. "I think when someone performs well in that position, he is promoted and appointed to be the head of the Society of Aberrations. There are a number of men here—all highly connected, all distinct possibilities."

"Including," I began, pausing for emphasis, "the previous Lord Atherton. . . ."

"As well as the Marquess of Herrington, the Marquess of Overstone, the Earl of Somers, the Earl of Warrington, and—well, the Duke of Harlowe."

We all looked at her at that one. "The Duke of Harlowe is . . . ," I said.

"Not open to new ideas," Mr. Kent filled in, rather diplomatically. It was impossible to imagine the aging, stubborn duke leading a society of people with extraordinary powers.

"Well, all right, I admit he is unlikely, but the others are possibilities. They could certainly be the head," Catherine said.

"Or Lord Atherton," I added.

"But that doesn't make nearly as much sense," Catherine said. "Why would the young Lord Atherton be appointed for the position just because of his father?"

"Inheritance," I answered. England's answer for most important roles in society. "Besides, he told me he had an important duty to the British realm."

I looked at everyone in turn. No one seemed to think that was noteworthy.

"Realm! No one says *realm*! No one except the head of the Society of Aberrations, who used the very same word in an order to Captain Goode!"

They stared more.

"Plenty of people say *realm*," Mr. Kent finally said.

"Who?"

"Why, lawyers, politicians, immortal men from the fourteenth century . . ."

"Evelyn," Miss Grey cut in softly. "What do you plan to do with the head, whoever it may be?"

"We will convince him to step down."

"And he will politely apologize and stop?" Camille asked, her words thick with sarcasm.

"Well . . ." I hesitated. "I think we should simply abduct him if it comes to that."

A heavier silence than before fell.

"Evelyn—" Miss Grey began.

"I like it," Miss Chen interrupted. She flashed her teeth in a vicious grin. "Why shouldn't we? You all don't know the half of the things he's made me do these past months. I say we tie him up."

I could almost see the visions of violence running through her head.

"Or, Mr. Kent, you could . . . influence him," I said stiffly, but he was already grinning like a little boy just handed an afternoon free from his tutor.

"Influence him, yes, surely, Miss Wyndham—now you couldn't possibly mean blackmail—no, no, I'm sure you didn't mean that."

I glared at him. "Extenuating circumstances."

"Ha!" He grasped his cane and raised it into the air. "I knew it."

"If we could return to the matter," Miss Grey was saying. "Evelyn, this seems extreme."

"And the Society's methods aren't? We know they will punish us. We know they are forcing powered people to join them, and we know they have imprisoned those who didn't deserve it. We have only so much time before Captain Goode realizes Mr. Hale is masquerading as his brother." I tried not to let my panic infuse the words, but it was true. We had to figure this out soon, or someone would get hurt.

"I think we should go confront Lord Atherton," I said.

"Except that it is very possible it's not him," Catherine interjected firmly. "I think we should focus on the things we do know. We know the head could be—or at least be connected to—any of these men, not just Lord Atherton." She gestured to the papers she held. "We know it's someone who does not have a power. We know it's someone influential in London society. We know he probably held this position in the Home Office. And we know it's someone very clever."

"So clever that he pretends to be the most boring, unimaginative man in all of London to hide his true identity," I countered.

"And what do you mean to do?" Catherine asked. "Go knock on the Athertons' door, all of us, and just ask? Take him from his own house while servants look on? What if you're wrong? What if there's a bodyguard? The Society will find out what you're trying to do."

True, it was not exactly the most elegant plan.

"Well, what do you suggest?" I asked her. Everyone turned and she cleared her throat, pink and nervous at the sudden attention.

"Your ball."

"My . . . ball . . ."

"It's the most obvious reason for all of us to be together, and it will be much less conspicuous. Your mother will have invited only the top of London society. You can look to be sure that the other men on this list are invited and we can quietly have Mr. Kent ask our potential suspects the correct questions. When we identify the head, he won't be able to do anything in the middle of a ball because he needs to keep these powers a secret. Then, at the right time, Mr. Hale can even bring us somewhere quiet."

A breeze swirled sand around us as everyone considered Catherine's suggestion.

"I have to say, that seems very sound," Mr. Kent said, throwing me an apologetic smile.

"And when is this ball?" Mr. Hale asked, frowning.

"In two nights' time," I said slowly, warming to the possibility. It was a good idea. We could corner Lord Atherton at the beginning and whisk him away early without anyone noticing. I could be sure these other men were on Mother's list as well.

I looked around. "Mr. Kent and I can question people. Miss Grey, you can try to dream about any powered people we don't know of in London. It's very likely this head would have a bodyguard like others have in the past—then you can come to the ball and let us know if you recognize anyone." Mr. Kent seemed pleased at the prospect of staying by my side and Miss Grey still looked ill, but my thoughts were galloping ahead of me.

"I know two other gentlemen who may have information about the bodyguard, too," I said, remembering Arthur and William. "I will visit them tomorrow. If there is a guard, Miss Chen, we may need you to create a distraction."

She flashed that wicked smile again. "Excellent."

"I will agree to none of this unless Miss Rosamund is kept out of harm's way." Mr. Hale stepped forward.

Camille sniffed and delicately stood at his side, her head held determinedly. "She is the highest priority. I will stay with her."

"I agree. Camille, after disguising Miss Grey, whom my mother would recognize, you should stay with Rose and Catherine at Catherine's house, just in case something goes wrong."

My stubborn friend opened her mouth to argue. "I can—"

"Please, Catherine," I said, glancing pointedly at Rose. Rose would not be comfortable with Camille at all and I suspected Catherine's presence would make it far more bearable. And she could keep an eye on Camille, making sure she didn't abscond with Rose.

Catherine took in the stiff-necked way Rose was looking at her former captors. "All right," she agreed.

"Good," I said. "Mr. Hale, we'll need you to check in periodically so you can take Lord Atherton—or yes, whoever the head of the Society is—off to a more remote location. Camille will stay with Rose and Catherine the whole time but of course you can go back and forth easily." He sighed but finally gave a reluctant nod.

"I suppose it's not the worst plan," Camille mused.

"That's everyone here," Mr. Kent said. "But I believe Mr. Myles would want to be included."

Miss Grey hesitated. "He is so young."

"But so helpful," Mr. Kent countered. "He could get anyone out of a tight spot. He proved that at the prison."

"He did," I said reluctantly. But I couldn't forget his injuries from today. I didn't want to force or coerce him into anything. I'd give him the choice and, if he wanted to participate, assign him a safe task. "He could watch from the floor above and deliver messages if there is an emergency. Is there anyone else?"

There wasn't. And if anyone had any Sebastian suggestions, they had the good sense to keep it to themselves.

"It's settled, then. I will work out the details and timing tonight. Mr. Hale, you will deliver letters with the plan to everyone?" He nodded. I felt a tiny bud of hope springing up beneath my bodice.

"But what then?" Rose said suddenly.

Everyone turned to her and she immediately looked like she regretted speaking.

"What do you mean?" I asked.

She swallowed and drew closer to Catherine. "What happens to the Society after he isn't running it?"

I looked around to see if anyone else had an answer.

They didn't.

"Well, I think we should let people decide if they still want to work for them, of course. And if enough people wish to stay, then we will have to find some common ground for what we want to do with the Society."

Camille did not seem to like the idea. "They are evil," she said, and gave a loud huff.

"Yes, but they could be *not* evil," I said, annoyed. "I think Captain Goode could be perfectly fair if he had better guidance." I looked at Miss Grey. "And Miss Grey, you seem to work very well with him. You could be that guidance." One line in her forehead softened as she took in the possibilities.

"And, Rose, I'd trust your judgment on all of it the most." I said. "You'd be integral—"

"No," Rose said, then bit her lip and looked downwards.

"What do you mean?"

An awkward silence prevailed. She refused to elaborate and no one knew what to say.

Mr. Kent finally broke in. "I think these are questions we can address after speaking to this head—whoever he may turn out to be."

"We have plenty we need to do before the ball—but we will certainly discuss it at length," I said, nodding at Rose.

I sighed. There was too much to do in too little time. I had to talk to Oliver, find William and Arthur, and disinvite Mae from the ball.

And keep Sebastian away from all of it.

"I will send you all messages tonight."

I shooed everyone else through the portals, asking Mr. Hale to give Rose and me a moment. "You can stand over there," I said, pointing him farther down the hot sand. I waited till he was far, far away, and there was no chance we would be overheard.

"Now, tell me what you're thinking," I said, taking her hand.

She scrunched her nose slightly, blue eyes full of worry and a flash of anger. "How can you think keeping the Society together is a good idea?"

"Because with the right people in charge, we could do good things," I said.

"I just . . ." Rose turned away, blinking back a tear. "I just want to be with Mother and Father. I want to go back to how things were, home and safe in Bramhurst. Not running around with these . . . these criminals!"

"But you couldn't wait to leave before!" I said, slightly stunned. "This is a way for us to use our talents."

She bit her lip and mumbled, "Your talent."

"Dear, your talent can be put to great use."

She pulled away. "Yes, I can make people do terrible things because they think they love me!" She swiped her hand under her eyes and closed them, speaking very tightly. "Within a day of finding me, you've brought together so many of these people to fight this terrifying Society. Everyone's suddenly putting themselves and their families in danger. I don't even know if my family truly loves me or if it's just this terrible thing inside me. Like how I took credit for what was clearly your skill with all our patients back in Bramhurst."

I was overflowing with excuses, gasping that she could think that, so I didn't think I was terribly convincing as I tried to reassure her. "Rose, dearest, we love you for who you are. These powers don't even begin developing until we reach about fourteen. We—Mother and Father and, Lord, even Robert!—we've loved you since you were born. You've been dear to us for ages—it isn't your power."

She had her back to me now, her thin shoulders trembling. I came up behind her and pulled her into a hug.

"I love you, Rose. For who you are, who you have been, and who you will be. It has nothing to do with your power."

"But you don't know that," she whispered.

"I do. And as soon as we figure out what to do with the head of the Society, I will have Captain Goode remove your power and I will prove to you that I love you despite it."

She sighed. "I just don't trust these powers or these terrible people. Do you really think it's a good idea to keep the Society running?"

"They aren't all terrible. And we can do so much good—we can help people all over the world. That's what you always talked about doing."

"I . . . The last time I tried to help someone . . ." Rose's voice cracked and she pressed her lips tightly together. "I wish we could run away."

I stared out in the same direction she did, my head on her shoulder, my heart torn from how much she'd changed. She was the decisive one, the one who always did what she thought would help others, the one who should have been pushing us to fix the Society of Aberrations and do some good. A fresh stab of anger for Camille and Mr. Hale and Dr. Beck hit me, making me plan elaborate tortures for what they did. For how they hurt her.

Rose's body stiffened in my arms. Mr. Hale was walking toward us, apparently our time alone was up. "I hate him," Rose said softly, but with conviction.

"I do, too."

"I want him to pay, after all this is done. He *should* be arrested."

"We will figure something out. I promise. Just give me two more days."

I held her tightly by my side as we crossed back through the portal.

Two days.

Two days and Rose would be safe. For good.

Chapter 18

ARTHUR AND WILLIAM'S gambling house was ablaze with electric lights. The floors gleamed, and the pockets of gentlemen playing French hazard, roulette, and baccarat were fanned out across the large room. Spots of color here and there signified the ladies present, and as I observed them, I was glad to have picked the right dress, for once.

"This is a dream come true, Miss Wyndham," Mr. Kent said. "You inviting me to a den of iniquity."

"So glad I could help," I said.

The crowd was noisy and genial. I carefully looked around to see if I could discern anyone else with powers. Of course, nothing was obvious. But we did discern the man who looked to be in charge of the place, pacing the room and scrutinizing all the tables and guests closely.

"Hello, sir," Mr. Kent said, stepping into the man's path. "Would you happen to know where we might find your proprietors?"

"I do," he said stiffly, answering Mr. Kent's question to its bare minimum.

"Will you escort us to them?"

"No. Not at the moment," the man said. "They are busy."

"They are friends with Miss Wyndham here," he said, gesturing to me. "I'm certain they will wish to see her immediately."

"They have many friends, sir," the man replied. "And they will see them when they aren't busy."

Mr. Kent looked annoyed for a moment, before he covered with a smile and I knew what was coming. "Very well. But before we go, what is the most horrible—"

"Thank you, sir," I said, seizing Mr. Kent's arm tightly and pulling him away. "We will wait for them."

"We'll be waiting all night," Mr. Kent said, once we were out of earshot. "If the staff at these places don't recognize you, they aren't going to take you to their bosses. They are rather careful with strangers."

"Then we'll find them ourselves," I said, scanning the assortment of gamblers. "You don't need to blackmail everyone for every little thing."

Mr. Kent sighed. "Fine. You know the men we are looking for, I believe," he said through a pleasant smile he wore. He was becoming quite good at phrasing questions so they didn't directly force anyone to respond.

"Yes, Arthur has tremendous hearing abilities and William can see through all kinds of disguises and at a great distance."

"I would appreciate a description of their looks," Mr. Kent finally said, having puzzled over the phrasing on that one.

"Arthur is very tall with a beard. William is shorter and has a great scar on his face."

"They sound like quite the duo," Mr. Kent said as we squeezed through the crowd. His eyes lit up. "Ah, there, how fortunate."

I followed him, wondering how he'd found them so quickly in the dense crowd. But he hadn't found anything, except for an empty seat at a baccarat table. Mr. Kent nodded to the dealer and sat down.

"This is definitely not what we were looking for," I whispered.

Mr. Kent pulled out a handful of money. "This will be much faster. And more fun."

I stared. "Sitting at a table and playing cards will help us find them?"

"Indeed."

I threw my hands up and left him there to have his fun as I walked a circle of the room. Cries at wins and losses rang out, but the entire scene was overwhelmingly cheerful. The clatter of dice on dice and the snap of cards on cards filled the air and I could see how easy it would be to get swept up in a game, betting more than you had in your pockets.

There was no sign of Arthur or William anywhere on the first floor, so I made my way up a staircase at the back of the room. On the second floor, billiard balls clacked on impact and glasses clinked all around the bar. I asked the bartender about Arthur and William and received a similarly condescending response that he would inform them after their meetings. They were very busy men, after all.

I made my way to the balcony, looking over the first floor from above. When I was unable to find either of them from the new angle, I searched for Mr. Kent, finding myself slightly more amenable to his blackmail approach.

But that was not who I spied, sitting with a familiar-looking, well-dressed man in his forties.

I ducked.

Not that it made any sense as he was not looking up, but ducking was what I was compelled to do when I saw my father in a gambling hall.

Blast. Why did every den of iniquity have to be full of people I knew? I cautiously stood back up. Lord Herrington, the man who had looked familiar, was next to my father, speaking into his ear. It felt like ages since I had healed his daughter, Lady Pippa, for the Society.

I didn't even realize how angry I was until I felt my palms digging into the balcony railing. How dare my father, who had only just recovered our fortunes, think to gamble away the money? How could he be so irresponsible?

Lord Herrington slapped my father's shoulder and laughed heartily. I glared down at them as my father threw more chips onto the table.

As I considered ordering a drink and throwing it at them, a disgruntled shout came from Mr. Kent's table. Somehow, he had already accrued a great deal of money since I had left him. And the croupier was whispering something to another man, who left his post in a hurry.

Oh, for God's sake. I couldn't leave him alone for five minutes. I hastened back downstairs, keeping one eye on my father, who wasn't moving from his table, and squeezed my way to Mr. Kent's side as I heard him ask his opponent, "Now sir, I don't want to force you. Only if you wouldn't mind sharing—what are your cards?"

"A king and a five," the man said, red-faced and very frustrated with his slip.

"How generous of you to say. I will take another card, please," Mr. Kent said to the croupier.

He smiled upon receiving his third card and when all the cards were overturned, he was declared the winner again. His winnings doubled.

I clutched his shoulder and tried my hardest to keep my

scolding to a whisper. "Mr. Kent, why are you just blatantly cheating? You'll get us kicked out and we really mustn't cause a scene. My father is here."

Mr. Kent looked up at me in surprise. "Your fath—"

"'Allo, sir," a familiar voice said. "My name's William Fitch. The owner of this 'ere 'ouse. Might we 'ave a word?"

Mr. Kent gave me a smug smile. "That's why."

I spun around. "William!" I said. "I'm so sorry about Mr. Kent here. He was trying to get your attention."

William's intimidating expression shifted to surprise, his eyes bulging. "Miss . . . Wyndham, uh, yes." It was hard not to feel the slightest bit of pride for surprising a man with extraordinary vision. I nervously looked to Lord Herrington, who stood from my father's side.

Mr. Kent rose out of his chair and held out his hand. "A pleasure to meet you, Mr. Fitch. My apologies. Your man wouldn't bring us to you, so this seemed to be the most expedient way to bring you to us. You can return my winnings to that poor fellow."

With a slow nod, William signaled to the croupier and then took Mr. Kent's hand. "I'll 'ave to set up a better system."

"William, my . . . father is unfortunately here. Terrible timing. Do you think we might talk in private somewhere?"

He nodded and led us out of the growing crowd toward the stairs. My father still sat at his table and as he threw back his drink, Lord Herrington was ready with another.

"Miss Wyndham, you have yet to congratulate me on my brilliant plan," Mr. Kent said.

"Why don't you ever tell me these things before you do them?" I whispered back.

"Because your reaction wouldn't be nearly as fun."

On the second floor, William turned a discreet door handle

that blended seamlessly into the club's wood paneling that surrounded the room. We slipped through, William scanning the room until he seemed satisfied that we had failed to catch anyone's attention. We were led through a narrow but clean hallway, up another flight of stairs, and out to the roof of the building, where Arthur stood guard.

"Miss Wyndham." He greeted me with a bow. "I thought that was your voice down there. I 'ope you are well. My condolences about your sister."

"Yes, we were very sorry to 'ear that sad news," William added.

I felt a brief moment of awkwardness, remembering that everyone else still thought her dead. As nice as Arthur and William had been to me, I had to simply pretend that was still the case.

"Thank you," I said. "She's . . . somewhat the reason I'm here. You are part of the Society of Aberrations, yes?"

"We are," Arthur said with a nod.

"Well, I joined because I wanted to help people as Rose would have wanted," I said. "But . . ."

"You don't believe the Society is 'elping, do you?"

I shook my head. "No. Not when they are threatening and imprisoning and hurting us when we refuse to follow their orders."

Arthur and William looked at each other.

"We'd started to 'ear rumors . . . ," Arthur said.

"But our work is just providing them with information," William said with disappointment. "We never saw a reason to refuse."

"Thought we were 'elping."

"I think we can help," I said. "There are enough of us who want to. It's just . . . the head of the Society. I think it's the Earl of Atherton—"

"It's not Lord Atherton," Mr. Kent interrupted.

"It might be," I shot back. "But we don't have any evidence. We were hoping you might be able to give us something. Anything about the head. Or his bodyguard. No matter how small, it would help."

Arthur and William stared at the sky and the rooftop, deep in thought. "Lord Atherton's as good a guess as any," Arthur finally said.

"But I'm sorry to say we don't know anything more about the 'ead," William put in. "No one seems to."

"The bodyguard, though," Arthur said, snapping his fingers, an idea coming to him. "'Ow about that knives woman?"

"Who is this knives woman?" Mr. Kent asked.

"Someone we'd 'ear 'bout e'ry once in a while," Arthur answered. "There'd be an attack, some poor wretch cut up all over by a woman with knives."

"'Cept the knives floated," William added, wagging his finger at Arthur. "Forgettin' the most important parts."

Mr. Kent's jaw tightened and I knew he was thinking the same thought. This sounded like the same person that attacked Laura.

"Anyways, we 'ad a suspicion 'cause the Society always snatches up the dangerous ones," William said. "But no one knows who this one is. She just runs free 'til the next story."

"Do you know anything else about her?" I asked. "Her name? Or her exact power?"

But William only shrugged, while Arthur shook his head. "If ya give us more time, we'll try to discover more," William offered.

"We don't have much," I said ruefully. Not with Mr. Hale impersonating Mr. Redburn. And his and Camille's worry over Rose. The ball was our only chance.

William peered closely at me. "You're not gonna do nothin' reckless?"

"No, no," I lied, grateful that it wasn't Mr. Kent asking me the question. "But thank you. Please send me a message if you do discover anything. And . . . please don't tell Mr. Braddock anything. I'm hoping to keep him uninvolved."

Arthur and William both nodded, understanding.

I stopped at the doorway and turned. "Do you think I might be able to ask that you . . . escort my father out? And not let him return?"

The men exchanged a glance and I could feel the burn of embarrassment on my cheeks. However, it wasn't *my* fault that Father had decided to do this.

"O' course, Miss Wyndham," Arthur said.

"Thank you."

In silence, Mr. Kent and I made our way back downstairs. Lord Herrington and my father had moved to the same table that Mr. Kent had occupied earlier. We steered ourselves to the other wall and slid outside. I sucked in a huge breath, relieved we made it down the long hall and out the door unnoticed. As we started toward our appointed meeting place with Mr. Hale, Mr. Kent slid his arm around my waist and I gasped as he pulled me against the building.

"Mr. Kent, what are you doing?" I whispered, not feeling particularly amorous.

"Why, Miss Wyndham, we never finished our discussion about our . . . moment in India."

"Now is not—"

"Miss Harding said you read the Agony Column. I'm surprised you did not see my many submissions. 'Desperately seeking the lips mine once touched'—there were many variations, but that was my favorite." He sighed longingly and I made to push him back, but he stopped me.

"Also, you said you wanted to keep Mr. Braddock out of this," he conceded.

"What does he have to do with anything?" I snapped defensively.

Mr. Kent peeked out of our nook. "He was coming down the street. We have successfully avoided him, but for your future knowledge, I've heard publicly kissing someone will keep others from even looking in our direct—"

"I thought that was you," Sebastian said, his voice dark and harsh.

I scrambled out of Mr. Kent's arms. "Oh! Mr. Braddock, hello."

The light from the gambling hall spilled over half his face and his great coat flapped menacingly. "Why are you here?" he asked, staring around me at Mr. Kent.

Mr. Kent laughed uncomfortably. "Why does anyone go to a gambling house?"

"To gamble," Sebastian answered.

"To find information for our plan," I muttered, Mr. Kent's power inadvertently affecting me as well.

"What plan?" Sebastian asked.

I glared at Mr. Kent. "Nothing, nothing at all."

"No one seems to understand what a rhetorical question is these days," Mr. Kent said to the skies.

Sebastian looked at me accusingly. "Miss Wyndham, what are you planning?"

"I don't recall saying anything about a plan," I said.

"You most definitely did."

"Don't worry, Mr. Braddock, I will clear this up," Mr. Kent

said, turning to me. "Miss Wyndham, did you say anything about a plant?"

"No," I replied honestly.

Sebastian frowned. "You just said *plant*. With a *t*."

Mr. Kent shook his head. "You must be mistaken. Miss Wyndham, did I say 'plant with a *t*'?"

"No, you didn't," I answered.

"Now, you just deliberately phrased that plant question—" Sebastian cut himself off and closed his eyes in frustration. "I just—Mr. Kent, would you mind giving us a moment?"

Mr. Kent smiled. "Of course, I'll give you a *great* moment. What are you brooding about, Mr. Braddock?"

"Miss Wyndham obviously came here to speak to Arthur and William and decided not to inform me," Sebastian answered, glaring at Mr. Kent. But he turned to me and continued. "I thought—after the other night . . . I don't know why—"

"One moment," Mr. Kent interrupted. "What do you mean, *the other night*?"

"When I spoke to Miss Wyndham in her bedroom," Sebastian answered with a groan.

"That's not at all what it sounds like," I put in hastily.

Mr. Kent's jaw hardened. "I fail to see the room for interpretation, unless *bed* and *room* are two separate words. Did you move your bed to the drawing room?"

"No, but it was a conversation that might as well have happened in a drawing room," I said quickly.

"Was anyone unclothed?" Mr. Kent said sarcastically, clearly not expecting an affirmative answer.

However.

"A bit," my uncooperative mouth responded and I tried to

cover it with a yelp. This was absurd. Both of them were absurd, tonight was absurd, and I was, assuredly, absurd. "Mr. Kent, stop asking questions. Mr. Braddock, there is nothing for you to worry about. Now, let us just part and I will see you both at my wretched b—"

I snapped my mouth shut.

Mr. Kent had his head in his palm and Sebastian was looking at me suspiciously.

He would not have known about the ball at all.

"Where?"

"Nowhere," I said and turned away.

"What is going on?" Sebastian asked us wildly. "Is it the Society? Did something happen?"

Mr. Kent had joined me at my side and we ignored him.

"Why would you keep me from this?" He sounded so utterly betrayed I almost bent. But this was for his sake.

"I didn't want to involve you," I finally said.

"You already involved me when you came to find me in Italy!" Sebastian said. "But now you insist on leaving me out of everything—"

"Except her bedroom."

"I'm trying to protect you!" I shouted. "I'm trying to make sure your intended stays safe and you don't have to run away again and you can just live a blasted happy life, for heaven's sakes!"

Sebastian stared at me. "My . . . *intended*?" His voice was approximately thirteen octaves higher than usual.

"Yes, your intended," I said, shooting a glare at a gaping Mr. Kent. "Your betrothed? Fiancée? Bride-to-be?"

Even in the poor streetlight, I could see Sebastian's cheeks were pink. "What do you mean?"

"I mean Mae."

He cocked his head to the side. "I . . . think there's some confusion here."

"You. Are. Engaged. To. Mae. Lodge."

"No . . . I'm not."

"You needn't worry. She told me months ago."

"I'm not worried, I'm—"

"I can't believe this," I said. "I can't even . . . comprehend how someone would actually be unaware of his own engagement. It's unbelievable. Mr. Kent, can you ask Mr. Braddock if he really had no idea?"

Mr. Kent had this faraway look in his eyes and I couldn't begin to figure out what he was thinking. But he regained himself and turned to Sebastian. "Mr. Braddock . . . Before today, did you ever have any idea that you were engaged to Miss Lodge?"

"No," Sebastian said, then frowned at me. "Are you certain that is what she meant?"

I frowned back. "She talked about your future together. And the understanding you two had. I'm certain."

"Oh."

I let out a heavy sigh. "So, you do remember proposing now?"

"I . . . still don't think I did," he said, his brow furrowed.

I dropped my head into my hands. My words came out half muffled. "You don't *think* you did? How do you not know if you proposed or not?"

"I will be sure to let you know when I find out," he said, giving me one last frustrated look. A glare at Mr. Kent and his footsteps faded away down the empty street.

An uncomfortable silence reigned for a few long moments. My mind was still blank when the quiet was broken by a crackle in the wall and the clearing of a throat. Mr. Hale stood in the portal, looking very much like Mr. Redburn, given his impatience. "Did you learn anything new?" he asked.

I didn't quite know how to respond to that. I felt a strange exhaustion, like I'd somehow used up all my words and had none left.

Mr. Kent finally answered for both of us. "Yes. I'd say we learned a thing or two."

Chapter 19

THE REST OF a night was a haze. I tried to concentrate on our plan for my ball, sending everyone their instructions and running over the variables as I lay in bed, unable to sleep. But mostly I was planning elaborate revenges upon Sebastian for distracting me so thoroughly. And for being such a nitwit.

By the time the visiting hours came the following morning I was dressed and more than ready to leave and spend the day with my sister. But before I could call for our carriage, I was informed that I had a guest.

I entered the room with bleary eyes and shaking hands. Even with recent tears proclaimed by her swollen eyes, the desperate wringing of her handkerchief, and the water that I could swear still shone on her cheeks, Mae was polite as ever. "I am so sorry to come over unannounced, Evelyn." She strode back and forth along the drawing room, sending me a weak smile.

I could feel guilt beginning to boil in my stomach and I sat down hard, trying to summon my own smile but failing. "You are always welcome, Mae. Please, do sit." She eyed the chair I gestured to as though it were a collection of snakes, but her perfect breeding prevailed and she sat on the edge, her foot pedaling up and down with excess energy.

"Mae, you're scaring me," I said with a laugh I did not feel.

She turned guiltily to me. "I'm sorry. It's just . . . I needed to speak to you."

"What about?" I asked, though I could guess the answer. She always had such control over her emotions, such calm, except when it came to one topic.

"It's about Sebastian."

"What did he do?"

"He came to see me this morning."

"Yes?" My voice was breathy and high and false and horrible.

"He told me things. Ridiculous things. He—he claimed to be responsible for my brother's death. For his parents' deaths. For my illness. He said he has some magical curse or something else just as strange, I don't understand, and frankly, he was scaring me."

She turned then, fixing her beautiful gray eyes on mine. "He said you have some strange power, too. That you can heal anyone with just a touch. Is this some story or joke? I—he—he's not gone mad, has he? Why would he say such things?"

But Mae wasn't asking me a question. She was begging me, from the depths of her soul, to provide a simple explanation, something that would reassure her about Sebastian, restore her balance when her world had been turned upside down. And I was tempted, so tempted to give it to her. But Sebastian had wanted her to know. Surely, now that he was aware of their engagement, he was declaring himself fully, telling her everything about him that he hated, letting her see the dark as well as the light.

And so, for his sake, I forced myself to speak the words. "I'm afraid, Mae, that everything he said was true."

She did not make a sound. Tears spilled over, running through already-worn trenches.

"He has no control over it, and I know it tortures him greatly.

But if he told you, it's because he wants nothing between you. He wants you to know everything about who he is." I couldn't say where the words came from, grinding out of my mouth like rusted cogs, turning, cutting tracks in my throat as I forced them out.

But Mae was still not responding, just staring at me. I began to feel trapped. There was no air in this room, only this girl I liked very much who happened to be marrying the only man I had ever had feelings for.

"Did he tell you anything else?"

"He told me about you and Mr. Kent. He said there were others."

"Yes, we are still learning what exactly causes it, and how, but it seems there are a number of people." I latched eagerly on to the topic, happy to be discussing something other than Sebastian.

"You healed me."

"Yes."

"With a magical power?"

"Something like that, yes." Mae was looking at me as though I were an extremely excited child who wished to convince her governess that the fairies *were* real, indeed. I sighed and picked up my fan, released the blade, and cut my palm. Mae gasped and shot out of her seat as I wiped the blood away and showed her the fast-healing skin.

She rubbed her eyes. "I'm seeing things."

"I'm afraid not."

She blinked rapidly and I decided that babbling on would be the best thing for it. "Mr. Braddock and I appear to have diametrically opposed powers—we cancel each other's out when we are in proximity. I was able to heal you when he was out of the room, but if he gets too close to anyone without my presence, they will fall ill."

"I . . . I know he's always kept his distance since his parents," she said. "But he wasn't like that when he returned this time."

"That's because we found a cure, of sorts. A man who can alter our abilities—enhance or remove them entirely, for a day or two. That's why Mr. Braddock came back from his recent travels. He can finally be with you without fear of harming you."

She gave a short shake of her head, her neck stiff and long. "I'm afraid you are mistaken. He did not tell me all this . . . this *madness*, so that we could be together." She was regarding me solemnly as a tear dropped off her jawbone onto the lace waiting below.

"But, to admit so much, he must truly—"

"He broke off our engagement," she said.

I stared at her. Those words did strange and horrible things to my heart. It was like it broke into two pieces and then tried to leap for joy at once.

"He told me all this as an explanation for why we would never be together. He said that he could *never* be sure that he would keep me safe. And he had promised my brother that he would look after me."

"But he's . . . not as dangerous anymore," I breathed.

Fresh tears were coming now. I waited, unable to do anything other than watch her fall to pieces—as simple and impossible to prevent as watching someone in the distance fall from a great height.

"If he is not dangerous, then I—I don't believe he wishes to be with me." Finally she sat, skirts settling gently around her perfectly erect form, even now, not sunken in disappointed dreams.

I stared at the wall, the stripes on the fabric warped together, doubling and separating under my dazed gaze. It would be so easy to confirm her fears. So easy to agree that it must mean he did not want to be with her. That, perhaps, he wanted to be with me. But when I looked at all of it with sober judgment, I knew it was not that.

Sebastian felt something for me. I was not a good enough liar to convince myself otherwise. But it was not the same ease and familiarity—the same constancy he had in Mae. He had told her everything. And then he told her he could not be with her. But he'd said nothing to her about their proposal being a misunderstanding. Nothing about not loving her. Sebastian only told her that he could not be sure he could always keep her safe.

This was the entire reason I had decided to keep him out of our plans for the ball. And he went and mucked it up.

The ridiculous, stubborn, infuriating, impossible fool. And here I was, with the chance to be as good and noble as him. As Mae.

I could feel a building, burning pressure behind my own eyes as I cleared my throat. "Mae, I believe he is just being his obtusely noble self."

She swallowed hard but her eyes did not leave mine. "He is not in love with me."

I forced myself to hold her gaze, hoping I sounded encouraging. "But I . . . I know how much he cares for you. He just carries so much guilt around and he is being martyrish. But I think he's also giving you the decision."

Mae was still in the way that frightened animals sometimes are, worried about doing anything to make things worse. Her lips barely moved but I heard her clearly. "What do you mean?"

"You have the choice to forgive him or not. He's giving you the freedom and the time to think about it without any promises to him. It's a hard thing to forgive—even knowing it was not something he wished. It's still your sibling. But if you do forgive him, you have to be certain. Otherwise, he'll never forgive himself."

She let out a heavy, wavering breath, considering my words. "I . . . hadn't thought . . . I don't know what I'd say to him." Alarmed, she snapped her attention up at me. "Will he be attending your ball?"

I watched her nervously bite her lip. This was the perfect way to keep Mae away.

"Yes," I lied. "He will be. I could ask Mother to disinvite him . . . ," I began, counting on Mae's infinite politeness.

She shook her head fiercely. "No, no, of course not. I just . . . I don't think I'm ready. Oh, I'm so sorry to miss it."

"The apology is unnecessary. You just need some time," I said, standing and taking her hand. "And believe me, I understand. I promise you won't miss anything of interest. It will be a great bore with a bunch of my mother's puffed-up friends."

At that, my friend nodded slightly and stood up as well. I hoped, for all our sakes, that I was right. I would be thrilled if the ball ended up being a great bore.

At least no one would get hurt.

Chapter 20

"Evelyn!" My mother's voice rang out through the house in perfect symphony with doleful thrums from the clock.

Seven. It was time to start. The guests would be arriving soon, among them Lord Atherton. The rest of our lives depended on the next few hours. The fates of people all over the world depended on what we did with the Society of Aberrations. And here I was, tensely waiting for my maid to finish tucking my elaborate curls just so under the light-purple ribbon.

"This is truly unnecessary, Lucy," I said. "There cannot possibly be another strand of hair left to pin."

"Your mother insisted on perfection, miss," she replied.

Indeed, she had. Lady Atherton had sent a note politely requesting that I wear one of the new gowns she had ordered. It was a terribly complicated, if lovely, lavender affair, with hefts of fabric tied up in bows flouncing down the skirts. It felt rather like I had donned armor, given the padding and constriction of the tight sleeves, with the row of pearl buttons at the wrists.

"Evelyn!" Mother called out again. Lucy gave me a nod and stepped back. I gave myself one last look in the glass, grabbed my dangerous fan, and made my way downstairs, where my mother and father were waiting in the largest drawing room, gilded, rich,

leather-looking red fabrics decorating the walls. Mother was dressed similarly to me, but in a dark-purple dress for half mourning. "Very nice," she told me.

She gave me a long, peculiar look, but it wasn't the usual critical one. Oh dear goodness, was that a look of admiration on her face? What was that doing there? And aimed at me?

"Lovely, lovely," Father said, looking larger than ever. He did not seem to really see me as he gave me a vague smile. Was his mind already on card games? I smiled up at him, determined that after this was over, we would talk as we never had before. There would be openness and truth and he wouldn't gamble anymore. Perhaps Rose could convince him if I couldn't.

Mother stepped forward, drawing me aside while Father poured himself another drink. "I want you to know how much I appreciate your efforts, Evelyn," she said. "Lord Atherton visited today and your father gave his permission."

"Oh!" was all I managed to get out.

"I know we've had our share of disagreements, especially about marriage," she continued with a sigh. "A great deal of it was because you reminded me of myself. I was just as stubborn about it when it was time for my Season."

"So you decided to force me to marry as revenge upon your mother," I said wryly.

She smiled and her eyes found Father across the room as he lit a cigar. "No, but I only learned to love your father after marriage. I know Lord Atherton plans to propose tonight, and I am sure you will find him most agreeable and, in time, grow to love him." Her voice lowered further. "But if not, there can be freedom, you know, in marrying a man whom you have advantages over." At the questioning look in my eye she gave a canny smile. "I know he is not the most . . . interesting man. But neither will he be demanding of your time and attentions. You will have security and your time will be your own. There have been many marriages built on less."

I inclined my head guiltily, suddenly very appreciative of her care. She had considered my feelings more than I would ever have thought. True, Lord Atherton was secretly a cruel, oppressive head of a secret society. But it was a kind gesture nonetheless.

"I know it has not been easy." Her throat worked a little and she dashed a finger under her right eye. "We all miss Rose terribly. And you were so close, ever since she was born."

"Even then?" I said, not sure whose voice was shakier.

"Oh yes. You were always at her bassinet, looking at her, babbling in some childish language." She caught my hand in hers and squeezed tightly. "She loved you very much."

"I love her, too," I said, forcing the words out.

My father, vacant across the room.

My mother, holding tight to the life she had, controlling as many aspects as she could.

We just had to get through tonight. Just tonight, and then we would ease—nay, *erase* all the pain my parents were going through. I squeezed my mother's hand back and watched as she blinked repeatedly. She coughed once and I wanted so badly to tell her everything.

But our first guests had started to arrive and my mother quickly composed herself and joined my father to greet them. Pretton announced their entrances in the great hall and his voice echoed throughout the room.

As planned, Miss Grey was one of our first arrivals. Disguised as an elderly matron by Camille so my parents would not recognize my old governess, she made her way in and stationed herself in a chair in the ballroom. We thought choosing someone who looked familiar but not an actual imitation of a specific person would force my parents and guests to nod politely, avoid her, and privately rack their brains for who, exactly, she was. She fussily pulled on a pair of pince-nez, as though she would be scrutinizing the guests for their correctness. Of course what she would really be looking for was the suspected bodyguard—and anyone else she might recognize from her dreams.

Oliver would be out in the mews with Miss Chen. When I told him our plan, there had been no stopping him from attending. He loudly voiced his hatred of the Society and told me he would do whatever he could to "be a thorn in their arse." Ignoring the colorful image, I told him to present himself to Pretton as an additional groom for the night. As soon as the majority of guests had arrived, Oliver would be sneaking inside and bringing Miss Chen with him to the floor above the ballroom.

More guests streamed in and I greeted all of them with more focus than I would have usually. Though I was sure the head was Lord Atherton, I couldn't help but wonder at every man from Catherine's list who kissed my hand and heartily shook my father's. By the time I heard the Atherton name announced, my eyes were beginning to cross and I felt sure that I had created two new, deep lines from smiling so hard for so long.

Lord Atherton and his mother swept in. Lord Atherton was as correct and boring as always, his suit smartly lined with the thinnest stripe of velvet, his hat perfectly perched on his springy hair. Of course, he took it off the moment he entered, handing it to one of the very ready servants. Lady Atherton's hair was very high, adorned with a number of flowers.

"Miss Wyndham, I promised you when we met we would take full advantage of the Little Season. And tonight this ball is all anyone can talk about," Lady Atherton said, coming forward to gaze around the room and claim credit for all of it.

"Indeed, you were correct, Lady Atherton" I said, curtsying. "Thank you."

"As the late earl said, 'The early bird catches birds of a like feather,'" she said.

I nodded, not even trying to understand how that would work. At the very least, the combination of proverbs made it somewhat original.

"Lady Atherton, Lord Atherton, a pleasure," Mother was saying warmly.

"We are delighted." Lord Atherton bowed stonily and turned to me as decorum dictated. "Quite . . . unique weather," he said.

I stiffened. Was he being his typical weather-fixated self or was this a reference to Miss Rao?

"Indeed," I said. "Unique weather for a unique night."

"Hum. May I have the honor of the first dance?" His words were as stilted as a tired actor's.

"I'm afraid I am engaged for the first, Lord Atherton, but the second is available?" He looked deeply offended but nodded over my hand, and I curtsied, trying not to crush my skirts in my clenched fist. There was something sinister lurking beneath the mask of that insufferable correctness. I was leaving the first dance for Mr. Kent so we could approach Lord Atherton together in the second. I was longing to confront him and hear his answers. I took a deep breath, reminding myself that it was almost over. He and his mother slowly disappeared into the ballroom and I steeled myself for greeting more guests.

Fortunately, the Kents arrived soon after. I was quite surprised that Lady Kent would have accepted the invitation, but Lady Atherton had so advanced our position in society, it would have been inexcusable for her to decline the honor. She did not meet my eye as she entered with her husband, Sir Peter, back from his travels. I could feel the waves of tension rolling off Mr. Kent as he stood just behind his hated family. After his explanation of how his father had treated his birth mother last year, I was not surprised.

When Mr. Kent greeted me with a gracious bow, though, his eyes brightened. "I will see you for the first dance," he said. "I've asked for a two-hour waltz. You'll love it," he said with a wink and disappeared into the crowd.

Slowly, our grand, empty house actually started to feel crowded. A woman's skirts bumped the base of a bronze bust and her husband lunged to catch the falling figure in time. Two girls who shared my first Season walked out of the ballroom, giggling over their punch. Servants darted in and out of the crowds, their shining trays held high above their heads. Anxiety was coiling in my stomach, turning my insides to mush. I looked back at the hall to the ballroom and saw Miss Grey standing, staring fiercely at someone. Had a guard just arrived?

"Hello, Evelyn."

Damn. Damn. Damn. I turned, took her in, and tried to contain a sigh. "Mae, what a surprise." Mae's eyes were outlined in red but blazing with determination.

"I decided that you were right."

I never thought there would be a time when I would dislike those words.

"I was?"

"Yes. He needs to know that I do forgive him and that I will stand beside him, be his helpmate and support. I did not think that was a decision that could wait." She looked fiercer and more ready for battle than any of us actually preparing to fight tonight.

Her words rushed into my head while my blood roared, and I struggled to rearrange them into something that made sense.

I shifted my fan and gave her hand a tight squeeze, feeling equal parts relief and guilt that Sebastian would not be here tonight. "Oh dear. Mae, I am sorry to say that I received word that Mr. Braddock will not be able to make it."

I had seen faces fall before, seen joy turn to a perplexed sadness before, but never so piercing as it was on her grave features. Her eyes tightened as she drew in a sharp breath, placing her hand on her stomach as though my words had been a hard punch, robbing her of air.

"Oh. I see."

"But, but you should certainly call on him tomorrow!" I said frantically, wondering how quickly I could get word to him if all went well tonight. Then, perhaps, he wouldn't be so worried about her safety. Then they could be together.

Mae did not even smile as she listlessly wandered into the ballroom, her purpose in coming quite spoiled.

When my mother finally nodded to me that we had done our duties at the entryway, I took a deep breath and entered the ballroom. It was grandly turned out, with enough greenery to impress the Queen herself. Lights reflected off the many-mirrored surfaces, but my mother had proved her excellent taste without veering into the territory of gaudy. There was no garish Oriental-meets-Turkish-opulence theme, just the beauty of her guests set among the many green plants that announced her new wealth more elegantly than any number of jewels would. She would have had to raid more than our conservatory, indeed *many* hothouses, for the beautiful blooms and potted trees, their scents mingling sweetly without overwhelming. I admired her hostess skills even while despairing of my own, which probably shouldn't involve kidnapping guests.

I caught sight of Miss Grey, staring pointedly at me from her chair in the corner. I slowly walked to her side, flapping my fan lazily.

"You recognize someone?"

"Behind Lord Atherton—that small woman with very plainly done hair. She's the one with the talent your friends Arthur and William described."

I shivered as I took in the woman. She had a thin face—not pleasant or unpleasant, simply not one anyone would take notice of. "And she is not a member of the Society we've seen before?" I asked.

"I don't believe so."

"Then please see if she stays with Lord Atherton," I said.

Miss Grey nodded and I felt a measure of relief. This proved he was the head.

We would end it tonight.

The first strains from the small orchestra sounded. Mr. Kent was at my side immediately, bowing deeply. He looked so very at home in his dark suit and trousers, nattily tied tie, and shining shoes.

"Shall we?" He expertly swung me to the center of the floor. I looked up at his familiar face, felt the heat of his hand lightly resting on my waist as we spun again and he pulled me back into his arms. Mr. Kent was as graceful a dancer as ever. We both tried to scan the room discreetly when he let out a quiet rumble of a laugh.

"What is it?" I asked.

"I just realized this is the first time you danced with me without me having to cajole you."

Mr. Kent smiled and a silence fell between us. I wondered if he was about to mention our kiss. I wondered if he was waiting for me to resume the conversation we had about our future. I wondered again why I couldn't simply be in love with my friend. With every turn, a jumble of emotions flew through my head.

But before I could identify any of them, we swung around again and my attention was completely arrested by Sebastian Braddock.

He was standing in the shadows, obviously, near a large fern that seemed set there expressly to show off how well his blasted eyes matched the deep green. Of course he had to be here. He just *had* to figure out we had a plan and come to help. He just *had* to interfere to do the kind, noble thing. He just *had* to give me more reasons to wish he were mine.

Oh, damn it.

"And here I thought you didn't invite him," Mr. Kent said.

"I didn't," I snapped. Sebastian eyed us then, and I watched as his hand clenched the stem of his glass hard, liquid spilling over the lip.

"What on earth is he doing here?" I breathed, and received a glare from Sebastian across the room and an icy reply from Mr. Kent.

"I suspect he is here for you."

I didn't respond. My stomach and mind were whirling faster than the dance and I was too busy thinking about how to get Sebastian out of here and also keep him in my sight forever.

"It's almost indecent," Mr. Kent said with a sigh.

"What is?"

"The way you look at each other." I did not pretend to misunderstand him.

"Mr. Kent—" I began, but he interrupted me gently.

"Lately, in order to win you over, I've been finding myself thinking, *What would Mr. Braddock do in this situation?* And it took me far too long to realize what that meant: I wanted to tell you that I would not be interfering anymore. I don't pretend to understand why it is that you would want to be with him, but even someone without my superior detective skills would notice how you gravitate toward each other."

Even as he spoke, I was perfectly aware of where Sebastian was in the room and where his eyes were trained—still directly on us as we flew across the floor in circles that even Mr. Kent's monologue did not disrupt.

"And more than that . . ." Mr. Kent's eyes were focused somewhere between my eyes and forehead. He looked suddenly less angular. "I no longer wish to pursue someone who does not realize how excellent I am."

I drew back, feeling threads of panic begin to run through my body. "Mr. Kent, you have been my friend for some time and I certainly realize how excellent you are," I said honestly.

"Yes, I know that. And you shall always have my friendship as well. But I do not wish to press anyone into loving me. The person who loves me will see me for who I am, good and bad, and say, *Yes, that's the handsome gentleman I have been hoping to meet all along, that handsome, charming, witty, disarming, genius, remarkable, dashing—*"

"Mr. Kent."

"See? That is not going to be you, Ev—Miss Wyndham. Which is why I will leave you to the most ridiculous man in London—who is made much less ridiculous by you. Indeed, I might even say he is tolerable."

I stared at him, wanting to smile and wanting to throw up. If I agreed, it would be the end of the future we had been tiptoeing around for almost a year now. I would not be able to change my mind and ask for time, for space, for the chance to keep the possibility of us alive. I'd be shutting the door on the safety that would come from being with one of my dearest friends, one who loved me enough to let me go.

"The dance is ending," he said, softly, gently. He had never looked so handsome.

"It is," I agreed.

I caught Sebastian's eye again. Whether Mr. Kent knew it or not, Sebastian was not for me, either. But no matter what, it wasn't fair to hold on to Mr. Kent. He *did* deserve someone who loved him for all the wonderful things he was, someone who would go to ridiculous lengths to make him happy, just as he did for me. He and I were never destined for more than a wonderful friendship.

"I am glad we shall continue to be friends, Mr. Kent."

Mr. Kent looked at me closely, a speculative glint in his eyes. "Are you absolutely sure you aren't having second thoughts on account of how noble I am being right now?"

"Mr. Kent!" I couldn't help but laugh trying to hit him with our entwined hands.

"All right, all right, just making sure," he said, holding me back. "No, no, very glad it's all settled and all that."

However, the dance was ending. Lord Atherton would be sure to claim his second. And Sebastian was walking toward us.

Drat.

Mr. Kent, no matter what he had said, was not removing his arm from mine as we reached the edge of the floor and Sebastian.

"Mr. Braddock, how unexpected," Mr. Kent said.

"Mr. Kent." Sebastian bowed stiffly. "Miss Wyndham."

"What are you doing here?" I said, heart beating swiftly. Talking to Sebastian, trying to enact our plan with Lord Atherton *and* look innocent, all at once, was too much to handle with equanimity.

"Arthur and William suspected you planned to do something tonight," he said, his voice low and urgent.

"I did not—that is—why are you—"

But before I could sputter my way through another question, Lord Atherton, grim and determined, came over for his dance.

"Miss Wyndham, we have the dance." And I was not sure which one of us was least thrilled at the prospect.

"Indeed, my lord." I curtsied and opened my fan, flapping it rapidly four times—the signal for Miss Chen to break my shoe's heel from her view above. A few steps toward Lord Atherton, and a satisfying crack made me stumble right onto Lord Atherton's arm.

"Oh dear," I said dramatically.

Lord Atherton held me upright with stiff surprise, as if I was an unidentifiable liquid spilled onto his arm. "Why, Miss Wyndham! Is it . . . the music? I've heard too much can be exhausting for ladies."

"No, I think my—" I looked down at my broken slipper and wobbled it about. "Yes, oh dear, my heel has broken. They were new, too!"

Mr. Kent was suppressing a smile, Lord Atherton looked appalled, and Sebastian was narrowing his eyes at me suspiciously.

"I . . . I'm so sorry, sirs," I said to the gentlemen. "Lord Atherton, would you please accompany me to the retiring room?" I did not give him a chance to answer as I pulled him along toward the exit. I shot Sebastian a hard frown as we passed him, hoping dearly that he would just leave.

I directed Lord Atherton out of the ballroom, back through the entrance hall and into a narrow corridor. I glanced behind me to see if the guard had followed, but the passage remained empty.

Lord Atherton looked perplexed by our direction, but I opened the door into an empty library before he could realize what was happening.

Mr. Kent entered through another door. And Sebastian was with him.

"My apologies, he followed me," Mr. Kent said.

"Really, Mr. Braddock, there was no need," I began, but he closed the door behind him resolutely.

Lord Atherton looked around nervously. "I say, Miss Wyndham, this is most improper."

"Lord Atherton, we know who you are," I blurted out.

"I should hope so," he said, looking offended.

"We know you are the head of the Society."

"Head? What society is this?" He looked at me as though I were very, very confused.

"The blasted Society of Aberrations," I said. Where was Mr. Hale? I was more than ready to throw Lord Atherton into a portal.

He looked at me with a convincing expression of bewilderment and concern for my state of mind. "What is that?"

Fortunately, before I punched a wall, Mr. Kent jumped in. "Lord Atherton, are you the head of the Society of Aberrations?"

"No," he replied dully. "I don't know what that is. I've never heard of it before."

I stared at him closely, sure that he was lying somehow. Mr. Kent hesitated before continuing: "Are you aware of the existence of extraordinarily powered people?"

"No, I don't know what you mean."

"Are you aware that there are people who can heal or kill another person with a touch?"

"No," Lord Atherton said, looking more and more uncomfortable.

Something was definitely wrong. "Ask him what he meant by his duty to the realm and his legacy," I said.

"What did you mean when you told Miss Wyndham about your duty to the realm and legacy?" Mr. Kent repeated.

"I, well, my estates. My position as an earl and my place in the House of Lords." He looked puzzled at the idea of my not having inferred that.

"Is your power still working?" I asked Mr. Kent.

"I don't know. Do you find me handsome?" Mr. Kent returned.

"Yes," I replied, following it with a growl.

"Everything is clearly in order here," Mr. Kent said. "Perhaps he is somehow resistant." He turned back to Lord Atherton. "What is your name?"

"Frederick Dalton Leopold Saddleworth," he answered.

"What is the most shameful thing you've done?"

"I once cheated in a card game against my mother," he said before his lips tightened in distress. "I've never told anyone that."

"My God, the man is a saint," Mr. Kent replied, shaking his head. "A boring, boring saint. Let's try one more. What is your darkest desire?"

"Sometimes, I wish I could be a humble meteorologist," he answered, looking aghast at his confession.

"Well, I think we can all agree that is a rather horrible thing for an earl to say. So it must be the truth." Mr. Kent said, throwing up his arms. "I don't know what's happening. Perhaps he is the wrong man."

"I . . . I'm going to go now," Lord Atherton said, rising on shaky legs. "I promise, I won't tell anyone what you . . . you were asking me tonight. Just please don't tell my mother."

Mr. Kent couldn't resist making the man more uncomfortable. "Tell her what?"

"That I cheated at cards and wish to be a meteorologist. Please, sir, have mercy! The shame!" With that, he rushed from the room, his composure utterly shaken.

The three of us stood, staring after him for a long minute. Oliver poked halfway through the ceiling, dropping a new pair of shoes into my hands. "That one . . . Not a lot going on up there, is there?" he asked, pointing at his head.

Sebastian finally turned back to us. "What on earth are the three of you up to?"

Chapter 21

As we returned to the ballroom, I quickly filled Sebastian in on our plan. He was quite angry that I had not included him in our scheming and I was equally angry that he had shown up uninvited. We found Miss Grey at the edge of the ballroom and told her that Lord Atherton had been a mistake. I was enraged and embarrassed. How should I have known that the man was truly that boring, thinking of his useless earl duties, instead of speaking obliquely about a position as the head of the Society?

Catherine had been right after all. I stood between Sebastian and Mr. Kent as we looked for the other lords on her list. The guard Miss Grey had pointed out earlier was nowhere to be found—was she off with her charge elsewhere in the house?

A sudden idea struck me. "Lord Herrington! He's not only on Catherine's list but he was the first person I helped with healing and now he's suddenly friends with my father."

"It's worth a try," Mr. Kent murmured, looking out over the crowd.

"The card room," I said, sure I was right, and turned to lead the way. We squeezed through the crush and down the corridor, twisting as I followed a trail of smoke. The door opened on raucous laughter, the clinking of glasses, and the smell of strong

spirits and stronger perfumes. It was small, though, and easy enough to find Lord Herrington . . . and also at his table, my father. Maybe we were finally on the right course. I carefully scanned the room to see if the bodyguard was also here. Nothing—but perhaps she was hidden, sitting low in one of the chairs near the fire. . . .

I took Mr. Kent's arm and we walked slowly to my father.

"Evelyn!" He stood up abruptly, looking entirely unsure as to what he should do, given the impropriety of my interrupting their game. I couldn't help but look down to see how much money was on the table ready to be gambled away.

"Hello, Father. . . ." I stopped, realizing I had no excuse for being here or needing to speak to Lord Herrington. "I . . . well." My mind was entirely blank.

"Evelyn, I think you should return to the ballroom." He was pink behind his ears, and I realized he was embarrassed that I was here.

"Actually, Father, I need to speak to Lord Herrington," I said sweetly.

Lord Herrington eyed me unattractively and I tried to tamp down the burst of hope. However much he didn't want to talk to me, he could not turn me down without appearing abominably rude.

"Of . . . of course, Miss Wyndham," he said, getting up from his chair in a smooth motion.

"I am sure Lord Herrington—" my father began, but Mr. Kent was already gesturing us toward a quieter corner of the room.

"Lord Herrington, wonderful to meet you, Mr. Nicholas Kent," he said, reaching for the older man's hand.

"Indeed, sir, now what is this about?"

"Miss Wyndham and I have the smallest question for you."

He smiled silkily. I turned slightly to see Sebastian hanging back, looking grim and brooding.

"We wonder, do you know anything about the Society of Aberrations?"

"Yes, I know of them" Lord Herrington said.

"I see, I see." Mr. Kent gave me a quick look. "And are you by chance the *head* of the Society of Aberrations?"

"No."

My stomach plummeted.

"Do you know who is?"

Lord Herrington looked perplexed and annoyed as the words came out. "I thought Miss Wyndham's father was the head of the Society of Aberrations." He turned to me. "Is that not why you helped my daughter?"

Oh for heaven's sake. I stared at Lord Herrington's baffled face. He was doing as terrible a job as we were at identifying the head.

I sighed. We were wasting time.

"Thank you, Lord Herrington, please make my apologies to my father." I gave him a tight smile and met Sebastian's gaze across the room. I shook my head slightly and he seemed to brood harder, if such a thing were possible.

"Now what?" Mr. Kent asked. His eyes were hard and cold.

"We keep asking," I answered, glad that his question had at least found an answer from me. I turned back to the ballroom. "We should see where that bodyguard is. Surely she wouldn't let her charge out of sight for long."

Sebastian caught us at the door. "Miss Wyndham, this is reckless."

"And necessary," I snapped. I marched by him and opened the door, taking a much-needed breath of slightly less-congested air.

The ball was bulging at the seams when we reentered. "Come along," I said, pushing Mr. Kent forward. "If we find that guard we can just ask her who the head is."

We looked out over the crowd and I tried to describe her to Mr. Kent, but neither of us saw her. My mind stuttered and fogged like an overworked engine, more time slipping through our fingers.

"Let's find those lords on Miss Harding's list—we can play it off as some kind of joke," Mr. Kent said finally.

I agreed, no longer caring if London society thought both Mr. Kent and me very odd. "Mr. Braddock. Please stay here and keep your eye out for anything that seems strange." He nodded and I caught those eyes for a long moment. I tried not to let the concern and exasperation I found there warm me too much.

Mr. Kent pulled me into the crush and began to insert himself into conversations.

"Excuse me, lovely to see you again, Lord Overstone—are you perhaps the head of the Society of Aberrations? No? Ah, no, a very new club—I thought for sure that *you* would know of it. . . .

"Lord Somers—yes, my father is very happy. No, no—look, Somers, a question for you—are you perhaps the mysterious head of the Society of Aberrations? No—I . . .

"Lord Warrington! My, we never see you at these things—is that because you're too busy being the head of the Society of Aberrations? Never mind."

As he grew increasingly blunt I grew increasingly worried. That was all the men we had suspected. I was getting desperate, ready to accuse a large man next to me, who was angry, drunk, or naturally ill-tempered, when a loud crash sounded.

Mr. Kent hissed in a quick breath as I spun around, along with most of the company.

A servant had dropped a tray of drinks.

"Oh no," I said, immediately recognizing the embarrassed soul. Laura Kent was here. Dressed as a servant. And dropping glasses.

Mr. Kent was already striding through the crowd. I followed as another servant began to help her pick up the shards of glass, and the party gave them wide berth, returning to their drinks and conversation.

"Kit! You are in the worst trouble," Mr. Kent was scolding in a whisper as he pulled her to her feet. Up close I could see that Laura had attempted some kind of disguise using kohl and rouge. It was not exactly effective, more comical.

"Nicky! Emily and I snuck out!" she babbled excitedly. I groaned and looked around, knowing that Emily wouldn't be far behind. Indeed, she was a few feet away and also dressed as a servant, subtly using her skills to push pieces of glass under a rug.

"Both of you, follow me," I announced, and turned on my heel.

Blast it. First Mae, then Sebastian, now these girls! Couldn't anyone quietly sit at home for one night? We didn't even know who the head of the Society was and they were running around willy-nilly, getting themselves caught up in things they did not fully understand.

I marched them into two chairs next to Miss Grey.

"Miss Grey, don't let them get up." Emily and Laura huffed into their chairs and made identical sulky expressions.

"We can help!" Laura said mournfully. "We don't want you to be forced to work for the Society."

"Hush," Mr. Kent said, his face blotchy with fear and anger. "How dare you do something so stupid?"

Laura shut her mouth as though he had slapped it shut. It was the harshest I had ever heard him speak to her, and I suspected the harshest she had heard as well.

"You will sit here. If Miss Grey sees either of you move—or any objects moving that should not be moving, Miss Kane—she will come get us," Mr. Kent said, then rounded on me. "If we don't find the head now, he will find us."

With that, he was stalking across the floor and I rushed to follow. We stood at the edge of the sea of people and I wondered how long it would take to question all of them.

"Damn, damn, damn." Mr. Kent was swearing softly, as rattled as I had ever seen him with Laura's appearance.

"Mr. Kent—"

"It's just been a very long evening, Miss Wyndham," he said, anticipating my inquiry into his state of mind.

My mother was staring daggers at me as I walked along on the wrong man's arm. Lord Atherton was standing just behind his mother, per usual, but he had a more desperate, nervous quality than before.

I had had enough of all this. "One moment, Mr. Kent. Follow my lead."

I marched over to my mother and the Athertons. "Mother! I have the most wonderful announcement to make. Do you think you could invite the entire party here for it? Every single guest?" I nodded significantly at Lord Atherton.

Mother looked rapidly between us. Lord Atherton appeared rather ill but I smiled widely. "You, ah . . . why yes, yes of course." Her face aglow, she started off, but returned to press my hands hard.

"You won't regret this, darling," she whispered. Her eyes were bright and the color was high on her cheeks. She looked so confident, so sure of me, and I swallowed down guilt. Once this was over, I would be returning a daughter to her. Surely she would forgive me then.

Mother rushed from the room. Lord Atherton looked like he

was trying to summon the courage to say something, but a glare from Mr. Kent kept him silent.

Lady Atherton was scrutinizing me but I refused to meet her eyes and looked out upon the crowd instead. The ballroom began to fill, the hum droning louder like a swarm of insects. The dancing whirred by in a frenzy that threatened to swallow us. The music felt sharper, more discordant with every wail of the violin, every moan of the cello. The walls seemed to close in with every curious guest that pressed themselves into the room, every face rendered sinister by the garish gaslight. My blood curdled. The head could be anyone. It could be everyone.

"Are you ready?" I said to Mr. Kent under my breath.

"Since birth," he returned.

"All right, darling, go ahead!" My mother was behind me, slightly out of breath. She handed me a small bell and I smiled. The music came to a stop. The guests were already looking around expectantly, confused, and it took only the briefest tinkle of the bell to make them all look my way.

"If you would, please," I said as everyone turned to me. "My friend Mr. Kent here has a question for all of you."

"Right," he said, clearing his throat. He hesitated, and I wondered if he, too, was thinking that this was the moment we would undoubtedly be turning our backs upon good society forever. If we even survived the night. "We would like to know, who here is the head of the Society of Aberrations?"

The question was met with dead silence.

Except for a furious, throaty voice.

"I am," said Lady Atherton.

Chapter 22

DUMBFOUNDED, I STARED.

Lady Atherton. She was supposed to be a mere friend to the Society! Someone earning her position! Now she was signaling to that blasted bodyguard across the crowd and hurrying through to disappear into the dining room. And we were letting her escape as Mr. Kent and I stood quite frozen in shock.

"A-another dance, shall we?" my mother announced, gesturing to the musicians. She turned to me and hissed quietly. "Evelyn, what is going on—"

"I must speak to Lady Atherton," I said, shaking off her grip.

"I will get Miss Kane," Mr. Kent said, darting off through the crowd.

I ignored Lord Atherton, who was beginning to make a protesting noise as I left his bewildered presence.

Across the room, Mr. Kent was admonishing Laura to stay with Miss Grey as he directed Emily to us.

I was gaining on Lady Atherton when Sebastian appeared by my side.

"Please, Sebastian, stay—"

"Not on your life," he growled, picking up his pace.

By the time we converged with Emily, we were into the empty dining room. Lady Atherton had nearly made it across that room when Miss Chen and Oliver dropped through the floor in front of her, blocking her escape. She spun around and hurried for the third exit. "Emily, can you stop her?" I whispered.

She nodded enthusiastically and gestured to the woman.

Lady Atherton was lifted off the ground, floating high up in the air, flailing to no avail. She let out a small "Eek!" and tried to keep her skirts down as she was held suspended in the air. We hurried past the dinner and dessert tables and I prayed that Mr. Hale would show himself. Was he not watching? The room was empty—it was the perfect place to take her away.

Instead, the sounds that came were a series of smooth snaps and rattling. All around the room, paintings and hangings crashed to the floor as the metal chains intended to hold them up broke off and flew toward us.

I turned to Emily, who looked distressed, and Lady Atherton fell slightly as Emily's focus turned to the door we came in.

"Emily, are you doing thi—"

A chain reached out and wrapped around my neck, dragging me across the room. A second later, another one struck my legs, pinning me hard to the wall. This wasn't Emily's doing.

As I gasped for air, restrained by two chains, I saw two figures emerge: the drab bodyguard, who waved her hand and ensnared Emily, Sebastian, and Miss Chen in more chains, slamming them against the floor—and a man who went over to help Lady Atherton back to her feet.

Another bodyguard. He was spectacularly mustachioed and blond—cheerful-looking even, like an overgrown boy.

"Thank you, Mr. Drake," Lady Atherton said, sounding just as commanding and unconcerned as she always had during our morning calls. How had I missed it? "Miss Miller, please hold them here; I will be leaving at once."

I struggled against my restraints, ignoring the pain of the metal digging into my skin. A series of sharp clangs rent the air, over and over, and my chains actually fell apart. I slid back down to the floor wondering briefly if I had developed some sort of strange new neck power . . . until I saw Miss Chen crouched in the center of the room, focusing on Emily and Sebastian's restraints, shattering them into hundreds of small pieces.

But Miss Chen needed time to focus, time our enemies were using. With more control than Emily, Miss Miller had somehow managed to collect all the silverware in the room and swirl it into a ridiculous sort of tornado that separated us from them. Mr. Drake was helping Lady Atherton limp toward the next room. I seized a small painting off the floor and a fire poker beside me and ran, charging at them.

As I stumbled across the room with my terrible excuses for a sword and shield, utensils clattered and thunked against my painting, ripping at the canvas, delivering small cuts to my arms and legs.

From the corner of my eye I saw Miss Chen staring hard at a chandelier above Miss Miller. But even as it fell, with a flick of her hand, Miss Miller flung it back toward my friends. Miss Chen reacted quickly, shattering it so it fell to pieces before it could hit anyone. Emily was using her powers to pull up a thick rug as a barrier against all the flying debris. I took advantage of the distraction and slipped by, hoping they would be fine on their own for a moment.

The next room was a billiards room, the air filled with the stench of whiskey and cigar smoke. I caught up to Lady Atherton and Mr. Drake, dropping my ripped shield and gripping the fire poker with two hands. I stepped quietly and swung as hard as

I was able to at Mr. Drake's head, feeling a fleeting bit of pity for the nice-looking man, but when I made contact, something struck my own head, sending me to the floor, my ears ringing.

Spots floated in front of my eyes and I felt blood run down my cheek for a moment before the cut on my head closed up and the ache faded away. As I dizzily stood up and regained my balance, I found Lady Atherton hurrying away on her own, while her guard stood between us. He seemed completely unhurt. He didn't even look irritated.

So I attacked again. I swung at Mr. Drake as he held out his arm to block the blow. Again, a searing pain hit me, this time in my right arm instead of his. He seized me by the throat as I dropped the poker. I thrashed around but he was a large man and he seemed entirely unaffected by my struggles.

Is this how I die?

But no. Oliver, climbing up through the floor, spotted the poker and grabbed for it. He gave a vicious swing at the guard's back and yelped, collapsing in pain, as if he'd been struck himself.

Mr. Drake, still squeezing my throat tightly, looked past me and gave a wet little chuckle. I kicked at him, feeling more pain in my own legs. As Oliver tried to rise to his feet again, Miss Miller walked into my line of sight, the dining-room door shutting and locking behind her. The fire poker in Oliver's hand lifted him up and then wrenched itself away. It spun around and tore into his shoulder with astonishing speed, propelling him like a rocket up at the wall. He managed to use his power before he hit it, but the momentum still sent him flying through the wall, way into another room.

A harsh cry was all that Mr. Drake's grip would allow, and I redoubled my efforts to get free. No, not Oliver—I needed to get to him. Now.

Metal rods floated and bent eerily in front of Miss Miller. "I'll restrain her," she said placidly. I struggled to open my fan, ready to fight the woman, when a voice sounded from behind me.

"You'll let her go," Mr. Kent said. He entered the room from the far door, holding Lady Atherton next to him with his pistol aimed at her head.

Mr. Drake's hold on my throat loosened. The dining room door shattered and Miss Chen, Emily, and Sebastian filed in behind me. Sebastian made to move closer, but I held out my hand, telling everyone to stop for a moment.

"You don't have to do everything she demands," I said, turning to the guards. My voice came out as a rasp, as though I were struggling with a cold. "They, the Society—*she* coerces all of us this way, pits us against one another. But if we all stop, she won't be able to fulfill their threats." I looked for a bit of reason from the two guards.

"She doesn't coerce us," Mr. Drake drawled. "She pays well."

"And if you followed their orders, you would be much safer," Miss Miller added. "You wouldn't be in this situation. Traitors."

Mr. Kent cleared his throat. "Excuse me, we seem to be forgetting a very important detail: You are the ones in a situation. I have a gun pointed at your head's . . . head."

Miss Miller glared and the barrel of Mr. Kent's gun twisted upward and back into itself, tying into a neat knot.

"Oh, for God's sake, that was a gift," Mr. Kent said, throwing it at them. "Fine, what are your blasted powers, the two of you?"

"My injuries get reflected back on my attacker," Mr. Drake said.

"I control metal," Miss Miller said.

"Splendid, and your biggest weaknesses are?"

"Being trapped," Mr. Drake replied.

"A room without metal," Miss Miller answered with a growl.

I shut my fan, not wanting her to see the metal blade. We looked about the billiards room. It was . . . quite the opposite of her weakness. It was practically a museum for medieval armor. Armor that could be used as painful weapons.

"Blast—" Mr. Kent began, but all at once the armor came to life, flying at us before we could react. A helmet struck Mr. Kent, allowing Lady Atherton to escape. A heavy chest plate knocked me over.

When I climbed back up to my feet, I saw Sebastian had managed to seize Mr. Drake with a wrestling sort of hold, but he winced in pain as Mr. Drake kicked him and slammed him into a wall, daring Sebastian to hurt him further. Emily was barely managing to keep Miss Miller's flying armor and weapon attacks at bay, while Miss Chen, peering at the cracking ceiling, was running out of wall hangings and light fixtures to drop onto Miss Miller, who managed to nimbly dodge them all.

Oliver had yet to return and I was worried I would find him dead. I dodged the flying armor as best as I could, shielding myself with a wingback chair, trying to formulate some plan. These two guards were too strong. They were too in control. They must have had years' more practice than all of us combined. They—

I heard a tear. It had come from Mr. Drake. His trousers dropped down in shreds. And not a second later, another rip sounded from Miss Miller as her dress fell apart and she shrieked. Miss Chen was looking more amused than I'd ever seen her.

"Never thought that would come in so handy."

These two guards were . . . not as intimidating anymore.

Snatching a wooden pool cue from the billiards table, I rushed at Miss Miller. Even distracted with her wardrobe problems, she managed to see me and sent a dagger into my shoulder and another into my stomach. I stumbled, trying not to cry out as I attempted to remove them, to allow my wounds to heal, but another struck my leg, sending me to my knees. I managed to pull that out and rise back up, but the second I took a step forward, another dagger was flying straight at my heart.

It passed through me like nothing. Oliver, sweating and pale, had slipped through the wall next to me and thrown himself on my shoulder, his touch saving me. I clung to the boy, relieved to see that he had managed to get the fire poker loose.

Miss Miller yelped in pain as a wound emerged on her shoulder. I turned around to see that her dagger had flown straight into Mr. Drake, still restrained by Sebastian, causing the wound to be reflected back on her.

"Keep hold of me, Oliver," I said, and he clung to my back as I spun around, closing the distance between Miss Miller and myself. I swung the stick at her and it struck her face with a satisfying crack. Oliver was jostled but managed to keep hold. I was about to swing again when he yanked me back, hard.

Above Miss Miller, the cracked ceiling finally opened up and I realized what Miss Chen had been planning, just as a massive wooden cabinet fell through, landing on top of Miss Miller, breaking heavily over her body.

"Ha!" A fully healed Oliver had leaped onto Mr. Drake's back and solved the problem rather efficiently by pulling him down halfway through the floor and leaving him stuck like that. To silence Mr. Drake's yelling, Miss Chen stuffed his mouth with the sad remains of his pants.

I finally took a breath. No one looked seriously injured. My own stab wounds had healed quickly and judging by Oliver's whooping taunts, he was feeling much better. Sebastian was cradling his arm, though, and I stepped forward, thankful that I could heal him today.

"Thank you," he said quietly.

"Where did Mr. Kent go?" Emily was looking around, color high in her cheeks as if she had enjoyed our adventure.

"He must have followed Lady Atherton." I hurried out of the room and into a massive gallery. There were five different doors and I didn't know which to take. Mr. Kent was throwing them open, calling down each in turn.

"Lady Atherton, have you gone this way?"

"Yes" was the distant reply at the third door.

"Oh, splendid, thank you."

We followed Mr. Kent down the hall into a moonlit glass conservatory, where Lady Atherton was looking for another exit. She sneered as we entered but didn't look terribly surprised to see us waiting for her instead of her guards. In fact, she looked as if it didn't matter one way or another.

"You reckless child," she said. "You don't have any idea what you are doing."

"I'm doing what's right," I said coolly, and she gave a harsh little laugh.

"The right thing? Who do you think is responsible for our country's safety? Strength? Comfort? The only reason you can have this life full of your balls and gowns and suitors is because of the Society."

"You think I would want that knowing how others will suffer for it?"

"Just as foolish as my husband was," she said, shaking her head.

I stared at her. "I thought you were following in your husband's footsteps," I said.

She let out a loud "Ha!" "That man had to be told exactly

where to step. He received credit for many, many things he should not have."

"Well, we knew that," I mumbled.

"The man only went into the Home Office with my prodding. All his policies, his promotions, were due to me." She eyed me coldly. "I thought you were clever at first, Miss Wyndham; I thought perhaps you could be the right wife to my son. Your healing power would ensure a long life for all of us. And a stable Society."

"I would never," I snapped.

She sighed. "Because you don't respect the duties required of you. You have vague high-minded ideals about doing what's right and helping people without an understanding of what you must actually do."

"We knew enough to get you," I replied and turned toward the rest of the group. Damn Mr. Hale. He should have been here by now. "All right. Where should we take her?"

"You will take me back to the ballroom," Lady Atherton interrupted. "If you all care about your families."

Her calm confidence sent a chill down my spine.

I kept my voice even. "We do care about our families, but we've already handled your bodyguards."

"All three of them?" she asked sweetly.

Mr. Kent didn't need my prompting. "How many bodyguards are at this ball?" he barked.

"Three. I was not lying," she said, pulling a green leaf off the pretty plant next to her and letting it fall to the ground.

"And what is the remaining bodyguard's power?"

"To manipulate bones. And she is currently using that power to hold your loved ones in place in the ballroom until I tell her otherwise."

"Then tell her otherwise," Sebastian said. He looked sick and

I wished, for the hundredth time this night, that Mae had not come.

"I will," Lady Atherton replied. "When I leave with my son."

"Is that true?" Mr. Kent asked.

"It is."

I could feel the stiffness among my friends. Every face, tight with distress, told me the same thing. We didn't have any other choice. We'd allow her to leave, track her, and catch her later.

"Fine," I said dully. "We'll make the trade. Your freedom for theirs."

Chapter 23

THE BALLROOM LOOKED eerily ordinary.

When we entered in our torn and somewhat bloody outfits, pointed glances and hushed whispers greeted us, but with a fake laugh from Lady Atherton, the dancing and flirting and gossiping still continued on, a strained attempt to preserve the normalcy.

"Don't let on, Miss Wyndham," she said through bared teeth.

"Kit," Mr. Kent muttered.

I followed his gaze to find his sister sitting in a chair in the corner of the room. She stared straight ahead, her hands folded on her lap, completely immobile.

"What did you do to her?" Mr. Kent growled.

"I told my guard to keep her firmly in place," Lady Atherton said. "They haven't been harmed."

And that was when I noticed my mother in another corner, frozen, sitting in the very same position. Miss Grey was across from her. And Mae was at the far end. Helpless dolls, unnaturally arranged around the room.

"We brought you here," I said, feeling the oppressive weight of the heat rising in the ballroom. "Tell your guard to let them go."

"Once my son and I are safely away, I will send someone to tell her," she replied, still smiling.

I turned to the rest of the group. "Check on them, make sure they are unharmed. Miss Chen, will you see to my mother?"

Mr. Kent hurried off with Emily to check on Laura; Oliver went to Miss Grey, Sebastian to Mae, and Miss Chen to my mother. As our group approached the captives, Lady Atherton gave a nod to the bodyguard, wherever she was in the crowd. I felt my heart stop for a moment, worried what the nod meant, but then I saw Laura responding to her brother's questions. Her expression was understandably panicked and her body still wasn't moving, but it looked like Lady Atherton had been true to her word. They weren't hurt.

"If I even suspect you are following me, I will order her to break their necks," Lady Atherton said gaily, giving another false little laugh. "Is that clear?"

"It is," I replied, imagining the twenty different ways I would murder her if she hurt anyone here. I was furious. Furious with myself for never guessing it was her. Furious that we had lost our one clean chance. Furious because everything that could have gone wrong, had.

"You killed him," a tight voice said.

I turned around and immediately felt as though I had been plunged into icy water. It appeared much, much more could still go wrong. For Captain Goode stood behind us, his hand shackled to my sister's.

She wasn't wearing her disguise. This was my Rose, my beautiful sister, the one I had missed and mourned for. The one who knew me better than anything. The beloved, the kind, the perfect sister I'd tear down empires for.

And she looked deathly pale. I let out a cry when I saw blood seeping through her dress at her waist. She shivered hard and winced.

"Rose," I gasped, reaching for her hand to heal her. "What are—what is going on?"

She shivered at my touch. "Catherine . . . and Camille and Mr. Hale. . . ."

Oh God.

"What did you do?" I hissed at Captain Goode, cold running through my veins.

Captain Goode said nothing. He looked over the ballroom, his usually placid expression had been replaced by a distraught, haunted look that altered his features entirely. Gone were the earnest eyes and slightly nervous demeanor. I barely recognized him.

"What did you do?" I asked louder, not caring who might hear and be shocked at my behavior.

"You killed my brother," he repeated, a dull shock threading through the words. His eyes narrowed in on someone across the way. "I want answers. And Mr. Kent will ensure I get them."

Around me, I started hearing honest answers winging through the air.

"May I have the next dance?"

"Heavens, no."

"What would you like to do?"

"I would like to stick my face in your bosom, madam."

"How are you?"

"Nauseated by the sight of you."

Captain Goode's face twisted as the truth filled the room. His power. He didn't have to touch us. He could alter our levels simply by looking at us. He'd kept it a secret this whole time.

"Now. You killed my brother," he said, rounding on me, pulling a little at Rose so she moaned in pain. I sucked in a breath. "Do you deny it?"

"I do," I answered.

"Then how did he die?"

"Camille suffocated him and Mr. Hale dropped him in the ocean," I said, the answer coming out against my will. As if Mr. Kent were asking me these questions himself.

"And you let them?"

"I did," I admitted.

"Could you have saved him?"

"Yes."

"You worked together against him."

"We did."

"Then you might as well have done the deed yourself," Captain Goode said.

"He would have killed Rose. Following her orders!" I said, pointing at Lady Atherton.

Slowly he turned to her, as if he were just realizing she was there. His lips clenched and he swallowed, looking very sick. "No, no, it's not her."

"It is," I insisted. "I told you they were lying."

"I—it can't be . . ." He was shaking his head madly. "*You?* You are the head of the Society of Aberrations?"

"Yes," she replied without hesitation.

"You have no power," he said, looking her over. "How can you run the Society without a power?"

"Just as the other heads have," she answered, tight-lipped.

His teeth ground together and Rose yelped as he twisted his wrist, yanking hers with him. I wrapped my arm around her shoulder, willing my power to heal her faster. A slight perspiration shone on her forehead.

"Then why does the Society exist?"

"To keep our country safe. To keep track of the undesirables like the lot of you and keep them tame."

Captain Goode was staring around in bewilderment and he

let out a long, guttural moan. "All this time—my God." He reeled back under the weight of these revelations.

In desperation, Lady Atherton turned to signal to her remaining guard.

"That won't work," Captain Goode said, fury making him almost vibrate. "I already shut off everyone else's powers."

He wasn't lying. Around the ballroom, I saw Laura, my mother, and Mae standing, in control of their bodies again. Mae was trying to embrace Sebastian, who held her back with one hand, glancing around fearfully. Oliver's power was shut off abruptly, trapping him and Miss Grey halfway through their escape through the floor, causing a commotion around them, and Mother was being held up by my father. Both were staring straight at Rose, their faces frozen in fear and awe.

I turned back to my sister, who was growing whiter by the second. Blood was continuing to spread along her dress. My power wasn't working, either.

"Captain Goode, please, turn them back on, just let me heal her—we can work together," I pleaded desperately. "I'm truly sorry about your brother. I wish it could have been different—"

"You killed him! And you thought I wouldn't know?" he shouted. Guests turned and no one seemed quite able to pretend that something fascinating wasn't happening. "You're the same as her," he jerked his head toward Lady Atherton, who was slowly beginning to back away until he fixed her with a fierce stare and she froze. "Look at you people—you're all the same. Lying. Manipulating. Using others to get what you want."

"We just wanted everyone safe, the same as you." I tried to sound calm. Rational. Tried to choke down the fear. "There was no other way."

"You play at altruism, Miss Wyndham, but the truth is that you decided your sister was more important than my brother. What you don't understand is that you don't just 'help people.' Any choice to help someone, hurts someone else. You want to help Britain? Then take from Egypt. You want to heal someone? Then you leave someone else in pain, waiting. You want to save your sister? Then you kill my brother."

He was fairly spitting the words now and I shrank back as he rounded on Lady Atherton.

"And you. You manipulative, atrocious woman. You used me. You let me think I was in control and you used me." His voice did not hold pity though. It was pure, unadulterated venom. "I followed your orders even when I did not understand why—and you thought you could control *this*?"

With that, he turned his gaze to the ballroom and gestured to Emily Kane, who was clutching Laura in fear, Mr. Kent tense and ready at their side. Shouts and cries started up all over the room. Objects floated up all around us. Jewelry, watches, fans, flowers, champagne glasses, and champagne itself. They all hung in the air like balloons. A strangled cry came from Emily as she floated up. Laura and Mr. Kent tried to grab her, but they rose up, too, unable to keep her grounded.

I clasped Rose's hand tightly. "What are you doing?" I growled at Captain Goode. "Please, just give me back my power!"

Rose tried to murmur something and swayed.

"Hold on, dearest. Just hold on." I clutched her to me as Captain Goode ignored me, still scanning the room. His eyes landed on Miss Chen, who was rushing over to Emily around the edge of the room, weaving in and out among the guests. Suddenly, the ceiling collapsed above a group of guests in front of her.

"No! Run!" Miss Chen yelled.

And then the room began to break apart. All the beautiful plants my mother had purchased were upturned, glasses shattering, gaslights exploding, tiles bursting as Miss Chen squeezed her eyes shut, throwing her arms over her face to try and control herself. The floor cracked and started to give way below her, but before she fell, Mr. Kent reached out and yanked her up in the air, where he and Laura still floated next to Emily.

"*Please!*" I yelled as I saw my father narrowly dodge a flying glass, holding my mother in his arms. Sebastian was in the middle of the room, swirling around Mae as he tried to deflect the many flying objects. Oliver was wrenching himself free, inch by inch, desperately trying to take advantage of the cracked floor.

"Stop this immediately!" Lady Atherton was spitting the words, her face red. Upon realizing Captain Goode would not listen, she spun around, trying to make her way to her son and the exit.

The loudest scream of all rang out, and I saw a hole blow open in the wall near Miss Chen. Guests tried to get out of the way, some slamming into walls and other people as the falling debris hit them. "No!" I heard Emily fairly bellow. The whole house began quaking. "*Laura!*" she screamed as the floor around them rumbled, building to something uncontainable. With Emily pulling him up, and Miss Chen unable to bring him down, Mr. Kent gave me one last, dreadful look across the ballroom. There was a thunderous boom and the four of them blasted out through the hole, falling toward the city streets.

"Please, please, you do not need to do this!" I said, but Captain Goode was looking at Lady Atherton as she dodged her way across the ballroom in the mayhem. Rose moaned again and I desperately moved my hand to the wound, pushing hard, hating that it made her cry out, but needing the bleeding to stop.

Captain Goode turned. The air felt sharp and acrid, and I sensed some greater danger to come. He looked down at me, his every word weighted. "You say you want to save people? I'll restore your power and give you a choice."

And then, as though watching through an impenetrable glass, I saw what he meant to do. His hand lifted, pointing straight at Sebastian, inky hair mussed, blood dripping from his cheek where something must have flown and hit him, and his eyes, catching mine, sliding to Captain Goode, registering what was about to happen with a glare of panic and sorrow.

"No!" My voice mingled with Sebastian's, a raw, tired sound as Captain Goode raised Sebastian's deadly power.

"Your sister's life for everyone else in this room. She's injured. She'll have a quick, easy death. Just let her go and everyone else will live."

Rose whimpered, "Ev." But I couldn't. I couldn't let go of Rose.

A coughing started, from Mae, and I turned to see her doubled over.

But I couldn't let go.

"You want to help them, Miss Wyndham! You want to do the right thing, you said!" Captain Goode's voice hit like a whip's lash.

Rose began sobbing. "Evelyn, our parents—"

"Please, please," I begged Captain Goode. "You don't have to do this."

But he said nothing, just looked at me and gestured at the ballroom, the conductor of this deathly orchestra.

Rose tried to jerk away, but I couldn't let go as everyone around Sebastian toppled like statues to the floor, radiating farther out. I couldn't let go as Mae, lovely, kindhearted, all-seeing Mae, slithered to the floor, as graceful in death as she was in life. I couldn't let go as Sebastian gave an inhuman howl, trying to find a way out among the bodies and debris. I couldn't let go as Lady Atherton and her son collapsed in fits of coughing. I couldn't let go as the Lodges and the Kents fell to the floor, choking, gasping for air. I couldn't let go as Oliver and Miss Grey slowly slumped over, the stubborn, heroic boy refusing to leave her. I couldn't let go as my parents stopped moving, so close to us now, their eyes never leaving Rose, never letting go of each other as they fell, panicked and bewildered, expressions that would stay on their faces for eternity.

"Stop, please, stop." The words poured from me in a torrent. I kept holding Rose to me. This must be a dream. Surely I hadn't just seen my own parents die.

"Let me go, let me go," Rose was moaning at me, and her voice snapped me to. I would not accept this horror show.

No. I would heal them and I would fix this. I instinctively unlatched the hidden dagger from the fan hanging at my wrist, and swung at Captain Goode hard. He tried to block my attacks, not expecting there to be a blade in my hand. He flinched back from the startling pain as I slashed at his arms, but he couldn't retreat far with his hand handcuffed to Rose. I maneuvered behind him as he tried to shield himself with her and fight back, but his injured arm was too useless.

I held the blade to his throat. "Turn his power off, and raise mine now!"

"You asked for this," he choked out.

My touch was canceling out Sebastian's heightened power and protecting us. But if the same logic held, I wouldn't be able to heal anyone, not without an increase in power.

I tore the dagger across Captain Goode's throat.

"Do it or you'll die," I snarled.

Blood poured out of his wound. He tried to say something but the words came out raspy and unintelligible. He choked. The gash opened wider. He fell to his knees, stubborn, refusing to give in.

Then I felt my power fill me.

He preferred not to die.

Chapter 24

S EBASTIAN WAS GONE.

The floor was littered with bodies that were not getting up. Bodies that were happily dancing minutes ago but lay crooked and lifeless now. Captain Goode had waited until it was too late. The warmth of my power mixed with the feeling of sickness in the pit of my stomach as I knelt down to touch hands and heads, hoping for a spark of life to stir them. Behind me, Rose's sobs came sharp and short, as if she didn't have the breath to cry.

I held my knife to Captain Goode's half-healed throat and pulled him and Rose toward the center of the room, stepping over legs and arms in suits and dresses.

"More. Give me more," I demanded.

"Have . . . given . . . you . . . limit," he rasped back.

I looked back to the bodies on the floor. No one moved. Every face was an awful, familiar one. That boy who barely knew how to dance, but wouldn't let that stop him. The girl who always gave me the sweetest smiles during the Season, but never had anything to say.

Oh God, our parents. Rose pulled us down, kneeling over them, hoping they might be different. They had crept closer to us, farther away from Sebastian and closer to my power; maybe they

weren't as exposed. I stared into Mother's open, vacant eyes as Rose grasped her hand, willing her up to her feet as if it were the simplest request.

"Mama. Please. I'm here, please come back," Rose whispered to her.

Mother didn't hear. Father was no different. He lay unmoving, his eyes closed. I turned away but there was no escaping the death around us.

Mae. Blue splotches all over her pale skin. Only this time, they refused to go away as I grasped her with my blood-covered hand.

Miss Grey and Oliver. Rose's sobs turned even more panicky and I felt bile rising in my throat when I found them slumped and motionless, Miss Grey still trapped in the floor and Oliver beside her, his fingers bloody from trying to free her. Miss Grey's arms were around him, her body half-covering his as though she had tried to shield him from death.

The darkest of rages flew through me and I turned, cutting at Captain Goode's throat again, bringing him down to the floor with Rose. As he grasped his neck with one hand, I bent over, wrenched his handcuffed hand out, and slammed my heel against his wrist to break the bone. As it cracked, he screamed in pain, the only sounds echoing in the room, until I set my dagger on his skin and started sawing over his protests, trying to cut faster than my healing could fix it. The dagger sank deeper and deeper, my hand slick with blood as Rose shuddered against me, pleading. In a daze I watched the blade cut all the way through, and the handcuff slid off his severed hand.

I left Captain Goode to bleed out on the floor and pulled Rose up to her feet. I had to get her to a safe place. I clutched her tightly to me and brought her out of the ballroom, through the foyer, and out the front door . . . where I found Catherine covered in almost as much blood as I was—but animated and alive and so very different from the horrible ballroom.

She threw her arms around both of us and hugged us with all her strength, which seemed to grow by the second. "Oh, thank God you're both all right. Something terrible is happening."

And that was when I noticed the dark, lifeless street behind her.

My hold around her went loose and I flinched back. There were more bodies, scattered about the sidewalk and streets. Horses pulled carriages manned by unconscious, slumped-over drivers. Captain Goode hadn't turned Sebastian's power off.

"Oh God. He's running through London now," I breathed.

"Wh-what? Who—was it Captain Goode?" Catherine asked.

I hurried past her to the sidewalk, checking the street in both directions, searching for movement. With a sickening sensation, I realized the multitude of bodies to the left told me the exact path Sebastian must have taken.

Catherine's hand grasped my shoulder. "Evelyn, what's going on?"

I spun back around and clutched their hands. "Catherine . . . God help us, Catherine. Everyone—so many people are dead. Just please take Rose somewhere safe and hide. I'll find you. I don't know who else is aliv—" I swallowed hard against the panic that I knew would overwhelm me if I stopped to contemplate it fully.

"Rose," I said, forcing her glassy eyes to mine. Her breath still came in tiny little bursts and I was sure she was moments away from fainting. "Stay with Catherine, I have to stop him. Wait somewhere safe and I will find you, all right?" I shook her a little, trying to get her to concentrate. "Rose! I will find you."

She gave the smallest nod that I would have to take as confirmation that she would be well enough for the moment.

"Evelyn, wait! What do you mean? Where are you going?" Catherine called after me.

"I have to find him," I yelled back, flying down the street.

As I ran along the awful path, bodies seemed to come to, people moaning and rising to their feet. My raised power seemed to be more potent than my touch had ever been. And these people had fortunately not been exposed long enough to Sebastian. But as I ran, dread still pounded through me. I didn't know how this would ever end. He had a head start and I already knew there was no way I'd ever catch up to him in a dress and slippers.

Unless there was an abandoned police horse on the street corner, waiting for a rider to do some good.

I hurried over, doing my best to get to him quickly and calmly without startling him.

"Easy . . . horse. I need your help," I said in a soothing voice as I grasped his saddle, stepped onto an upturned crate, and pulled myself up with a groan. My bustle poked into my back awkwardly and my skirts were at my knees but I was stable enough. With a tight grip on the reins, I ordered the horse forward, hoping I could learn the secrets of riding astride.

He was fast. As we flew through the dark streets, with only the moon and streetlamps for guidance, my heart stayed firmly in my throat and I prayed nothing would stop the beast and throw me from the saddle. But despite the risk I didn't dare slow down. I could get up from any fall. I gave a gentle dig with my heels to encourage him to fly, steering around stranded carriages, aimless horses, and unconscious bodies so fast that they became blurs, but I heard shouts and turned to see people rising to their feet.

"Good, good," I murmured over and over—a litany to keep back the dread, the sorrow, the knowledge that there were so many people who would not be rising again.

Soon, a jolt of familiarity ran through my body as I turned onto one thoroughfare in particular. I had ridden down this road before, months ago, when we had been searching for Rose. I didn't need to follow the trail of bodies anymore. I knew where Sebastian was going. Dr. Beck's old laboratory passed in a blur, the horse's hooves clattering onto that wooden bridge where Sebastian had almost bled to death.

And there he was. Farther down, toward the center of the bridge. Around him, I saw carriages veer off course, drivers and pedestrians coughing, losing energy.

"Please, run!" he shouted at them. But as they doubled over he hurried toward the railing of the bridge, to the slight break in the barrier where nothing stood between him and the water.

I started to lift myself off my horse before he even came to a stop. Sebastian heard the heavy tread as he reached the railing, and his head shot up in wild panic. He held one hand up. "Stop!" he shouted. "Don't come closer! I'll hurt you."

I leaped off the horse and stumbled from the momentum, but I climbed to my feet in the next motion, refusing to stop. I approached him slowly, hoping not to startle him. "It's me, Sebastian. You won't hurt me!" I said. His breath was coming in weak pants and I didn't think any of my words penetrated the wild panic engulfing him. "Look at me. That monster gave me all the power possible. You can't hurt me. Everyone here is safe. Come back over here. Please."

He dropped his panicked grimace and instead his face became a skeletal picture of horror and pain. I was close enough to see he gripped the broken edge of the iron railing with trembling hands.

"Oh God."

I was close enough to hear his whisper now.

"What have I done?"

"Sebastian, please, please, come back here," I said, trying to keep my voice soothing and succeeding not at all.

He shook his head without hesitation. "This is all my fault."

"No, you didn't do this," I said.

"I did, Evelyn. This horrific thing that I am . . . God." He turned wildly, looking out over the half-frozen river. His feet were inches from the unfinished edge. "I can't let this keep happening. . . . I can't, I can't." He repeated it on a terrifying moan, wrenched from somewhere dark and desolate.

"This was Captain Goode," I insisted, my voice coming too quickly, too harshly, and I forced myself to calm down, taking a slow step forward. "He did this. Not you. He heightened your power and he is the one who deserves every imaginable punishment."

Sebastian looked down at the murky water of the Thames below. "It's . . . still my power, my responsibility. I was still here for him to use. I *let* him kill everyone—"

"Not everyone," I interrupted, sick with despair. I couldn't lose one more person tonight. Not him. *Please, not him.* "I am canceling you out right now and all the people you passed on the way, I saw them get to their feet. You didn't kill everyone."

There was the slightest glimmer of hope. "At the ball—were you able to heal them?"

I wanted to lie. I wanted to wait until he was less panicked. But my momentary hesitation was enough.

The hope died and his lips let out a tortured groan. "H—how many?"

"There are survivors," I said desperately. "I—Rose. Rose is safe."

"Out of a hundred? More?"

"Sebastian, please . . ." I could feel my mind slow, the horror of the night slowly stealing over my body, a numbing cold ready to swallow me whole.

The traffic rumbled merrily by us, oblivious to our bubble of misery. Sebastian shivered in the unbearable cold. He gazed out at the city beyond, which looked bruised black and blue in the faint moonlight. His hair was disheveled, his lips quivered, and he felt so far away he might already be gone.

"This hideous thing, I thought it could be fixed. . . . I shouldn't have come back. I should have stayed in the woods forever," he said, his voice dead and flat. I could feel him shutting me out.

I shook off the cold, taking another step closer, to within an arm's length of him, trying to find the words to reach him. To make him stay with me.

"I should never have trusted them and I'm so, so sorry. But this isn't your fault. You have tried so hard. You have sacrificed so much to try and keep people safe."

"And still I hurt them." He glanced back and I looked directly into his eyes, saw his heart breaking as clearly as though he had pulled it from his chest and handed it to me. "Too many."

"I know. I can't imagine how much pain you are in." I pressed myself against the railing, creeping closer to him along it, letting the chill seep through the folds of my gown. "This awful power . . . it should have turned you bitter and angry and cruel. But despite everything it's done to you, you're still kind; you care about others more than yourself. You're good, Sebastian. You do the right thing as instinctively as I say the wrong thing. You make me better—you make everyone better."

He shook his head tightly. "I don't. I've killed so many—and I can't hurt anyone else. This is the only way."

"It's not. I promise you. There is no cure, but there is a way to control this—I've seen it. It's slow, but we will do it together. Day by day. And I will stay with you for as long as it takes."

His chin trembled. Tears rolled down his jaw, dropping into the water.

"We can't let him get away with this. And I need you to stay with me. I need you to fight alongside me, Sebastian. You are going to help so many people."

He turned back over the water. His face was masked in the shadows. Our powers were so heightened they seemed to whirl together even without contact, so intertwined I couldn't tell whose blood was running through my veins.

He let out a light breath and his hand left the railing. I didn't know whether that was a good sign or a bad one.

I didn't wait to find out.

I made a wild lunge, slamming myself into the railing, skidding closer to the broken edge as my fingers dug into his wrist, his weight almost enough to pull me after him. Rubble crumbled to the water below. His feet slipped further forward. *"Evelyn!"* My name was ripped from his throat and with a great heave I flung him back, slamming us down against the wood instead of into the dark waters on the other side.

I was stunned from the impact, from the heavy weight of him on me, from the overwhelming sensation between us. It brought fire and ice to my veins, it brought a scream and a whisper to my throat, it brought hope and despair to my heart. I pulled him up till his head rested on my chest and my arms went around him, holding him fiercely to me as he tried to push himself up.

"Let me go. Let me go." He repeated the words desperately and I could feel his heart battering his chest as I clutched him harder. My mind whirred as the truth of the night overwhelmed us both. My mother. My father. Mae. Oliver. Miss Grey. All those poor people. My breath began coming in gasps but I could only hold on to him; there was no one else left to save. So I clung to the one person I could still help, the one I could not let die.

"Sebastian. Sebastian. Sebastian. I'm here. I can't let you go. I can't let you go."

His body shuddered with huge racking sobs that shook us both. I held his face against mine, wishing I was big enough to cover him. To hide him away. I finally gave in to my own choking, breathless sobs and our tears mingled, running down our cheeks as we pressed together tightly, as though maybe, if we just poured enough of ourselves into each other, it could wash away some of the guilt and horror. His lips were near my throat and I didn't hear but felt his muffled words through my skin. Felt the wretched truth that doomed any chance we had at happiness together.

"When Mr. Kent's powers were raised . . . She said she loved me. And my—my last words to her were that my promise to her brother was to protect her, not marry her. That I loved . . . you. And she . . . I broke her heart. And then . . . then she fell—"

"No, that wasn't your—" I croaked, my voice all but gone, pulling his eyes to mine, needing him to understand. "You aren't to blame."

And it was true. I meant it with every fiber of my being. Sebastian hadn't come back on his own. He hadn't put all his loved ones in danger. He hadn't taken on the Society without fully understanding the consequences. He hadn't chosen one life over a hundred others.

I had.

Epilogue

A LITTLE SMOKE STILL rose from the grand, broken house at
43 Belgrave Square. It had been two days since the mysterious tragedy, but onlookers still gathered across the street at all
times to whisper about the "Belgrave Ball" in tones of horror and
morbid glee.

Their whispers seemed to center around two topics of discussion. First, there were the words scrawled across the facade of
the house. An angry tangle of red letters, some thickly painted,
some fading, as though a quill had begun to run out of ink, or
more accurately, blood. The metallic stink that mingled with the
dead bodies proved it to be true.

"Must have been a monster."

"It's blood—I'm sure of it."

"What's't mean, Ma?"

In the back of the crowd, hidden behind her veil, Rosamund
Wyndham squeezed Catherine Harding's hand and quivered as
she read the words, over and over again.

We will find you

She knew exactly what it meant.

"That's the fifth this morning," a voice said behind her.

"Naw, seven."

"You're all wrong; I've been here since dawn and only counted six."

"Can you even count past six?"

The other topic of discussion: how many bodies had been removed that day. Hospital men mixed with volunteers, carrying another shrouded body on a stretcher and dropping it into a waiting carriage. Even after two days, corpses were still being found buried under the rubble of the crumbled walls and collapsed ceilings.

"We shouldn't have come here," Catherine whispered.

"I just . . . I needed to know it was real," Rose said numbly.

She needed to know that her home was truly gone. That her future had been ripped away by a man intent on destruction, a man with a power more terrifying than any she had seen yet.

Standing here, across the road, was the closest she would ever get to returning to her mother and father. After that one unsatisfactory, fleeting glimpse of them from across the ballroom, in the haze of her injury, as they collapsed to the floor. She still didn't know whether she was hoping or dreading that she might see them one last time, being carried out on the next stretcher.

"Will you buy a flower for the dead, miss?"

A group of young girls took full advantage of the tragedy, trying to sell their flowers, white and still fresh in the early-morning air. Their thin faces were hard, stripped of youth. Rose shook her head, wishing she had a coin to pay them. But she and Catherine barely had enough, between the meals and the inn.

"Let's go," Catherine whispered.

Rose took Catherine's arm and it almost felt like the only thing holding her up, keeping her on her feet, stopping her from melting into a puddle. They began to walk west. The wind was harsh and their borrowed cloaks were thin. The streets became more crowded and the noise more overwhelming. The farther away they walked, the heavier Rose felt. Even though there was nothing there for her, it still felt like the last link to her family and home.

"Where are we going?" she asked, finally.

"The Harevian Society," Catherine said. "I took Evelyn to a lecture there last Season and it was one of the few she did not sleep through."

"A medical lecture?" Rose said with surprise.

"I seem to recall her saying something about giving the notes to you." Catherine did not look at Rose, exactly, and somehow that made it even harder. Rose missed Evelyn, feared for her, needed her here, and wasn't sure how long she could keep herself in one piece without her sister.

"And she'll remember that?"

"I don't know. I hope so."

It was that desperate hope that seemed to drive most of these attempts to find Evelyn. After reading the news about Captain Goode's message the previous morning, they'd decided that it was foolish to return to any of their houses and announce themselves. Those would be the places he would be watching. And Evelyn wouldn't risk it, either. Their best hope was to settle on a neutral location, connected to an intimate memory or shared secret.

The only problem, Rose thought, was that she and Catherine knew Evelyn too well. There were too many possibilities. They'd walked all over the city, trying libraries, theaters, museums, tea shops, every place Evelyn had declared to have the best cakes—which meant whichever she had visited most recently. But Evelyn wasn't to be found in any of them and they didn't know whether they might have just missed her, she might have just missed them, or she was simply waiting somewhere else that they hadn't tried.

The worst part was the not knowing. Rose couldn't help but wonder if Evelyn had felt this hopeless during her search last year.

Guilt squeezed at her, even though there was nothing she could have done.

After a half hour, they finally found themselves in front of the Harevian Society building. The sight should have filled Rose with joy. It would have a year ago, when she'd dreamt of becoming a member of these medical societies, attending the latest lectures and one day, perhaps, even presenting a discovery of her own. Now the building was simply another place to discover more disappointment.

"Their weekly lecture is starting in fifteen minutes," Catherine said, pointing at a sign as they passed by the front. "If Evelyn thought of this place, too, I'm sure she'd try to be here for the start of the lecture."

Indeed, Catherine had timed their arrival to coincide perfectly with a lecture that, according to the sign, had a last-minute change in topic. The subject was no longer blood transfusions; that had been postponed to the next week. Now, it was the more pressing concern of speculating on the causes of death at the Belgrave Ball. It seemed to be all anyone wanted to talk about.

Rose and Catherine waited across the street. They watched the Society entrance and scanned the rest of the area for places where Evelyn might watch the entrance herself. Rose heard snippets of theories as doctors walked by, speaking with their colleagues about bombs, poisoning, suffocation, and diseases. Soon, they all congregated inside, while Rose and Catherine continued to shiver outside. The lecture started and there was still no sign of Evelyn.

Finally, Catherine let out a sigh. "She must be somewhere else," she said, leading them back. "Maybe the Royal Academy. It was the last place we went."

"What if she's—what if Mr. Braddock hurt her?" Rose asked, putting voice to her greatest fear.

Catherine shook her head doubtfully. "We would have heard about it."

"Captain Goode might have her."

"And he might not."

"It's already been two days."

"Which means, Evelyn's probably being as careful as us."

"I . . . worry we are going in circles."

Catherine's cold hands clutched Rose's. "We will find Evelyn. I promise."

But would they find her soon enough?

Rose didn't like imagining what might happen if her powers returned and Evelyn wasn't there. She still had a little more than a day left, but she already found herself flinching at every passing glance, dreading every little act of politeness. Would strangers fall in love with her and want her for themselves? Would another misguided person kidnap her in an attempt to protect her from the rest of the world? What would it do to Catherine? Was she already affected? Rose didn't know what she hated more: her own power or her own impotence.

She couldn't get the images from that night out of her head. The things everyone did for her. The sight of Mr. Hale meekly complying with Captain Goode's threats to keep him from hurting her. The sight of Camille's true form, an ancient-looking woman, when she'd died trying to guard Rose. The sight of Catherine fending off Captain Goode and nearly dying from being thrown out the window. And the sight of Evelyn refusing to save an entire ballroom full of people. For Rose's sake.

The tears came without warning. Rose was thankful her face was covered. She felt nauseated, like a knife was twisting into her stomach. She'd ruined everything by coming back. Evelyn was moving on, ready to do something great, ready to help the world. And then—

"Mayhem!" a newspaper boy shouted. "Mayhem at the Belgrave Ball! Numbers rising! One hundred and twenty-two found dead!"

Both girls stopped, watching the boy make his way toward them, waving a copy of *The London Times* above his head.

"It can't be that high," Catherine breathed.

But Rose's pinched face and shallow breathing suggested it was not as much a surprise to her. She managed to find her voice by the time the boy reached them. "Please, may I see it?"

The boy held his hand out. "Threepence, miss."

"I don't have any. I just want to see for a moment," Rose pleaded, her voice rising.

He pulled his hand away and grunted his dissent. "No coin, no paper."

"But, but it's my fam—"

"Here," Catherine said. She pulled a silver coin from under her glove seam and gave it to the boy. Rose took the paper and turned through it as they huddled together in a spot under a doorway.

"No," Rose was whispering, looking at the horrific image that dominated the page. Her parents' ballroom, crudely rendered, a stage for slaughter. Looking below it, her eyes could only catch flashes of words before the tears welled up again.

Dead.

Sickness.

Plague.

Poisoning.

Murder.

Rose closed her eyes and let Catherine take the paper from her. She squeezed her palms against her face, trying not to let the panic overtake her.

"Rose—"

"I know. I know," Rose said, reaching for some kind of calm.

"Oh heavens, the Agony Column," Catherine muttered to herself. "How did I not think of this until now?"

"Of . . . of what?" Rose asked. She reached under her veil and mopped the rest of her tears with her sleeve.

"'The baker is grieving'—no, 'hundred-pound reward'—no." Catherine was reading the front page of the paper, her finger moving down the second column.

Rose looked up at Catherine, her voice a rasp. "What are you doing? Why—"

"There!" Catherine exclaimed, jabbing her finger at a particular entry. There was a shadow of a smile on her face and Rose trembled as she took the paper from her. It was a short note—to most it would appear commonplace in its absurdity, but Rose gasped as she read it, her hand flying to her mouth.

Evelyn.

In search of stolen friends—brilliant enough to solve the impossible, charming enough to win over a room, brave enough to face their ghosts, clever enough to find the truth, loyal enough to follow us anywhere, fierce enough to destroy it all.

Friendship for each, and faith to all,

And vengeance vow'd for those who fall.

    Find me at my favorite poet's statue.

    All Good things must end.

    —E.

Acknowledgments

E VERYONE TELLS YOU how hard a second book will be, but for some reason we thought it would be different for us.

Hahahhhahahahahahahahaaahahhahahahahahhahahhhahahhahaha-hahahaaahhahahahaahhhaahahahahaha.

We will spare you the stories of our shouting matches and slumps, the highs of thinking we had it all figured out, and the lows of realizing we did not. Suffice to say, this one didn't exactly come easy. And as we wrestled with this book, we were probably not the easiest people to be around, so we have some people to thank:

To our respective roommates, who didn't mind our long phone calls, weird writing hours, and jumpy bleariness whenever we emerged from our rooms. Who gave us food and tea and made us take much-needed breaks: thank you. We are lucky to have such wonderful people in our lives.

To all our friends who told us they missed us, understood when we rescheduled for the fourth time that month, did not get mad when we had to bail on yet another play or party or trivia night: thank you. We missed you too. We can't wait to hang out. Stop rearranging the bookshelves now, the employees are going to hate us. (But we love you.)

To Dr. Elliot Handler, thank you for always enthusiastically answering all our panicked medical and psychiatry questions. We'd be lost without your help.

To the Sweet 16s: You're a wonderful group of people and we are so thankful we had your support, guidance, and joy as we navigated through

the debut year. A huge thank-you to the admins who were tireless and excellent. We are a little bit awed and entirely grateful.

To the bloggers and booksellers and librarians and reviewers and critics and booklovers and book clubs and conference-goers and to anyone who read *These Vicious Masks*—whether you loved or hated it—thank you, from the bottom of our hearts. We are inspired by your enthusiasm, critiques, threads, shout-outs, features, top-tens, staff picks, and all the wonderfully creative ways you promote books. Thank you for taking the time to pick up ours.

To our parents: How do we ever thank you enough? We know it's impossible, but we can try. You have given us so much. Years of support as we pursued careers in the arts, cheerleading when we wanted to give it up, firm pushes uphill when things were hard, and so much love. Thank you for never doubting. We love you.

And to Swoon! Oh, Swoon. We swoon for you, Swoon. The hugest of thank-yous to Emily, for giving us brilliant ideas and enthusiasm and making us believe in this book. To Lauren, for your never-ending fangirling and love for Mr. Kent. To KB, for our gorgeous cover. To Jean, who helms the ship so skillfully and is such a genius. To Kat, who makes us crack up whenever we look at Swoon's Twitter. To the wonderful marketing and Fierce Reads crew: You are the most fantastic. We still can't believe we ended up working with such an extraordinary team.

And finally, we have to thank Holly West. For, well, um, *everything*. If it weren't for Holly, there would never have been a book two. We would have hid away and said "What trilogy?!" to anyone that asked. But Holly coaxed us into finding our story, sorting through our more sleep-deprived ideas (What if: ZOMBIES!) to find the heart and truth of Evelyn's journey forward. Thank you so much, Holly, for helping us tell this one. Where would we be without your brilliant brainstorming sessions and kindest, non-panicked responses to our most desperate e-mails? Thank you for taking us on two years ago. We hope we get to work together on many more projects to come.

To anyone we missed, it's because we haven't slept in a year. We love you. Good night.

Tarun and Kelly

FEELING BOOKISH?

Turn the page for some

Swoonworthy EXTRAS

From the Diary of Laura Kent

February 5, 8:00 a.m.:

Nicky is being most mysterious and I think it has something to do with Evelyn, who has been missing. He will not tell me what his secret is, but I have the most brilliant plan that I daren't put to paper!

February 5, 8:05 a.m.:

I can keep nothing from you, diary! *I am going to follow Nicholas like a spy!* He will be so wonderfully impressed!

February 6, 9:30 a.m.: Oh, diary, wouldn't it be wonderful if I dressed as a boy?

February 6, 11:00 a.m.:

Tuffins caught me searching for clothes in the footman's belongings and was unfairly cross with me. I will have to settle for wearing black.

February 6, 11:15 a.m.:

And a veil!

February 7:

Where do I begin? Nicholas found Evelyn and there are more people with all these special powers. And most important, I have the most marvelous new friend—her name is Miss Emily Kane and we are already sisters and she is staying with me as my companion. Best of all, she can speak with ghosts! They fly objects all over the room and it's simply _wonderful_! I am wondering what my special gift is! I am sure it is something magical!

February 11:

Emily was very shy at first, but today we saw Mr. Edwards in the park and got revenge for the awful things he said about Evelyn by asking the ghosts to lift his hat and float it along the ground, and we laughed until we almost fell over as he ran around trying to catch it!

February 15:

Mother has always refused me coffee, but Emily managed to ask a ghost to sneak some during a morning walk! Today will be such an exciting day!

February 16:

Tuffins is extraordinarily skilled at fixing many types of broken things! I wonder if he has a special gift?

February 18:

I have asked Nicky if he thinks my mother might adopt Emily and he was not terribly encouraging. Perhaps she can simply be my companion forever? I will have to find a husband who also has a companion for her to marry.

February 20:

Nicky had another secret rendezvous tonight! I wanted to follow but Emily suggested we ask the ghosts to fly us around my room and we had so much fun!

February 21:

I am not myself today, diary. A man hurt me today. He threw me down the stairs and Emily's ghosts were all that kept me from dying. Only, it turns out she doesn't have ghosts. It's all inside her. I am very happy for my friend, but I am tired now. Good night, diary.

February 22:

Mother is miraculously healed! She has been so quiet, though.

February 25:

I think Nicky and Evelyn are planning something. I wish I could go to Evelyn's ball but Mother never lets me go to balls no matter how much I beg! I must try another tactic: I will show her I am a sensible, well-behaved woman.

February 26:

<u>Emily and I have the most wonderful plan. We are going to sneak into the ball dressed as servants!</u>

From the Diary of Frederick Dalton Leopold Saddleworth, Earl of Atherton

February 1: The weather is surprisingly mild.

February 3: The weather has turned cooler.

February 4: It is still chilly. Today was also a very wet day.

February 7: Mother has indicated her choice for my wife: Miss Evelyn Wyndham. She is too tall with brown hair and a face.

February 9: An amusing misunderstanding occurred this morning. For breakfast, I asked Elmsley for some eggs. A few minutes later, he brought out a plate of figs. I told him that I had asked for eggs. He apologized for the mistake, explaining that he'd misheard me, and returned with a plate of eggs.

February 12: Somewhat cold today.

February 18: I attended the Royal Academy Winter Exhibition last night with Miss Wyndham. Her behavior was abominable, but I must do my duty as a son.

February 20: While I was reading the newspaper this morning, I noticed a misspelling in the fifth line of the Egypt story. I wrote a letter to the <u>Times</u> editor immediately.

February 21: My health has been very good this winter. I suspect the wool waistcoat.

February 23: The weather has taken a turn. It is very cold for this time of year. Hopefully the winter will end shortly.

February 24: Met Pearson for dinner at Verrey's. He agrees that the weather's been rather cold lately.

February 25: I have indicated to Miss Wyndham that I will be making an offer.

February 27: My last day as a bachelor. I've no regrets. I've lived my life to the fullest.

A Coffee Date

with authors Tarun Shanker and Kelly Zekas
and their editor, Holly West

Getting to Know You (A Little More)

Holly West (HW): What books are on your nightstands now?
Tarun Shanker (TS): *The Dark Days Club* by Alison Goodman, because of course.
Kelly Zekas (KZ): *Flashfall* by Jenny Moyer. Just finishing it and it's great!

HW: What's your favorite word?
TS: *Susurrus*. Kelly made me cut it out of *These Vicious Masks* and I'm still bitter about it.
KZ: *Limerence*. I think it's gone out of style a bit, but it's beautiful.

HW: If you could travel in time, where would you go and what would you do?
KZ: Absolutely would go to Victorian London. I want to travel those streets and peer into the world so badly!
TS: Can I say the future? Every time I consider a place in the past, I can't help but think about how bad it probably smells or how quickly I'd probably die. I just want to go one hundred years forward, play with all the cool technology, and see how it's changed the world.

HW: Does your co-author have any strange or funny habits?
TS: She writes on the subway. It's . . . weird.
KZ: He is weirdly obsessed with making books perfect. :-)

HW: In the book, Catherine brings Evelyn the perfect gift back from her travels. What gift would you bring back for each other?
TS: Judging from the amount that Kelly plays with a fan during our brainstorming sessions, a dagger fan would probably be the perfect gift for her. Maybe some Band-Aids, too.

KZ: I love my fan! I'd love a dagger fan more. I'd buy Tarun a solitary writer's cabin in the remote woods, with a secret address. I'd stock it with chai and fast Wi-Fi.

TS: Okay, now I feel bad that you bought me an entire cabin. We really should have set a limit.

The Swoon Reads Experience (Continues!)

HW: What's your favorite thing about being a Swoon Reads author so far?

KZ: Well, not to sound like a broken record, but probably the amazing team at Swoon! We love every single person in the amazing group. Our books would be nothing without the wonderful people who make our books better (especially Holly).

TS: I second that. Especially our online brainstorming chats with Holly, Lauren, and Emily. I've been used to writing being a solitary, getting-way-too-stuck-in-my-head-type activity, so it's been great to come up with fun what-if scenarios for our characters with them. A lot of our favorite moments in this book wouldn't exist if it weren't for those talks.

HW: Awwww . . . Thank you! We love brainstorming with you, too! I know you are both active in author groups online. How do you think the Swoon Reads community affected your experiences as authors?

KZ: Swoon basically alerted me to the fact that there WERE writing communities online! It just wasn't something I knew to look for. The feedback we received for our *These Vicious Masks* manuscript when it was up on the site was invaluable. It's been so great finding other authors and feeling the support of a whole group of people behind you.

TS: Yeah, it's been incredibly motivating, both having a community as interested and excited about our books as we are, and seeing all the buzz other Swoon books have been getting. I never get tired of seeing those tweets where people declare their love for Swoon Reads as a whole. It feels like we're part of a nice cozy nook.

HW: Do you have any advice for aspiring authors on the Swoon Reads site?

KZ: Read the open edit letters! I read each one, at least a few times, and go back through my work to apply it. Keep putting up your manuscripts—there are definitely authors who were not selected for their first one but they didn't give up. Give generous comments to other writers.

TS: Try to find at least one person you trust with whom you can talk about your writing and creativity and struggles and frustrations. Having that second perspective is so important for even the smallest things.

The Writing Life

HW: Second books are notoriously difficult. What was the hardest part about writing *These Ruthless Deeds*?

KZ: Everything. My God, this one was a LABOR. We couldn't believe how many corners we had walked ourselves into, plot-wise, by the end of book 1.

TS: Agreed. It was everything. There was this constant second guessing going on because we were always trying to find a balance between the other books. Whether it's too similar or too different from book 1. Whether we're solving too many problems or pushing too many of them back to book 3. It just feels like the messiest place structure-wise because every decision we make requires simultaneously thinking about three books.

HW: What was the thing you were most excited about going into the sequel?

TS: More powers! Both in the sense of introducing new ones and also finding new, unexpected uses for the ones we're familiar with.

KZ: I couldn't wait to reveal that Rose didn't die.

HW: What are your writing processes and how does working with a co-author change them?

TS: I'm an intense plotter and brainstormer, to the point where I'll get down to outlining every dialogue topic and emotional change in a scene rather than have to actually start writing it. It makes me so slow on my own, but Kelly basically forces me to just get something down so we have something on the page to edit and discuss. Or she'll just jump in and write something in an hour that I've been stuck on for days.

KZ: My writing process began as Tarun's . . . helper, basically? I had no ambitions to be a writer, but since working with him it's become the thing I love most. However, I did write a play without him and I pantsed it so hard. Very freeing after working with a plotter for so long! But looking back, I could see where the structure didn't quite work, and I am pretty sure an outline would have clarified some things as well. Tarun definitely helps remind me that to get the great, explosive moments I love between two characters, you have to build them a great plot.

HW: What do you want readers to remember about your books?
TS: Everything is bittersweet.
KZ: Fight for what and who you love. Never stop.

These Ruthless Deeds
Discussion Questions

1. The title of this novel is *These Ruthless Deeds*. Which deeds do you think it is referring to?

2. Captain Goode believed that there was a purpose to everyone's power. If you developed an unexplained power, how would you interpret it? Would you seek out the reason for it? Or would you use it however you wished?

3. Mr. Redburn can copy anyone's power for his own use. If you had the choice of any extraordinary power, what would you choose and why?

4. The Society of Aberrations was very insistent on hiding powered people. Why do you think they prefer to keep the true existence of these powers a secret? Would life be better for the powered people if the world knew of their existence?

5. Evelyn chooses to keep Sebastian out of her plans to fight against the Society of Aberrations. Was she right to leave him ignorant? How much would you have involved him?

6. Rose's power charms people into loving her and doing what they feel is best for her. Is this a power you would want? What would you do with it?

7. Near the end of the novel, Mr. Kent comes to the conclusion that he and Evelyn are not right for each other. Do you agree with him? Explain why or why not.

8. Mr. Hale can travel across the world in the blink of an eye. If you had his power, where would you want to go and why?

9. Lady Atherton reveals that the Society of Aberrations was created to protect England from powered people, while using them in service of

the Crown. If you were the head, what would you change about the Society? What would you keep the same?

10. Captain Goode forces Evelyn to choose between her sister's life and the lives of all the other guests at her ball. Do you think she made the right decision? What would you have chosen?

**In which a lady and a law clerk find themselves
entangled in the scandal of the season.**

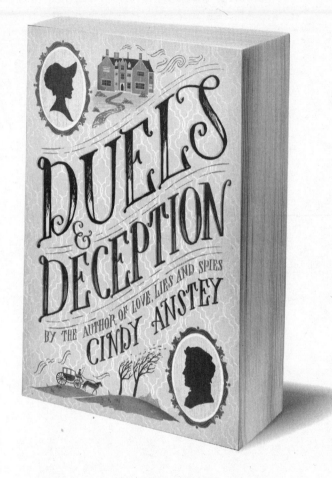

A young heiress and her lawyer are caught up in a
devious plot to destroy her reputation and
steal her fortune in this Regency YA novel.

KEEP READING FOR A SNEAK PEEK.

"**F**ROM MR. ALFRED LYNCH."

Lydia's hand went out instantly, but she slowed it just enough to take the letter with great dignity and solemn interest. "Mr. Lynch of Bath? My solicitor?"

"One and the same."

The letter was not long and took mere seconds to peruse. "You are Mr. Newton? Mr. Robert Newton? Mr. Lynch's clerk?"

Mr. Newton leaned forward, looking down at the paper as if he were going to read it upside down. "Clerk? Is that what he calls me?"

Edging back, Lydia instinctively pulled the letter to her bodice. "Are you not his clerk?"

"Well, I am. But he offered me an apprenticeship just last week. Though I will admit he did not state exactly when it was to begin. Still, he might have referred to me as an apprentice-in-waiting."

"A somewhat unwieldy title."

"True enough. Though it's more likely that he forgot."

"Seems unlikely. The man's mind is as sharp as a tack."

"Been a while since you've seen him?"

"At my father's funeral, three years ago. Not that long."

"Yes, well . . . a lot can happen in three years."

Lydia thought about how much *her* life had changed and reluctantly agreed—though silently. "Mr. Lynch's letter does not explain why you are here to visit us."

"No, it does not."

Lydia waited for him to continue, but he didn't seem disposed to enlighten her. "So why have you come all the way from Bath to Roseberry Hall, Mr. Newton?"

"Bath isn't all that far. It only took me a couple of hours." He glanced over at his gig and shrugged. "Would have been faster on horseback, but Mr. Lynch did insist. Thought it looked better. More official."

Lydia's heart skipped a beat, and she swallowed with a little difficulty. "Do you *need* to look official?"

"In some eyes, yes, I would say so."

"You aren't being very clear, Mr. Newton. Rather cryptic."

"Mr. Lynch said you were clever."

And so it was that Lydia stood on the side of Spelding Road just outside her own gates, observing that the day had grown chilly and that the splash of the rill was rather boisterous, in a less than charming manner. Had she been of the right disposition, she might have snapped at Mr. Newton for his uninformative conversation. She was now overburdened with thoughts of tardiness and broken wheels while her solicitor's emissary thought nothing of being mysterious.

Perhaps Mr. Newton didn't realize that an official visit from a solicitor had preceded the retrenchment of several households in the area. Or he might not know that Mr. Pibsbury, the estate land agent, had just retired and that a ninny had been hired in his stead. Still further, he might not know that arriving without an invitation or warning was highly irregular and boded ill.

And as those thoughts passed through her mind, Lydia hit upon another possibility—a reasonable and nonapocalyptic reason for his visit. It was just a seed at first, but it grew until it blossomed in the form of a smile and brought out the sun again. "My letter about Mr. Drury—the new land agent. Mr. Lynch sent you in response to my letter."

"In part, yes."

The sense of relief was such that Mr. Newton's hesitation barely registered.

"Oh, excellent. Most excellent. Come, Mr. Newton, let us wend our way to Roseberry."

With a quick step back to the gig, Mr. Newton grabbed his satchel, pulling it free. Joining her by the estate entrance, he half-raised his arm toward her and then, likely realizing they were too newly acquainted to offer such an intimacy, he dropped it back to his side.

However, Lydia found that she was not disinclined to take his arm; in fact, the prospect was rather exciting, in a daring sort of way. Feeling somewhat roguish, she stepped to his side and placed her hand in the crook of his arm. He smiled down at her in a manner that caused a strange flutter in her belly, and then he led them through the gates.

Check out more books
chosen for publication
by readers like you.

Mild-mannered assistant by day, milder-mannered writer by night, **TARUN SHANKER** is a New York University graduate currently living in Los Angeles. His idea of paradise is a place where kung fu movies are projected on clouds, David Bowie's music fills the air, and chai tea flows freely from fountains.

tarunshanker.com

Tim Goodwin Photography

KELLY ZEKAS, a New York University graduate, writes, acts, and reads in New York City. YA is her absolute favorite thing on earth (other than cupcakes), and she has spent many hours crying over fictional deaths. She also started reading Harlequin romances at a possibly too-early age (twelve?) and still loves a good historical romance.

kellyzekas.com

These Ruthless Deeds is their second novel.